NIGHT CROSSING

NIGHT CROSSING

A NOVEL

Don J. Snyder

ALFRED A. KNOPF   NEW YORK   2001

Library of Congress Cataloging-in-Publication Data
Snyder, Don J.
Night crossing : a novel / Don J. Snyder. — 1st ed.
p.   cm.
ISBN 0-375-40906-8 (alk. paper)
1. Northern Ireland—Fiction.   2. Intelligence officers—Fiction.   3. Political violence—Fiction.   4. Bombings—Fiction.   I. Title.
PS3569.N86 N54 2001
813'.54—dc21   00-062008

For Cara, with love

Winter 2000

NIGHT CROSSING

Chapter One

August 1, 1998 . . . In the quiet harbor of Inishowen, which faced east to the Irish Sea, Captain James Oliver Blackburn stood on the bow of a sailing sloop waiting for the men from Group Four to arrive. After more than a year of American-brokered negotiations between the warring factions in Northern Ireland, the chance for peace was in grave jeopardy. A drastic measure to save the Good Friday peace accords was to be set into motion this morning in a secret meeting of senior intelligence officers in the North Channel of the Irish Sea.

Blackburn, an Englishman from Lancashire, was a tall, gangly man, forty-three years old, narrow-waisted, with the thin, slightly bowed legs of a schoolboy. He had sideburns that would have been fashionable in another era, high cheekbones, and piercing blue eyes that were narrowed against the cold morning rain. It was the first of August, but in this remote part of Northern Ireland, summer had already begun to fade.

Blackburn shivered, but not from the cold. What was going to take place in the next several hours would set in motion an atrocity that the civilized world, and God, and he himself would forever condemn. There would be no forgiveness. But he was a part of it now; there was no turning back. And what was worse—maybe this was what made him shiver—he was eager for it to happen.

The alarm on his watch went off, he checked the time—seven—and just as the watch stopped beeping he looked out to the mouth of the harbor. In seconds he heard a motor off to the west. And then a corresponding sound to the south. He waited as the boats appeared. He checked his watch again: 7:03. *If nothing else, we are precise,* he thought.

The boats were purposely unmatched, one a Grumman 34 trawler like those used by cod fishermen out of Portsmouth, the other a Keisling Fury, twenty-five feet along the waterline from bow to stern, with a two-ton keel. He knew that there were two snipers on board each boat, fore and aft, armed with Italian-made Carlino long-range rifles, silencers screwed into the barrels, their scopes fitted with infrared filters for night vision. The skippers of both boats, men who would not be identifiable by either the British government or the IRA if they were caught, had been smuggled into the country three days earlier. They had traveled from Rome under false French passports, and Blackburn himself had sailed them here from Stranraer, Scotland. During the meeting this morning they would be in constant voice communication, via satellite, with Carl Landry in an unmarked office at the rear of a record shop on Bathe Street in Belfast. Landry was a good man, brought up through the ranks of counterespionage by the Thatcher administration. His obsessive personality made him perfect for this operation. He couldn't leave his office at the end of a day without straightening the Oriental rug in front of the tall windows that looked down on Bridge Street and lining up the pencils on his desk in ascending lengths. Sixteen years ago, Landry had been stationed at Dublin Castle, and on occasion

Blackburn had been his doubles partner in agency badminton tournaments. Those were the dark days of the Irish Troubles, when it seemed a passageway to peace would never be found.

Peace, Blackburn thought. He had imagined it luxuriously and hungered for it the way a man hungers for a woman's touch. And in the last year it was finally there, in the wind and in whispers. To Blackburn it felt like a vindication of everything he had believed in from the time when he had volunteered before his twentieth birthday for transfer from his first post in the ranks of the Royal Guard on Downing Street to the Special Services in Northern Ireland. *How odd,* he thought, *how terribly odd,* that now, in order to have the peace at last, he would betray the British government he honored and the army he had pledged himself to.

Watching the observation boats take their final positions, Blackburn plotted the course he would sail this morning. A westward tack to clear the mouth of the harbor and then a broad reach into the channel. In the harbor the water was as still as a mill pond, but half a mile from shore there was already a light chop, which he knew would build through the morning. Calm on the Irish Sea was virtually nonexistent, but the sloop he was skippering today had a high freeboard and plenty of weight underneath to hold her steady in rough seas. In Blackburn's mind she was as safe as a church pew, but the three officers joining him—Paul Norney, former head of Ways and Means for Internal Operations in Winchester, England; Nelson Orr, allocations specialist trained at the observatory in Portsmouth; and Timothy Nichols, communications chief of the Wolfe Council twenty-five years ago when headquarters were in Churchill's old war office—were landlocked fellows who'd never had salt water up their noses. If it got too rough, he would take down the mainsail and put up the storm jib to keep the boat from heeling over, and the three of them from throwing up.

After checking his watch once more, he fiddled with both halyards and loosened the bowline so that when the others arrived they could pull out of the harbor as quickly as possible. When he was satisfied, he stood up and, out of habit, tapped his shirt pocket with his right hand for the cigarettes he had quit smoking ten months earlier. It would have been nice, he thought, to light up in this dismal rain and take a deep drag.

He walked to the stern and glanced at the shore, where residents were beginning to appear in the village under dark umbrellas. He saw a red telephone booth, a white church steeple, and piles of granite blocks from an old dock that had washed out decades ago in a winter storm. He took in these details thoughtlessly, and then as he was searching for signs of anything unusual he noted a woman hanging wash on a line in the garden of a newly painted cottage. Her laundry consisted of small articles of clothing, small enough to be doll's clothes, Blackburn thought, and he assumed that she had a baby in her midst. A smile spread across his face. He had been with the British Army in Northern Ireland most of his adult life, and the sight of this young mother reminded him of his early days here when he had first been struck by the beauty of the Irish women. Not the physical beauty so much, though that was appreciable, but the brilliant light of their spirit and the music in their voices. Here was a population of women who held on to a desire that the contemporary world had declared unfashionable, the desire to have one baby after another and to spend their days at home with them. Something in this had appealed to Blackburn's sense of promise and order and filled him with hope.

And there was also the romantic readiness of the Irish women and the persistent optimism even in the face of hardship and loss. A young mother hanging out her family's laundry in the morning rain symbolized for the captain the patience that was so steadfast in this country's women.

He watched her until she had finished and disappeared inside the cottage. When he saw a light go on in an upstairs room, the baby's room perhaps, he told himself that it was the ordinary and plain acts in a life that convey the dignity of our intentions and mark our presence with holiness. This holiness was what he had poured his life into protecting; he had given himself so completely to the task that he had missed out on the chance for a wife and children of his own, but sometime after he turned forty he grimly accepted it as his destiny and began burying himself even deeper in the work to bring about a peaceful resolution to the conflict here.

Today it seemed to him that he had always known that never very far from the restorative routines and the comforting symmetry of mornings like this was the brutal violence that had destroyed those things in the thirty years of troubles in this country—pubs and cottages blown to bits, lights in children's rooms put out forever, dreams ripped apart by the awful killing.

Long after she had gone inside the cottage, Blackburn was still wishing he could have stood beside her for a moment and told her that soon he would meet the three men who had secretly helped him plot the last remaining way to save the fragile peace process. The last chance to bring Protestants and Catholics together, guaranteeing a new political order in the country, which would include representation by Unionists and Republicans. Here it is, he would tell her, a recompense to the Irish people for all they have suffered.

He allowed himself one last glance at the faintly lit room. Didn't that room hold all that a man needs in the world? Shelter from the cold. A woman to love. A child to be remembered by.

Unless the man is at war, he told himself.

That thought was lingering in his mind when the car arrived and the three men made their way down the dock toward the sloop. As part of the deception, their car was a junker and they themselves were camouflaged in the clothing of local fishermen. Blackburn was just beginning to settle into the steely demeanor he had always brought to covert operations when suddenly he saw the same demeanor in the three men making their way toward him. He felt a hollowness settle in his lungs. *This is going to happen,* he said to himself. *And I am going to let it happen.*

The stocky man in front was Paul Norney, whom Blackburn had known for eighteen years, ever since Army Intelligence had transferred him to Northern Ireland from Helsinki. Nelson Orr came next, limping on a right leg made of wood, compliments of the war in the Falklands. He and Blackburn had worked side by side for sixteen years, all of those years under the command of Timothy Nichols, who walked just behind, one hand holding a fishing cap on his head.

The three men were silent as they boarded the boat. No greetings were exchanged, not a word was spoken. When they were under sail, tacking across the harbor, the rain increased and Nichols's gold-rimmed glasses were fogged when he turned to Blackburn. "Have you got her all right, James?" he asked.

He took off his glasses, and James nodded.

"Well, then," Nichols said as he drew his lips tight. "As we all know, this will be the last meeting of Group Four. When we return to shore, no trace of Group Four shall remain in existence. Everything is in place, gentlemen."

Orr, the one quickest to anger, spoke next. "The bastards got Mountbatten on a sea just like this. Let's not forget that."

"That was a bad day," Paul Norney said gruffly.

Blackburn remembered it as well as anyone. August 27, 1979. The same afternoon the IRA set off bombs at Warren-point in County Down, killing eighteen British paratroopers. It was a turning point. Margaret Thatcher visited Warren-point the next day and immediately adopted a battle cry from the 1930s, declaring that the terrorists could be defeated by the army only if the politicians showed the necessary will to declare an all-out war against the IRA.

"Everything goes back to that day," Nichols said grimly. "We're out here today in the rain, bobbing around on this cork because of that day."

True, Blackburn thought, and somewhere in this world were the broken souls of those Irish citizens who lost loved ones on Bloody Sunday, when British paratroopers shot dead thirteen anti-internment marchers in Londonderry. He remembered the statement issued through his office after that massacre saying it was perfectly legal for the army to shoot anybody who obstructed or got in the way of the armed forces of the queen because getting in the way made you the queen's enemy. This went for children and the elderly, too, anyone who was simply too *slow* to get out of the way.

Jesus, somewhere along the line it had all gotten out of hand, Blackburn thought as he watched a gust of wind from the northwest rush across the water. He pushed the tiller away from him, bringing the bow of the boat into irons to spill the gust. When the mainsail began flapping, Orr looked up at it anxiously.

"Here's a pleasant thought, gentlemen," Orr said. "If we're caught, the loyalists and the IRA will argue over who gets to hang us."

Norney laughed without expression. "No. Downing Street will hand two of us to the Catholics and the other two to the Protestants. And that will be the end of it."

Blackburn, surprised to hear himself speaking, said, "If we're uncovered, there won't ever be an end to it."

A silence fell over all four men.

At last Nichols spoke, stating what was obvious to them, but what they were grateful, nonetheless, to have articulated. "If anything goes wrong, it's each man for himself. Our government will discredit us, our army will—"

He paused for several seconds, then resumed with his head bowed as if in prayer. "We have done disagreeable things in the past so that the people in this pitiable country"—now he looked up—"people like the woman I saw you watching this morning, James, aren't crushed in the end. We do these things in order to prevent the destruction of everything that is decent."

A strange silence fell over them; it seemed to possess a weight of its own, a weight that Blackburn could feel through the boat's rigging. There had been plenty of evil before, enough of it committed in the torture chamber of the prison at Long Kesh to send every British intelligence officer, bureaucrat, and politician to hell for a long time. And an equal sentence awaited the IRA, and the Unionist fanatics.

Blackburn looked at the deep lines on Nichols's face, and his thinning gray hair. He remembered that when Timothy was just starting out, he had possessed the looks of a movie star. Espionage work has one moral principle: It is justified by results. These results had aged many good men beyond their years. But there was something more about the four of them, and each of them knew this. Each man in his own way wanted an end to this war the way only a soldier could want it. No politician in London or Belfast or Dublin or Washington was willing to do what these men were going to do to finally stop the killing.

The meeting was over quickly, and when the sloop began heaving in the rising swells and two of the men started throwing up over the gunwales, Blackburn felt his own stomach turn, not because of the sea but because of the secret plan that the four of them were now pledged to. It was a murderously simple plan: The current peace negotiations must reach fulfillment at any cost, and everyone involved knew full well that they were doomed to fail in the end because the IRA would never agree to decommission its weapons. Unless, as Timothy Nichols had put it at their first meeting seven months ago when they formed Group Four, "we can succeed in turning the Irish people against their own army. We make the people hate the IRA and demand that they lay down their arms."

The one certain way to achieve this was clear: The next time a bomb warning was called in by the IRA, the warning would be reversed, sending the innocent citizens of this country *into* the bomb area rather than away from it. There was no way of calculating in advance when the next warning would come or how many people would be killed or maimed, but Orr had told the group that his informers believed the IRA was planning a large incident before the end of summer.

As Blackburn maneuvered the sloop back to her mooring,

he thought again of the woman hanging out her clothes. Maybe someday he would return here and meet her. There would be peace then, and he would tell her how it had been achieved. Unless, of course, she was in her grave by then, one of the innocents sacrificed in order to bring this to a close.

"And we're certain there's no other way?" he asked, though he knew the answer plainly enough.

Only silence again. All three men looked at him and then away. It was Nichols who had the last word. "We've set our course to do the thing that governments and politicians cannot do," he said. "I think it's best if we remind ourselves that in this bloody business you can never be less evil than the evil you oppose."

Chapter Two

Across the sea, on a shore three thousand miles from Northern Ireland, Nora Andrews was waking in the summer light outside Boston to the sound of her husband shaving. The water running. The sound of him tapping the razor gently against the marble sink. His handsome face in a shaving-cream beard. In their early days together she would call to him, "Good morning, Santa," and he would set his razor down and come back to bed, crawling under the covers at the bottom and slowly working his way up so that she would be breathless when he reached her face.

He turned and smiled faintly. "We have the Wainrights' party tonight, don't we?"

Nora heard the discouragement in his voice. "We can skip it if you want."

"Maybe you can," Steven said. "Not me." Meaning, of course, that the party was about work and politics.

"Jesus," he said, and in this single word Nora could hear the anger rising in him. "Do you know what it is that's killing everybody, Nora? It's the new death in America. The new American *death by loneliness*. Christ, it's awful."

She had married a morning person, and somewhere in their twenty-three years together they had stopped making love in the mornings, which had resulted in sermons, diatribes, pro-longed filibusters, soliloquies in the first light of day. She took a deep breath as Steven squared himself in the threshold of the bathroom. He wore a loose-fitting T-shirt with the call letters for their local public radio station emblazoned on the front. A year before, when he had begun gaining weight, taking on a thickness around his middle, he stopped sleeping shirtless. Self-conscious of the roll of fat, Nora knew.

This morning she motioned for him to come back to bed. She was thinking she might hold him before he went downstairs.

He walked toward her, but stopped short and sat down on the bed. She watched him looking around the room as if he'd misplaced something. "Here it is," he said. "We've got the blinking red light on the answering machine. And there, the cell phone recharging for the day. The fax machine. What else? E-mails waiting on the iMac. That's the illusion, Nora. The great numbing illusion that we're connected with each other, that we're close, that we're not alone. But we are. We're all so fucking proprietary about our space, our goddamned space, that we're—I don't know. We're so afraid that we'll be accused of something if we get close to anyone. They'll know too much about us, or they'll get us on a video camera or a tape recorder, or their brother will be a trial lawyer—hell, Nora, death by loneliness. The new American death."

She said the first thing that came into her mind. "Ireland. We should take a trip. Go back to Ireland. I was talking with Marge Anthony the other day. She and Mike took a trip together to Rome. She told me it was wonderful."

She didn't tell him the rest, how Marge had said that the time together, just the two of them, had reminded her *why* they had fallen in love in the first place.

Nora might have told Steven this, but he wasn't really listening. "What happens," he said with such resolve that she knew he had been thinking his way through this for some time, "what happens in this modern life is we ratchet everything up, we keep raising the ante. Christ, look at us. Two cars, two houses, all these empty rooms. I never really knew how we got into all of this. The children? When did we ever decide together to have two children?"

"You wanted children," she said softly.

"Yes, I guess I did. But no one ever told me how expensive they would be, and, oh, hell, Nora, you're not lonely like I am. You don't feel it the way I do. I can't breathe." He stood up then and marched into their walk-in closet.

THAT NIGHT AT THE WAINRIGHTS', Steven dragged one of his young golf partners across the living room to show Nora his new wristwatch. No ordinary watch, this was equipped with a beeper that sounded at the news of worldwide catastrophes and then spelled out the disaster in red electronic letters. "Only those disasters that influence the world's currency markets," the young man declared enthusiastically.

Steven glared at the watch, then turned to Nora and said, "See what I mean?"

There was something in his voice, something close to despair, but not despair. Resignation, she thought. A ghastly resignation.

LATER IN THE EVENING, Paul Livingstone, a vice president at the publishing house, like Steven, stood with her in the Wainrights' library, telling her that he had found the secret to happiness. It was a long story. He and his wife had recently had a baby, and he told Nora how he loved just spending whole days in bed, the three of them, taking naps when the baby fell asleep. "The first time through, Nora—I mean with Muriel—I was too busy earning money, too busy to get close to our three children. It was all just a blur. For fifteen years I was nothing more than a glorified money machine. Seriously, from the time we got married when I was twenty-six, until I turned forty, it was all just making money."

But this time it was different. This time his eyes were wide open. He had left his wife for a girl half her age so he could experience it all over again. The years of making babies and having babies, as he put it to Nora, those were the best years by far. He had met his new wife when she was working behind the counter at a 7-Eleven store. He went in one night for some Pepto-Bismol and there she was. The moment he laid eyes on her he knew that he would gladly trade away everything for the chance to start over with her.

"I'm forty-five now, Nora. Much too old to be practical any longer." He went on with mounting excitement, "I don't have any illusions about how long this will last into the future. I have this time with Carolyn, a few years, ten at best, and then I'll practically be ready for a nursing home and she'll go on and live another life. It doesn't matter. All I care about are the sweet individual moments with this girl and with our child. I can't ask for more than that."

SOON AFTER THAT PARTY Steven began drifting away from her. He began spending his weekends at the office. When he was home he spent his time lying in bed with his arm folded across his eyes and the curtains in the room drawn. And this was when the true loneliness set in for Nora. The loneliness Steven had spoken of. It was a loneliness with dimensions. Like rising water, it was sweeping away everything that was superficial, leaving her alone with only the profound and essential matters of life to consider. To dwell upon them with nothing to distract her. And she saw clearly how unfair the chronology of life was. Twenty or twenty-five years with one man, raising children, came to a definite end when the children moved away to step forward into their own lives. And it was true that the best part of those years was when they were making babies and having babies, those beginning years when everyone adored one another. A woman understands that those years end and cannot be re-created. She gets on with living the rest of her life even though she knows in some part of her that nothing will ever be as good, that there will be a certain emptiness to accommodate. She accepts this. But a man didn't have to accept it. He could discard the first woman, as Paul Livingstone had, find a girl who was barely a woman, and start over again, living these times more fully the second time around.

IT CAME ON HER SUDDENLY that summer, the determination that she would do *anything,* anything within her power, to prevent this from happening in her life. Their daughter, Sara, was twenty-two now, and their son, Jake, was twenty-one. There would have been a third child; she and Steven had tried for four years to conceive before they'd given up, and now she began talking with Steven about trying again. When he didn't oppose her, she took it to be a consent of some kind. Start over again with me, she seemed to be saying to him when she stood in front of him the first time wearing the hooker's clothes.

WELL, SHE THOUGHT NOW, *give me an A for effort. And forgive me for being so ignorant.* She was driving this morning from their home in the Boston suburb of Watertown to their summer place in Maine, where Steven was not expecting her to arrive for two more days. It was the twelfth of August, and from the moment she had awakened that morning, certain that she had to make this trip, she had begun to commit the day to memory, the cast of the pale gray light outside her bedroom window, the pitch of the whistling teakettle in her kitchen. It was peculiar, the way the day already seemed to belong to her *memory* of it rather than to itself, as if it were already finished and behind her, and she was traveling through it only to see things clearly enough so that when the time came to tell the story of this day she would know what to leave out.

FOR EXAMPLE, she might never tell anyone that when the morning traffic outside Boston slowed to a crawl, surrounding her in a sea of businessmen on car phones, she imagined briefly that they had picked up her scent like hound dogs and were calling their confederates from the office to tell them about this pitiful woman in the northbound lane who was traveling with two plane tickets to Ireland, a four-week-old fetus the size of a grain of rice in her belly, and a bag of lingerie from Victoria's Secret in the trunk of her car, fishnet panties and a bra with little diamond cutouts for her nipples.

"Hooker's clothes," Nora whispered to the man beside her in the Ford Expedition, sitting so high above her that he might have been a judge in a courtroom.

"Yes, Your Honor," she said as she smiled back at him, "I am guilty as charged."

She was forty-two years old, she had raised two lovely children and graduated from an Ivy League college herself, she had given immoderately to the poor and kept her figure and fought the zoning board when it would have been easier to walk away, and somehow she had become a woman whom no one touched and no one needed.

"The things we do for love," she sang softly when a truck loaded with canisters of propane rolled up alongside her. It had been a long summer. Steven had agreed to try for a third baby after she convinced him that there was no more exciting way for them to spend the twenty years before they became senior citizens than to lose themselves in a child's world, but it turned out that after twenty-three years of marriage, her husband had lost interest in her. She could have given up then.

The cashier at Victoria's Secret had looked at her with a kind of sorrowful expression in her eyes, Nora thought. But the hooker's clothes had worked. Which led to the grain of rice in her belly, the appointment tomorrow morning at the Women's Health Clinic in Wellesley, and the plane tickets to Ireland. "We're old enough to be grandparents," Steven had reminded her when the little kit from Stop and Go confirmed what Nora already knew. He left her on the white couch in their living room to go open a bottle of wine while she called to make the appointment.

He handed her a glass of Chardonnay and watched her push it away. "Come join me in Maine," he said.

After the abortion.

He'd left her alone to take care of this while he went to the summer place to repair the boathouse ramp.

Tomorrow, after it was over. Tomorrow, not today.

"But I have one more trick up my sleeve," Nora told the driver of a small red sports car that crept up behind the truck. She had been waiting at the door of Tour and Travel when Peter Rowe opened for business this morning, and she bought two plane tickets for Ireland before he had a chance to turn on all the lights in the office. While he was going over the itinerary, she pictured the whitewashed cottage on the Rathdrum road in County Wicklow where she and Steven had spent one winter with their babies when they were just starting out. In Ireland, she might be able to convince Steven to let her keep this baby.

AT LAST, when the traffic began to move, Nora thought of turning the car around and going back home. This time tomorrow it would be over. Maybe what kept her heading north to argue on behalf of the grain of rice in her belly was the memory of driving Steven to the Maine house for the first time, twenty-five years earlier on a gray morning like this one. They weren't engaged yet. As they traveled north that day along Route 128, creeping past the ruined textile plants and the splendid new electronics manufacturers, Steven had sat beside her on the front seat, content to have her drive. He seemed to read her mind when she wished that he would move closer to her; this happened often in the beginning, his anticipating her desire for him. Soon he was feeling inside her sweater, and then her laughter fell away to a slow sigh as he reached under her dress. He was testing her, she seemed to know this. He was carefully measuring her resistance to him, and when she felt him slide her dress up her thighs she almost drove them off the road. He was unrepentant, with that boarding-school grin of his. He leaned back in his seat, appraising her like a man looking at a meal spread out before him on a table.

WHERE DOES IT GO, she asked herself today. The closeness. *How is it squandered?* You hold a baby in the first days of its life and cannot conceive of a time when you will be separated by a storm of silence. A boy holds your face in his hands when he kisses you, as if he is worshiping you, and the years pass quietly while he becomes a man who just gets on top of you, and then doesn't touch you at all.

From the beginning she had surprised herself in her competence, her passion for Steven, what she allowed him to do to her in bed. He had told her that he would never tire of taking her to bed, and she had believed him.

She remembered how eager he had been to help her get back into shape after Sara was born. He had bought her a rowing machine, and each morning he wrote a workout schedule for her on the shirt cardboard that he left on the bedside table. *Should I have known then that I wasn't going to be good enough?*

What she knew now was that marriage was like the natural environment; marriage can take a direct hit like the Exxon disaster. It is the slow depletion that dooms it.

Chapter Three

The Maine house had belonged to her father. It was a house with many rooms that faced the ocean, a summer cottage with a sleeping porch whose ceiling was painted enamel blue. There were hand-carved half models of wooden sailboats on the fireplace mantels. Crushed scallop shells in the driveway. A handsome, sprawling place in a seaside colony of summer mansions where nannies had once arrived by train. They came from across the sea, contracted through a Salt Hill broker. There was a wreck one night in June 1913, less than a hundred yards from the harbor, and sixty-seven young Irish girls had drowned. All summer long their corpses washed up onto the beaches, colorless, yet somehow still pretty, undressed immigrant girls implanted in the wet sand in every imaginable position. Sometimes headfirst, with stiff legs sticking straight up in the air like starfish turned hard as wood in the sun.

At night from the east windows of her father's house she and Steven watched stars drowning on the bay and cargo ships blinking red and green in the distant shipping lanes along which they made their way toward the city, "as thoughtfully as someone turning the pages of a book," Steven once remarked. From the boathouse you could see all the way to Bar Harbor, its tourist carnival of gift shops and the mansions of J. P. Morgan and David Rockefeller all shimmering in the haze.

It was just after noon when she arrived. Before she turned into the half-circle driveway of crushed shells, Nora acknowledged for the first time that Steven wouldn't let her keep this baby. He would tell her again that their *children* were the ones who were supposed to have the babies now, not them. She was suddenly certain of his reaction. A closet full of hooker's clothes, the rest of their lives in the whitewashed cottage on the Rathdrum road wouldn't change his mind.

Still, she decided to park the car in town so her surprise would be complete. As she walked back to the cottage she allowed herself to imagine taking him to bed this afternoon, telling him about the tickets in bed. "Surprise," she heard herself saying.

Maybe love is over when it can no longer surprise us.

THE DOORS WERE OPEN and the windows were up, but she found the house empty. In the library a fire had burned down to a few coals in the hearth.

In the kitchen two fresh tomatoes sat on the windowsill above the sink. A bottle of wine was opened on the long oak table. She stood pouring herself a glass (one glass couldn't harm a fetus the size of a grain of rice, could it?), noticing that the leaves on the maple tree by the back porch had already begun to turn color. Then she heard geese honking overhead. She opened a window and craned her neck to watch them make and break apart their black chevron passing south across the sky, leaving a season behind in advance of winter. The urge to survive is instinctive, she thought. And what of the other urge, the urge to wait for winter and to go out in the snow and lie down and sleep? She thought of this, wondering what it would be like to lie down in the snow, to sleep through the long winter ahead, sleep curled up like a bear, in a kind of suspended animation, and then wake to find that this decision had been made for her and it was over, all of the unpleasantness of an abortion had fallen away, behind her.

She brought some wood in from the woodpile on the back porch and sat in front of the fire in the library for a while.

An hour passed. Then another, and he still hadn't returned. She climbed the front stairs, thinking she might take a nap. After a summer of humidity the varnish on the banister was sticky beneath her fingers. She skipped the twelfth step, the loose step with the squeak that had always betrayed her during her adolescent summers here when she stayed out beyond her father's curfew and snuck home late.

At the top of the stairs she glanced into the sewing room just across the landing and saw the Boston rocker where she had sat with her babies when they awoke during the night. It had belonged to her mother, and the sewing room had been her dressing room when Nora was a girl.

When she walked across the threshold she could feel her mother's presence. For a few moments Nora was a little girl again, standing at the window, watching her mother brush her hair as she rocked in the chair. She had loved her mother's long black hair. And watching her paint her nails. How calm she had always been, and how smooth was the world she created around her. As smooth as ice. Baking on Mondays. Laundry on Tuesdays. Grocery shopping Wednesday evenings. Party invitations finished weeks in advance. She was a woman who skated through life. She kept conversations light, and Nora could remember the times her mother had dispatched her from the dinner table for frowning. Her philosophy was that when bad things come along, you take them in stride, manage them, and get on with life. She had always moved through the world with such confidence and style that when Nora's father left her and she fell apart, Nora was devastated, as if her mother's loss had been her own. Today in the mirror in her mother's dressing room she caught a glimpse of herself. She studied the reflection of a woman who was once the center of someone's attention, a woman who had expected a certain kind of life. A sensible, ordered life.

In her mother's dressing room, sitting in the Boston rocker, Nora remembered how she used to sit here as a girl, her feet not reaching the floor, while her mother polished her tiny patent leather shoes, polished them as bright as glass as part of the Saturday night ritual, preparing her wardrobe for Sunday mass.

Now the chair groaned under her grown-up size, under the weight of a woman who could no longer be sure of her husband's love. She thought of herself as a brick heated in the oven and then carried upstairs to the old bed on winter nights. She had always been there for Steven, her body spreading its flame, radiating its heat for him. Her idea had always been to create a closeness in her family, an intimacy composed of love and loyalty, weaving them all together in such a way that the misfortune of one—a loss, a pain, a failure—would register in the others. But that idea had begun to fall away once her son and daughter had begun their own lives.

She looked around her mother's dressing room. As a young girl in this room Nora had begun preparing herself for love, the love of a boy. She had reached into the bureau drawers to touch the cool lace of her mother's underclothes. She had stood before the mirror trying to figure out how the lingerie went on and what it was made to conceal and to reveal. In the folds and creases of the garments was a trace of her mother's perfume, hidden like a secret.

Nora had tried to picture how these things looked on her mother. Now, as she waited for her husband to arrive, something came into her mind—a revelation. Those women standing at the glass counter in Victoria's Secret, laying down their credit cards as if they were credentials, must have known what she hadn't known until this moment: The things women do to entice men, the things she had done, they are less preparations for love than precautions against being left alone.

She was afraid of this, wasn't she? And hadn't she always been conscious of how much more she needed Steven than he needed her? He was one of those people who march straight ahead through life, leaving everything but their work unattended to. His things were always thrown all around the house, behind the couch, under the car seat. It was as if there was no irony in Neil Young's old song "A Man Needs a Maid." Nora had to be careful not to let herself think he was doing this on purpose, out of disrespect for her. He was the kind of man who could never say for certain where his Social Security card was. He needed a woman—or a wife, or a servant—to follow him around, to take care of the daily business of getting through the day without too many accidents. He needed to be cared for, like a child. Someone had to be there to remind him to change out of his suit and tie before he mowed the lawn. But, to his credit, he always had the power to transport their children when they were small. He had the most wonderful reading voice. He sat on the floor and they listened with their heads propped on his thighs, rapt, delighted by his imagination. At age nine, on Christmas morning, their daughter composed a play for him about a handsome prince who leaves his princess after warts grow on her forehead.

THE LOWERING SUN fell on Nora's knees. Its warmth was gone. A cold night approached, and she shivered as she got into the hooker's clothes. My uniform, she thought. And how strange life was; if she managed before this day was through to persuade Steven to keep this baby, who could say what the future would bring? This child might turn out one day to be a Supreme Court justice who owed her existence to a black silk bodice that weighed no more than a handful of butterflies.

She got down on her knees at her mother's window, folding her arms before her, resting them on the sill. She was a face at a window. Her breath clouded the pane of glass. She wrote his name there with her finger, the letters holding for an instant as if they would crystallize. Her husband's name. It was the only name she knew to write.

Chapter Four

When he came at last, he was not alone. And of all things, they arrived on bicycles. The girl was out in front, leading the way. Steven had the wicker picnic basket balanced on his handlebars. Their hands and their cheeks were marvelously colored from the sun and the cool air. The girl looked like a dancer, her shoulders were wonderfully erect. She was dressed like a schoolgirl, a pleated woolen skirt, quite short, and practical shoes, boots actually, laced only halfway up. And above the boots the red tops of woolen socks. Her body seemed small beneath a bulky sweater. She was one of those girls that men love to hold.

She could have passed for Nora's daughter. She did a cartwheel in the grass for him, her skirt turning inside out. Her legs were lean and strong. She landed on her bottom in the grass. Her hair caught the sun the way a painting catches light. There was an innocence about her, a vulnerability. She was someone to whom he could tell things for the first time. It would all be new to her.

He walked over to her and touched her and Nora shivered as if *she* were touched. He placed his hand on top of her head as if baptizing her. She took his hand and pulled him down onto her lap, between her pretty legs. He laid his head back, smiling. She seemed supple, weightless. She had a girl's grace.

A moment later she leaned forward and kissed him, folding at her waist like a puppet. Nora watched. It was like the magic trick she could never watch as a girl, the trick where someone lay down inside a trunk and the trunk was sawed in half. Her life was being sawed in half. It was no trick this time.

Nora's knees were red from kneeling at her mother's window. A Catholic woman's knees, she thought. Perhaps the church could have saved her from this. If she had managed to get Steven into church now and then, the fear might have rubbed off on him. God would be watching from a window of His own. He would hold Steven accountable.

These thoughts passed slowly through her mind. Was she to blame for this? Was there something more she should have done to satisfy him at home, to please him? Had she given herself away too easily?

She had only done her part, she had let no one down. When she was called, she had answered. She puzzled no one. She was unambiguous. When she was asked for—her lips, her breasts, her heart—she gave these away. She held nothing back. She gave the full gaze of her eyes, the whole heart of her thoughts. She hid nothing. She was a woman who uncovered herself, who let herself be touched and turned, and then awoke as if from a dream to find things suddenly out of place.

This was only the beginning—somehow she knew this. The beginning of uncertainty. With every shift of air from now on, a new thought, a new apprehension. The uncertainty reached ahead as far as she could see. What of this? What of that? What about the things she would have to leave behind? In her absence, her exile, who would care for these things that she had treasured? The trees she had planted in their yard, the plants in orange clay pots. The beach stones she lined her perennial garden with.

At the window she barely moved. There was no recourse for what was happening. The air outside the window seemed heavy as rocks. The man and the girl moved slowly in it, as if caught by its texture. He opened the wicker basket and took out a camera. He urged her into position, motioning her toward the swing that hung at one corner of the porch. She sat on the swing and looked off into the distance, smiling wistfully for his photograph. What can she be thinking? Nora wondered. She knows nothing about the houses over whose rooftops she's gazing. This is all foreign land to her. She couldn't know that in the hallways and rooms above her, a girl had passed through her youth expecting her life to turn out a certain way.

As she swung she disappeared beneath the porch roof. Nora could see only her legs from the knees down, then nothing, then her legs again. She watched Steven snap the picture. He took several shots while she performed for him. There was something boyish about her, Nora thought. She looked as if she might have grown up with brothers, arm-wrestling, sizing up their anatomy.

They moved toward the front door. They were holding hands. She was smiling tenderly, wanly. Then Steven hurried into the house, his hand still grasping hers.

NORA QUICKLY PULLED ON her jeans and sweater. Boards creaked, the rafters sighed, the rusty pipes cracked their joints. Nora waited for what seemed to be a long time, then went down the corridor. She reached their door, took the crystal knob in her hand, breathing heavily.

She paused as she heard the girl's voice: "When you die, will you leave me behind for your son? Who was the writer who left behind a mistress for his son? Was it Wells?"

"No," Steven said.

"Who, then?"

"I can't remember."

"It must have been Wells."

"No, it wasn't, it wasn't Wells, I'm sure of that."

"I know," the girl said triumphantly, "it was Dumas."

"Right! That's right," Steven blurted out.

Nora lingered in the darkening hallway, then on the stairs as she made her way down. In the empty foyer she paused on the checkered tiles and listened as their voices faded away above her.

She walked into town, where she had left her car. In a few more weeks the shopkeepers would flee south in advance of winter, their store windows boarded up with unpainted sheets of plywood. On the village green the bandstand would also be sheathed in wood, a dull green canvas hood tied around the face of the clock so that it stood like a man condemned to execution.

LATER IN THE TWILIGHT, as she drove home, many cars were backed up along Route 128. There was a popping noise in the air, at first faint and then louder as her car crept nearer the spot where a tractor trailer had overturned. Through the half-light the scene came into focus. There were hundreds of sheep wandering along the roadside. The state troopers were trying to herd them into a rest area. The ones that ran back out into the highway, threatening to cross the median into traffic coming up the other side, had to be shot. There were bleeding sheep all around her, their long noses in the gravel, some moaning as they died.

Chapter Five

She tried to steady her hands on the steering wheel to keep the car from drifting off the road, and to focus her mind upon what lay ahead of her. Ahead of the bedroom where she had slept during her girlhood summers, ahead of the sound of their voices on the other side of the door, and her own hand on the cut-glass doorknob that she couldn't turn. These things were part of her life now, they were real to her. *So, this is who I am,* she thought, *a woman with a grain of rice in my belly and a cheerleader in my bed.*

Night began to fall, and she knew she had to stop thinking that this was the night she had planned to try once more to overpower her husband's indifference so she might convince him that they could be close again, close enough to welcome a baby into the world. This no less a bribe than the plane tickets to Ireland.

A cheerleader in my bed . . . a grain of rice in my belly.

Foolish. She felt foolish.

If she couldn't drive these things out of her mind, then the car was going to spin around on its own and she was going to find herself driving back to Maine, where, in the moonlight, she would either end up on her knees begging Steven to work things out or set fire to her father's house.

She turned on the interior light of the car and held out her right hand. She watched it shaking until a car blared its horn as it flew past her. She pushed down hard on the accelerator. And then harder, until it was flat against the floor and she had caught up to the passing car. She wanted to run right up the back of this car that had blown its horn at her, up the back and over the roof and down the windshield, screaming at the driver the whole time.

It came to her then, before she could move her foot from the gas pedal to the brake: Without Steven she wouldn't know what to do next.

In the glare of her headlights she could see the driver of the car in front of her turning his head to look back at her.

"When I get home," she said to him, "I'll do my laps at the YWCA. I'll stop at Emery's Market for some Ben and Jerry's ice cream. Cherry Garcia, which Steven doesn't like."

Just saying these words calmed her.

She eased her foot off the gas pedal. She pushed her hair back from her face and pictured herself walking through the empty house, climbing the front stairs to her bedroom, taking her bathing suit from the drawer, grabbing a towel from the bathroom. It should be easy, back down to the car, a two-mile drive to the Y. But there were the family photographs on the wall along the staircase. She tried again and again in her mind just to get into the house and out, into her bathing suit and into the pool, where the rhythm of her laps would distract her until she was tired enough to sleep, but it was no good. And so, coming into Watertown, she took the exit off Route 128 south, and pulled into the parking lot at Wal-Mart because she knew she would not be recognized there, no one from her circle of friends shopped there. And because she knew that

Steven would be appalled. He had declared a family prohibition against the store from the day it opened its doors for business. She could see him shaving and telling her how the same Stanley fifty-foot carpenter's tape measure cost exactly twice as much at the local hardware store owned by Felix Kaye, but if people bought enough tape measures at Wal-Mart it was only a matter of time before the local hardware store vanished. "There's a whole subculture of people in this country living from paycheck to paycheck who can only afford to buy crap, Nora. So we get Wal-Fart, a store full of crap for them to buy."

Heaven help his cheerleader if he ever caught her shopping there.

Or perhaps the cheerleader would call the shots. Maybe she was such a thrill to him that he would let her shop wherever she pleased. Maybe she would buy him a bathrobe at Wal-Mart and it would hang on the brass hook inside the bathroom door with its Wal-Mart tag displayed for the world to see.

Something told Nora to mark where she was parked so that she could find the car when she came out of the store. A straight line from the last row of yellow-and-green sit-down lawn mowers on sale outside.

The parking lot was full. Maybe it was always full. She took note of the faces of the people walking to and from their cars. "Dazed" was the word that best described them, a little weary, as if they had spent a long day walking among the exhibits at a convention of shoppers. Just ahead of her, the last people before the glass doors opened to her were an elderly couple, husband and wife, the two of them moving the shopping cart together, husband in back pushing, wife in front pulling, like exhausted soldiers moving artillery into position. The only item in the cart was a big white square package of diapers.

Nora caught herself smiling at them, thinking how nice it was that these two people were taking care of their grandchildren, changing diapers again after so many years, happy to be back inside the busy orbit of little children. Nora kept smiling at them, smiling at the tops of their heads until she saw that the diapers were for *them*. On the package she could see the smiling face of a white-haired woman and the word "Depends" printed in a jaunty script.

Steven would have laughed at her for this. For the way she assigned romance to everything, rather than acknowledging the cold reality that ran through life, just below the surface.

And now he had a cheerleader to change his diapers when the time came. If she stayed around for the final act.

Nora turned and watched the elderly couple walking out into the vast parking lot, which was now ablaze with lights as bright as searchlights in a prison yard.

THE WOMEN'S BATHING SUITS were the colors of painted Easter eggs. Long rows of skimpy two-piece and backless numbers. Bathing *costumes* is what her English neighbor called them. Costumes, indeed. All she was looking for was a black one-piece without the thighs cut up too high or the neckline too low, like the one she had in the bottom drawer of her bureau in the bedroom. In the bedroom where Steven had given a speech one morning about the death of passion. She remembered this now, a sign she had failed to interpret at the time. He had told her that the reason 50 percent of all marriages ended in divorce was that women, once they have their babies, are no longer interested in attracting a man. In fact, they go about the solemn business of trying to make themselves physically *unexciting* to men. He recalled how, in the first few years of their marriage, Nora eagerly spent whole weekends in just panties and one of his Brooks Brothers shirts, and he would come up to her anywhere in the house, lifting her onto the kitchen counter, leaning her against the refrigerator. He remembered vivid details of what he numbered in the thousands of encounters like this, when Nora hungered for him to take her to bed. Now, he claimed, she had become matronly. (A word that Nora looked up in the dictionary to grasp its precise meaning.) The trouble, according to Steven, was that men never changed at all; they went about constantly searching for the barefoot girl in panties and a man's dress shirt whom they had fallen in love with so long before.

She bowed her head over the bathing suits and took a deep breath. It all came back to her now. She had seen a kind of hard truth in what he was saying. And she had had this truth in mind when she went to Victoria's Secret thinking maybe she *could* do something to bring them closer. And maybe she would get her third baby in the bargain. He might agree to it after all. She imagined him gazing at her in her pregnancy as he once had, thrilled by the sweet curves of her breasts when they filled with milk.

A third child, she thought now. The joy of it. A new friend in the world to walk beside her when she grew old. To keep her company after her husband left her for someone who promised never to become *matronly.*

An entire rack of black bathing suits, but not a single one that was plain enough. Plain enough for what? To conceal rather than reveal.

She stepped up to a mirror. She grabbed a handful of hair and held it close to the glass, where it looked more silver than black.

Count to a hundred and I'll be an old lady.

The cheerleader would be fixing Steven his supper by now. He would be sitting at the kitchen table watching her. She would be standing at the counter in just her panties and bra, knowing that he was watching, sizing her up, just biding his time until he could take her into his arms again. This lovely girl, barefoot in the kitchen where Nora's mother had taught her how to roll out piecrust. The cheerleader in her underwear. Steven would be pleased with himself. And thankful. Yes, thankful. He was a man who said his prayers at night before he fell asleep, thanking God for the good things that came his way. For healthy children, and for his personal possessions and achievements. For things he could lay his hands on. The cheerleader's breasts, each one as heavy as an apple in his hands. The nipples faintly rough against his thumbs. When he put his lips on them he would feel the cheerleader's breath quicken.

Oh, God. Maybe what Nora wanted to wear was not a bathing suit at all but a long black robe. A nun's habit. A graduation gown. Congratulations, my dear, you have graduated to the ranks of *matronly* women.

Chapter Six

In the locker room at the YWCA she had just opened the Wal-Mart bag and taken out the black leotard, the white bathing cap, and the Mountain Dew beach towel and laid them on the varnished bench when, as God would have it, two pregnant women came in. Their bellies huge, like they were going to pop at any moment, they moved as though they were pushing wheelbarrows.

To her surprise they made her feel self-conscious. Here she was, alone, the Mountain Dew beach towel, the Wal-Mart bag with its big yellow smiley face. Didn't she appear to be a card-carrying member of that army of suspicious-looking strangers that these mothers would make their toddlers promise never to accept a ride from?

She began trying to win their approval and trust by asking them their due dates and if they knew whether they were having a boy or a girl. In her nervousness she began talking about her own deliveries like an old veteran recounting tales of combat. Like war, labor had its specific vocabulary, and she easily found the old words—the water breaking, five centimeters of dilation—as if she had brought her own babies into the world just yesterday.

Swept away by the wonderful connection she felt to these pregnant women, Nora felt no reluctance at passing along some advice. "The most wonderful thing is how everything slows down. The whole world seems to stop for a newborn baby. Until the baby learns to walk, the best thing you can do, so that you never forget what a miracle it is, is learn to live in the present. That's where a baby lives. And each moment is a gift."

"That's very sweet," one of the women told her.

Nora couldn't help going on. "The thing that I miss is how compressed life felt then. I mean, being enclosed within a baby's world, being so completely needed, it's . . . well, there's nothing else in life that matches that feeling. You never have to wonder if what you're doing is important. I mean, you take a whole morning for an outing to the library. It's the way we're probably meant to live our lives. Thoughtfully and slowly."

Suddenly one of the women interrupted her. "You must have stayed home with yours, then."

"Oh, yes," Nora replied.

The women looked knowingly at each other, then told Nora that they didn't have that luxury. They worked all day, nine or ten hours a day, often six days a week, and planned to keep their babies up until ten or eleven o'clock at night so they could spend a few quality hours together each day.

Of course it dawned on Nora then, exactly how foolish she must seem to these modern women. What planet did she inhabit anyway?

And then she saw that they were indeed looking at her as if she had come from outer space. Both of them were staring at her and trying not to look at her at the same time. It took a few more seconds before Nora realized that she had taken off her sweater and pants and was standing before them in her hooker's clothes.

She quickly wrapped the beach towel around her, sat down,

and began to dress. They were some distance from her when she dared to look up again. She watched them waddle toward the door of the pool. How old were they, she wondered. Early thirties? Maybe they were twelve years younger than she. When you thought about the vast sweep of time, a dozen years was only a heartbeat. But in this world where things were changing so quickly that there was now a new generation every five years, the passage of time could cut you off from those just a few years behind you. To them the world where a mother spent a whole morning taking her child to the library belonged to some long-forgotten civilization. Sitting on the locker room bench, Nora wondered if this made it easier at the end; maybe we finally let go of life in our old age because the world around us has become unrecognizable.

She began to feel exhausted, too tired even to put her swimsuit on. She looked down at her bare legs. They were from her mother's side. Irish legs, the skin as white as paper all winter long and then, after a summer day on the beach, the same color exactly as those hot dogs injected with red dye number two. She shook her head, sighed hopelessly, and then smiled as she remembered how she and her best friend in college, also an Irish girl, had once created a sorority skit that made fun of their Irish legs. They played the roles of two college graduates entering the job market for the first time and presenting themselves as ideally suited for a job that required them to stand behind a counter. Desk clerks in a hotel. Ticket vendors at a movie theater. *We're looking for high-paying counter work.*

It was funny to Nora, but never really that funny. She always had the feeling that her friend was better equipped than she to skate with equanimity across her deficiencies, if you could call them that. It wasn't that Nora's father, who had told her for four years of high school that if she lost ten pounds off her butt she would be a knockout, or that her two dear brothers, one who called her Fatso for her bottom and the other who called her Flatso for her chest, had sent her to a psychiatrist's office or into the bathroom to throw up her dinner. She had the psychic stamina to take the criticism in stride, but what she lacked was the resignation to laugh at herself and at the absurdity of her body's disintegration. She remembered a family Thanksgiving where her eight-year-old niece had asked her why her breasts weren't "perky" like her sixteen-year-old cousin's.

Perky. Standing in the empty locker room, she said this word out loud and then laughed at the sound of it. It might have been the silence after her laughter, the stark emptiness of the silence that made her start to cry.

Chapter Seven

Without consciously taking a step, Nora was back on the highway, driving south again, with her bathing suit and cap and the ridiculous beach towel on the front seat beside her. Outside the passenger's side window a three-quarter moon was sailing over the open fields and the shopping malls, as if it were racing her. She glanced at it and pushed down on the gas pedal until it slipped slightly behind her. Then she let up on the gas and watched the moon catch up. She felt herself drifting away into the hum and the motion of the car. It was as if she were falling into a trance. She thought of her daughter, Sara, out of college now and working at a summer stock theater on the Cape. And her son, Jake, running his coffeehouse in San Francisco. The last conversation she'd had with Steven was about Jake. She was trying to remember how that conversation had ended when out of nowhere came the murderous blast of a truck's horn. She looked into a flash of blinding light in the rearview mirror and then shrank down in the seat as the truck charged past her with its engine groaning. The driver, just a blurred figure wearing a baseball cap, shook his fist in the dimly lit cab.

Jesus, God, she thought in the quieting darkness, *is this what my new life will be like—danger at every turn?*

She pulled off at the next exit and came to a stop beside a Dumpster in a Dunkin' Donuts parking lot. When she turned off the engine, there was that same empty silence again, as if someone had closed a heavy door between her and the rest of the world.

Her hands were shaking when she walked up to the counter. There was only one girl on duty, a blonde maybe twenty years old, with a gold ring through her nose and the straps of her bra falling off her shoulders. She glanced at Nora, then flirted for a moment longer with a boy at the drive-through window before she walked to the counter. When she licked her finger to wipe a smudge off the glass counter Nora saw that she had another gold ring through the tip of her tongue.

"I was almost killed on the highway," Nora said just above a whisper.

"Did you say honey-dipped?" the girl asked as she turned to the slanted shelves of doughnuts.

Nora bought a cup of coffee and burned her fingers and the palm of her hand carrying it back to the car.

She sat there for a few minutes, motionless, with her head bowed. In the heat of this August evening she felt her thighs sticking to the car seat.

From the parking lot she watched the cashier for a bit longer while she continued her conversation with the boy at the drive-through window. At last the cashier raised herself across the counter to kiss him. Nora felt a little guilty for watching. It was a long kiss and Nora leaned over the steering wheel to see more clearly. In their eagerness the girl climbed up onto the stainless-steel counter and the boy seemed to be trying to pull her across the counter and the space that separated them, out the square drive-through window and in through the window of his car. Nora had not been kissed like that in more than twenty years. Even in her hooker's clothes. Kissing had vanished somewhere along the way.

At last the boy released the girl. Nora felt a terrible emptiness when he gunned the engine and sped away.

THEN SHE WAS DRIVING AGAIN, driving faster with the coffee running through her like an electrical charge. She felt her home falling away somewhere behind her as she passed the tractor trailers heading south. She imagined their metal containers filled with clothing from China, shoes and coats sewn together in sheet-metal warehouses in that country that would one day take over the world, and this made her feel small. Except for Ireland, she had never really gone anywhere. The truth was she didn't sleep well in strange beds, and she wondered now if the events of this day would make her even more dependent upon things that felt familiar to her. Perhaps when she drove home she would lock the doors and pull the curtains and die from starvation once she had eaten all the food in the refrigerator and the pantry. Too frightened to go outside her house.

She was taking an inventory of the pantry shelves when she drove beneath the sign for Cape Cod.

In half an hour, when she came upon the Bourne Bridge, she knew exactly where she wanted to go. Maybe she had known this back in Maine, known it the moment she had seen Steven coming around the corner with the girl.

She took her foot off the gas pedal and felt the weight of the car pulling against her. She slowed down near the center of the bridge and waited for a car to pass, then rolled her window down. There were stars above her beyond the skeleton of green steel. She saw where the girders were welded together, and she felt the iron frame of the bridge swaying gently in the wind as it had the first time she went to Cape Cod with Steven. It had been a night journey then as well, and she remembered him rolling down the car window and the scent of the sea air rushing in. She began to recall details from that night. He had asked her to marry him on a beach near Hyannis, and in her memory this had overshadowed the other moments that were now returning to her. For one, he had been playing Bob Dylan tapes all the way down from Maine, where he had picked her up at her parents' summer place. The big clumsy eight-track tapes that seemed like an electronic miracle in 1975. She lay across the front seat, her head in his lap, looking up at his handsome face as he drove. Lights from oncoming cars flashed on his glasses. *I was all right until I fell in love with you,* he sang to her. He had told her then that boys had their hearts broken again and again, first by girls who flew away and then by women who grew tired of them. She must have loved this about him—his humility, the way he seemed to understand the phases of love. He warned her that he was not going to be easy to please. "You've heard of those old widows being interviewed after their famous husbands die and they say occasionally, 'He was a demanding lover.' I'm going to be that way to the end of my life. I'm always going to need you to love me as passionately as you do right now. And to believe in me this way."

With the scent of the ocean, and the wistful lyrics of Dylan's music, it had seemed that this would be a cinch. Nothing would change her love for this boy or his love for her.

Tonight she listened to her tires on the steel planks of the bridge. She felt the wind throw her hair back. Below her, ships of all sizes made their way through the dark water. That trip to Cape Cod with Steven. Hadn't she known by then that she would give herself away to him? Her plans for graduate school. Her old dream of traveling across Europe with friends. On the bridge tonight she wondered for the first time in her life if she had begun giving these things away, along with herself, long before Steven asked for them. Wasn't it her mother's breakdown after the divorce that had sent Nora rushing into the embrace of convention? Something must have happened to her the first time she awoke in the night to the sound of her mother weeping. That was the first and, until today, the only storm she had ever faced in her life. It might have made her determined to hold on to herself, to hide herself away, to swear off marriage and children, to clear her own path through the world. But it had the opposite effect. *I will love a man better. I will love him more. And I will never be cast out into darkness.*

When she came to the traffic circle she veered to the right on Route 6-A, toward Hyannis. Would the world take note of this and call her a lunatic? That on the same day when she watched her husband take another woman in his arms, she returned to the place where he had asked her to marry him?

SHE DROVE FOR MAYBE HALF AN HOUR to the Post Road turnoff. She heard seagulls crying overhead when she slowed the car down, and off a little ways the sound of the breakers pounding the sand. It was not difficult to remember her desire for Steven when they had come here the first time. Her sweaty palms, her racing heart. She felt the breath rush out of her when he pressed against her. And when he rode her sundress up her thighs and she felt his hands on her skin, there was that brief moment when the meaning of life seemed clear and she was certain of her destiny for the first time, a destiny that established her in a world apart from her mother's shattered world. Tonight, for the first time, she acknowledged that more than loving Steven, she might have loved the *idea* of being in love with him.

Tonight the waves were tall rollers coming at her out of the darkness, lit by the moonlight only when their tops broke off into white foam. The ground vibrated under their concussion. She felt the spray on her face and arms. She tried to concentrate on remembering what she had loved about Steven that night when she answered, "Yes, I will marry you." Suddenly it was important to her to remember this. She loved his irreverence for the ruling class that she had grown up in, the summer aristocracy that measured a person's worth by achievements and possessions. Taking Steven's hand, allowing him to push inside her that night on this beach, was her way of throwing away everything in her parents' world. It was her declaration of independence. Odd that surrender should have felt like independence.

While she stood there, trying to get a clear picture of what she had wanted then and what she had found in Steven, she watched the black water wash over the sand at her feet and then recede. It surprised her that her recollections were grounded only in the physical memory of him, the way his body fit against hers. The anticipation of his touch.

The wind picked up, blowing spray from the tops of the waves against her skin. She felt the shore shudder beneath her feet and some new desire rise up inside her. Maybe it was nothing more than the desire to gain some courage. The courage to be alone and unafraid.

It took her only a moment to decide that this was the time

to begin. She turned her back to the ocean and walked to the car. Inside, she undressed. Rather than putting the Wal-Mart bathing suit on, she stayed in the hooker's clothes. *Let them find my body and think I'm a whore from the city,* she said to herself.

She was aware that swimming in the ocean at night, alone, might be the first crazy thing she had ever done in her adult life. She considered the possibility that this might become the first in a long list of crazy acts she would commit and that people who had always known her to be a careful woman would now say that she had gone off the deep end when she learned of her husband's affair.

Steven would get the credit for her craziness.

This thought made her angry enough to slam the car door behind her as she made her way back down the beach with the Mountain Dew towel draped over her shoulders like a cape. Against the soles of her bare feet the sand felt cold, damp and hard, exactly like a basement floor. *She lost her husband and she went completely crazy,* is what she heard inside her head underneath the crash and boom of breaking waves. When she raised her head, she could see in the moonlight that the waves were taller than she. It was an angry, raging sea that she was facing. She was one of those people for whom heated hotel pools are never warm enough; from the time she was a girl she always went into the water like a coward—one toe, then two toes. But tonight she knew that if she was actually going to do this, she had to charge straight into the sea before her fear could overtake her. She let go of the towel and the wind ripped it from her shoulders. She looked up at the moon and briefly thought of saying a prayer, The Lord Is My Shepherd, maybe. Instead, with her right hand she made the sign of the cross, then plunged into the sea. Yes! Like a soldier, she thought.

Bayonet shining in the moonlight! *She saw her husband with his mistress and she went completely crazy!*

The first wave knocked Nora off her feet the instant it struck her. She landed first on her bottom and then the next wave drove her flat onto her back. She felt a burning, stinging sensation where her back scraped against the clattering pebbles and broken shells. She held her breath, rolling onto her belly and then up onto her knees. When she stood up she caught sight of another wave rising above her. This time she quickly laid herself on the bottom so the wave broke above her, thunderously but harmlessly. It was a small, simple act, but she performed it competently, and this was enough to send a rush of adrenaline through her.

She began swimming beneath the waves straight out from the shore, taking measured, powerful strokes that carried her across the ocean floor, through the twisting crosscurrents of the sea and the turmoil of this long day. She went as far as each breath would take her, then surfaced quickly before diving back down again. Finally she sensed that the sea had flattened and that she was out well beyond the breakers. When she came up and opened her eyes, the first thing she saw was the Big Dipper, each star shining brightly as if it had just been polished. The sequins on her bra shone in the moonlight. It was strange, the feeling that came over her then. The feeling that she had swum a long long distance, back across time, before the start of her present life with her husband, back to the narrow space in time just after she had left her mother's broken life and just before she had entered Steven's. It was the only part of her past that belonged to her. Out on the dark ocean, she floated on her back, looking up at the stars as she tried to recall that time. Her dormitory room in Prospect Hall, the red Ford Mustang her roommate drove. The antiwar march through Philadelphia. The steps of the college library covered with autumn leaves.

Lying on her back in the rolling sea, she could feel the salt drying on her forehead. When she closed her eyes to the stars, a picture of the whitewashed cottage on the Rathdrum road in County Wicklow emerged from her memory. Suddenly the sea grew still around her, and the whitewashed cottage and the road smelling of roses seemed to belong not to her past but to her future. So what if the tickets to Ireland had been no more than a bribe? So what? She thought that if she could walk that road alone in a country where no one knew her name she would figure out what to do next. She thought of this and, for the moment, of nothing else.

Chapter Eight

Here is Ireland, Nora thought when she boarded the plane—nuns in their summer habits and stewardesses with freckled arms.

The moment the plane took off Nora fell asleep. She slept until dinner was served, and then fell asleep again after eating everything on her tray. Sometime in the night a snoring nun awakened her. She turned and stared at her across the empty seat meant for Steven. Her head was back and her mouth was open. Her hands were folded with a rosary in her lap. The skin on her face looked new, like an infant's. Not one wrinkle. Her reward for a life without a husband and children, Nora thought. It is romantic love that scars us, cuts us open, tears our hair out.

She thought of what she had in common with this woman. Like a mother who creates safe little worlds for her children, the nun created little worlds as well, worlds of ritual and mystery to spare us from the crushing betrayals and the random cruelties of the real world. The consolation is ours for the taking; all we have to do is the hardest thing of all to do—we have to believe like little children, cast away all that we know by our reason to be true, close our eyes to the overwhelming evidence. *My husband still loves me. I just have to try harder to please him. I must create a world for him, a world of lingerie from Victoria's Secret, romantic dinners, a kitchen full of steaks and chops.*

Nora watched the nun and wondered what her sins were. Maybe she had none. Maybe she never took change from her mother's purse when she was a little girl, or told a lie so she could stay out late with her friends when she was a teenager.

When the airplane bumped through some turbulent air, the nun's eyeglasses slid down her nose and landed on her lap. She stopped snoring for a second or two, then started again, her chest rising and falling so peacefully that Nora imagined laying her head on her breasts and telling her every sin she had ever committed, from the time she was six years old and stole half of Ellen O'Malley's peanut-butter-and-jelly sandwich from her lunch box. How restful it would be, Nora thought, to lay her head there and whisper her confession. But when she tried to compose a list of sins, her mind went blank. Serious sins were what she was trying to recall, and there weren't any. No affairs, no horrendous lies or grand deceptions, no devious scheming. She wondered what this said about her, and what it meant that she had become another person in the world who believes in good things and lives life the best she can and then gets up one morning to find that nothing is the way she always thought it was.

When the movie started, Nora walked to a bathroom in the rear of the plane. She locked the door and a light went on above the mirror. She leaned over the sink and looked at her reflection in the glass. There were tiny beads of sweat on her forehead. She had always known that her beauty was varied and conditional. In the wrong clothes or the wrong light it vanished. But catch her in the rain when her hair curled naturally, and she was pretty. From her teenage years she had thought of herself as possessing the prettiness of a camp counselor, pretty enough for a convenient summer romance, but then easy to forget. Plain. Average. She had to work at it a little too hard, blush on her cheeks, mascara on her eyelashes. A nicely shaped body but not a head-turner. Still, pretty enough to bring the world close to her and to elicit a kind of heat from most men.

She pulled away from the mirror, leaning back against the padded plastic wall. *I am going to know what to do when I get to Ireland,* she said to herself. *If I had canceled this trip, the cheerleader would have won. This is my trip. This is my decision.* She wondered what it was going to be like to be old, beyond vanity. She wanted to become one of those women who simply didn't care anymore, who were finally able to do, and say, and *look* however they pleased. A stocking sagging below her knee. Watching old movies on TV with a bowl of popcorn between her thighs. Not giving a damn.

She wondered, if she kept this baby, what she would tell this new child about love one day, how love must take you in, it must break your arms, your back.

WHEN SHE STEPPED OUT of the bathroom she found the golfers gathered there in the back of the plane. Men in their fifties, laughing like little boys. A convention of potbellies. They had left their wives at home. She noticed the one who didn't have a drink in his hand. She watched as he turned away from the others and bent down low so he could look out the window at the darkness. *That's me,* Nora thought. Always keeping watch, never letting go completely, afraid the plane will go down. Afraid her children will slip behind in school. Afraid of someone dropping by and finding her kitchen in a

mess. She remembered hitchhiking in a blizzard from Philadelphia to Amherst College in her sophomore year to see
Joan Baez in concert. Two years later she had become a careful person. After her mother's disintegration. Careful. Cautious. Afraid to be cut off from the life we all agree is to be so
earnestly desired. And then even more careful, more cautious
once the babies arrived? She had lost herself in her children,
she would have to admit that, though she had not really been
aware of it while it was happening. It happened by small
degrees, like the way we lose our youth.

While she was still looking at him, the man at the window
turned, smiled at her, looked away. But when their eyes met
again Nora could see a sadness in his face, as if he had just discovered while looking out the plane's window how small he
was in the black sea of night. All her life she had dwelled on
what was good and positive. What was broken in the world,
and in those around her, fell beneath her comprehension. It
was not that she didn't care about the struggles some people
were up against; it was just that she was moving forward in
the furious progression of her life, always forward as effort-
lessly as if she were skating across time, her arms out at her
sides, the wind behind her.

SHE HAD BEEN ASLEEP for just a little while when she was
awakened by some sort of disturbance up ahead of her. One of
the golfers had brought the nun to his row of seats. She was on
her knees in the aisle, holding someone's hand in hers. Two
more of the golfers stood just behind her, looking down and
then helping the nun to her feet while she still clung to the
hand. On her face there was a tender expression that might
have been meant to console a child.

It was the golfer with the sad look in his eyes, the one who had been peering out the dark window. He stood up slowly. The nun released him into the embrace of his friends, who walked him carefully to the rear of the plane. Nora looked back and saw them helping him into the bathroom.

When the nun returned to her seat Nora smiled at her and asked, "Is he going to be all right?"

"Cancer," she said. "His friends are taking him golfing in Ireland. To cheer him up, I suppose. Isn't it remarkable how you can look at men at a certain age and see exactly how they looked when they were little boys?"

A wistful smile fell on the nun's face.

It was later, just before the first blades of sunlight struck the plane, when Nora followed the golfer to the back of the plane. Because it was so unlike the woman she had become, she forced herself to say hello to him. He stopped and looked at her before he opened the door to one of the bathrooms. She put her hand out for him to shake. And he took it as he looked into her eyes.

This is my new life, Nora said to herself. *This is who I will become now.* "The sister told me," she said to him.

He smiled at her and took something from his shirt pocket, cupping it in the palm of his hand and then showing it to her. It was a joint. "It's the only thing that works," he said. He pushed open the bathroom door and invited her to join him.

She was thinking that maybe it is possible to make yourself into a different person in one minute by doing the unexpected. Yes, she had been a girl who was going to go somewhere—the Peace Corps, Africa. Then on to medical school; she had the grades. But the divorce made her frightened, washed away her resolve, her internal courage. She fell into Steven's arms, then gave herself away completely.

They were pressed together in the tiny compartment. He

bolted the door. Because she was nervous she began at once to talk about her children, telling him a story about the day she and her husband dropped their son off at college.

"When we got back home, I went up to Jake's room and found that he had cleaned out all his junk. Everything was in trash bags at the foot of his bed. For some reason I went through all of it, and I found this little wooden box that I'd given him years before. It was just a little box. When I opened it I saw that all of Jake's baby teeth were inside. I'd saved the teeth and now he was throwing them away."

"You kept them," he said.

"I couldn't help it," she said.

She noticed that he was wearing a prism on a silver chain around his neck, and she recalled reading somewhere that some people believed these had healing qualities.

She felt remarkably calm in the presence of this stranger, until he began taking apart the smoke detector and telling her that he had become an expert at disassembling them. Suddenly he gave off a dangerous glow. She reached for the door handle, telling him that she had to go. "I'm sorry," she said. "I hope that—"

"What? That things turn out okay?" He sort of sneered at her. Then he said he was sorry.

A few minutes later when he came down the aisle from the bathroom he stopped and sat down in Steven's seat. They shook hands like golfing buddies. He began speaking right away. He said, "People say that at the end you regret every chance you had to touch someone but didn't."

He waited, looking into her eyes, then away.

"There was this plane crash years ago," he said. "A Japanese airline. The people were told that they were going to crash.

They had, like, twelve minutes to prepare. When they went through the wreckage they found two bodies in every bathroom. Men and women making love."

Should I believe this? Is this what I should do, something unpredictable, something for myself? Something I might have done long ago.

Despite the hissing stream of cold air, he was very hot. She watched beads of sweat appear on his forehead.

She asked him how he had kept himself from giving up.

He thought a moment, then said, "I think I'm just too selfish to believe the world will ever go on without me. But do you want to know what's strange? I was always behind all my life. Behind the bills, I mean. I could never earn enough money. I think a lot about finally being set free from that rat race. No more sweating over money."

She told him she was going to have a baby.

He looked into her eyes. "Lucky you," he said.

"Lucky me," she said.

"When will this baby be born?"

"In the spring," she said.

He started to say something, but then he bowed his head. *If I were braver I would run away with you,* Nora was thinking. *Because I'm lonely and because my husband betrayed me and because I'm on my own for the first time since I was in college, and because you seem to want me.*

Of course she knew that this was crazy. But all around her in the metal compartment there was evidence of craziness, sheer lunacy in the physical universe—people were sleeping and dreaming and eating and calling home as if it were *not crazy* to be soaring through the night sky, thirty thousand feet above the black Atlantic Ocean.

She saw tears rolling down his cheeks, and she began to

miss home. She had spent most of the day yesterday fighting the urge to drive back to Cape Cod, to tell her daughter everything that had come to pass. Steven's cheerleader. The grain of rice in her belly. And now as she sat beside a dying man, she thought of never leaving the airport in Dublin. When the plane landed she would find a place to sit and wait for the first flight back home.

AFTER THE GOLFER RETURNED to his friends, Nora fell asleep. When she awoke and found the nun sitting in Steven's seat, many hours seemed to have passed and the orange light of morning was streaming through the cabin. The nun smiled at her and leaned over her knees to look out the window. "We'll see land soon," she said.

In the half hour before they landed Nora told her what had happened. "I really don't know what to do," she confessed.

The nun told her that she should go back to Steven and try to patch things up. Her words, "patch things up." "It's a man's world, there's no getting around that," she said with a smile, "but after what I've seen in my life, the horrible things people do to one another, what your husband has done—well, in the scheme of things, it seems you might want to forgive him and try to heal the tear."

"And if I can't forgive him?" Nora said.

"You'll need a way of healing this wound," the nun said. "And the only way of healing I know is to heal someone else."

Chapter Nine

The thing that kept Nora from taking a return flight was a notebook in a magazine shop at the airport in Dublin. It was an inexpensive spiral notebook with a simple black cover that was embossed with a small silver shamrock in the lower right-hand corner. She held the notebook in her left hand, turning through the empty lined pages. Pages to fill, like the twenty-one days ahead of her. A story to complete. Emptiness to turn into something. A story even if it wasn't completely true, if she were to leave out the truth.

Waiting to pass through customs she wrote on the first page. *Day One. Dublin. The sun is bright in the sky.* Here was her chance, she thought, to keep a record of this time in her life, if for no other reason than to make herself observe everything carefully. Looking at the words that she had written conveyed to her the thrilling sense that she had now begun a journey.

"Purpose of the visit, ma'am?" the customs official asked as he opened her passport. His necktie was crooked and he looked weary.

I should tell him all the grim details, Nora thought. "Just a visit," she said.

He hesitated before he asked for her return ticket.

"September fourteenth," he read. "On holiday, then?"

"Yes."

"Well. Enjoy the country," he told her as he stamped her passport.

SHE TOOK A TAXI to O'Connell Street and overpaid the driver because she couldn't remember the value of the Irish coins. Then, as she was waiting at track number 7 for the train to Wicklow, the skies opened in a sudden downpour that soaked her to her skin.

She went into a rest room with both her suitcases and tried to dry her hair with paper towels. She inadvertently placed the suitcases in front of the door to one of the stalls. When a woman inside the stall tried to open the door, Nora apologized and hurriedly pushed them aside with her foot. The woman's face was dirty and she was scowling at Nora.

Stupid. I'm so stupid, Nora said beneath her breath.

A few moments later, standing in line for a cup of tea, she noticed a barefoot child sitting alone on the planked floor, surrounded by pigeons.

By the time the train for Wicklow had been announced and she had boarded, Nora felt as if she had mistakenly wandered onto the stage set of a Dickens novel where the actors had been instructed to look forlorn. Around her was a world where everything was just slightly off: the man in front of her in the dining car was dressed well enough, but his trousers were an inch too long, so that he was walking on the cuffs. The little child in the window seat across from her had a horrible bruise on her forehead, and her mother was drinking something from a brown paper bag.

Nora closed her eyes. Maybe it was her. The flight over the ocean, the snoring nun, the dying golfer, the long night. She let herself lean back into the motion of the rocking train and wonder what was going to happen next. It was the sort of thing she had seldom wondered during the twenty-three years when her days as a housewife and mother were mapped out and almost identical.

She watched a man in a tweed coat walk his son down the aisle to the bathroom. They wore identical black rain boots and tweed caps tilted at the same angle on their heads, and like the people in the train station, they appeared dispossessed and gave Nora the vague sense that they had been placed in her path to remind her how lonely and far from home she was.

If Steven had been here beside her, she would have felt none of this, of course. Now, as she closed her eyes, Nora imagined a time in the future when she would recall this day, perhaps opening the notebook and reading her own words: *I returned to Ireland because I believed that once I was there I would know the right thing to do. The right thing for me. Not for anyone else.*

SOON THE TRAIN GATHERED SPEED and there was only open countryside along the tracks. A soft light lay evenly on the green hills. There were the clusters of tan sheep that she could almost recall pointing out to her children when they had ridden this same train twenty years ago. She smiled at this memory. Gradually, as she neared her stop, she felt as if something was being returned to her, something fine that she had not allowed herself to remember.

Maybe it's time, she thought. This time in her life would not belong to anyone but her. If coming here by herself was selfish, then too bad, she thought. This was the first selfish thing she had done since before she was married.

IT WAS RAINING AGAIN when she stepped off the train in Wicklow. She climbed a steep hill to the main street and stepped inside a pub that shared the shop front with an undertaker.

She sat at the bar, straddling a tall stool, something she had never done before, and ordered a bowl of potato soup, bread, and tea. Then she changed her mind about the tea and ordered a pint of Guinness instead. (Hadn't someone told her long ago that Guinness was actually good for pregnant women?) When the bartender nodded to her, she told him that she had been here twenty years ago and that was the last time she'd drunk Guinness.

"You've waited long enough," he said pleasantly. "You must be parched."

She put two one-pound coins on the bar, and as she watched the man set the pint glass under the tap and pull the long handle that drew the beer from its keg, she crossed her arms on the bar and put her head down. She felt as though she could fall asleep to the murmur of the voices behind her. One man was talking about his cows. Another had just visited a friend in the hospital. She thought about buying drinks for everyone in the place. She had taken all but twenty-five dollars out of her money market account yesterday, sixteen thousand and· thirty-four dollars. It was a joint account, and she'd forged Steven's name on the withdrawal slip. Not that it mattered, but she could sign his name so that it looked exactly like his signature.

AFTER TWO PINTS Nora began a conversation with the bartender. He said his name was Neil. He had one daughter, who had moved to California when she was nineteen.

"You have to learn to live without them," he said as he wiped the bar with a damp, filthy rag. "They leave you," he said, "and then you're alone."

Nora surprised herself and told him that she had once dated a boy from California.

"A surfer?" he asked with a smile.

Nora laughed.

"I used to listen to the Beach Boys," he said. "When my daughter was small, I used to sing Beach Boys songs to her. So I have only myself to blame for losing her to the state of California."

When he left his place behind the bar to wipe the tops of the tables Nora closed her eyes. Two pints of Guinness had set the room turning. Not spinning, just turning slowly, pleasantly. More men entered the pub. She heard their rubber boots on the wood floor, and when they began speaking, their voices seemed to carry a song.

THE AFTERNOON WAS OVER and Nora still hadn't walked back out into the street and down the Rathdrum road to the whitewashed cottage. A man with a lovely tenor voice was singing a heartbreakingly beautiful ballad about returning to the town where he had once been young, only to discover that the place no longer held the beauty he had remembered across the years. During the final chorus Nora joined in. Then she bought him a pint when he had finished and drank another herself.

It was the next pint, or the one after, that made her swoon when she stood up to walk to the ladies' room. The bartender put his arm around her and ushered her through a door behind the bar that opened to the kitchen of his attached house. He called out to his wife, "Annie, love, take care of this dear traveler, will you?"

Annie took over from there, guiding Nora to a musty old couch where she lay down and fell into a deep sleep.

SHE AWOKE TO THE SOUND of the Beach Boys singing the song she had danced to in high school, the slow song called "In My Room." And soon Annie was helping her to her feet and telling her, "Dance with me, love, it will help."

And so they danced back and forth across the worn linoleum on the kitchen floor while they talked. Annie had raised five children without a washing machine. She had boiled the dirty diapers outside over a stick fire. "Seven years of that," she said happily. "We saved our money until one day we had enough to buy a machine. Johnny took me to Wicklow. We were walking to the appliance shop when I saw a lovely, gorgeous ring in the window of a jewelry store. Johnny hadn't the money for an engagement ring when we married, and when I saw this ring, I said to him, 'If it's all the same to you, Johnny, I'd rather have the ring.'

" 'Are you *mad,* woman?' he says to me. Oh, I'll never forget the look on his face."

Annie's story, for some reason, prompted Nora to tell her not about her own husband but about the boy from California. She had been nineteen years old, he was a year younger, one year behind her in college. He came from California to Penn with long hair and an electric guitar. From their first date he seemed to have been born with no other ambition in mind than to run aground her father's admonition that she save herself for the man she married. During her freshman year, her promise to her father was safe, protected by a set of strict dormitory rules. No boys were allowed any farther than the lobby, where girls were not permitted to even speak with them unless they were chaperoned by the dorm mother, an elderly, scowling woman who was said to be the sister of General George S.

Patton. She would sit in a Queen Anne chair, directly across from the boy and girl, no more than six feet away. There was no holding hands. No touching of any kind.

Nora went home for Christmas at the end of her first semester, and by the time she returned, all the rules had been abolished and boys moved into the dormitory like an occupying army.

"But I was a good girl," she told Annie. "In my sleep I dreamed of the next time he would touch me. I dreamed of how much closer we would come the next time to breaking my promise to my father."

"I thought all you American girls were taking the birth control pill anyways," Annie said.

"Not me," Nora confessed. "I would have felt too guilty. I used to think that if I took the Pill I was planning to break my promise. Which seemed worse to me than if it just happened." It was all preposterous, Nora had told herself years ago. He had pushed her, all boys did then, as if it was as much his duty to push as it was hers to say no along the way. He turns off the light. She turns it back on. Like a path leading into the woods. Little lights along the way, lamps under pale green shades, she turns them on, he turns them off, one at a time. Who would have blamed her if she followed this boy a long way down the path and couldn't find her way back? But in the end, his lack of convention frightened Nora. She imagined the two of them ending up living on the West Coast, in a station wagon that she made monthly payments on by working at a Dairy Queen, brushing her hair each morning in the rearview mirror.

Thinking of him now, she was pleased that she had never told Steven anything about him. He belonged only to her.

"And it did happen?" Annie asked hopefully.

"No," Nora said. "And I went on and married the wrong man. I know that now."

In the sudden silence Annie said, "Well, then."

Nora caught her looking into her eyes as if she knew there was more that she wanted to tell her.

In the end Nora told her everything. "I'm not sure what will happen now," she said. "If I walk down the road, back to the cottage," she said, "I'm going to want to keep this baby. A part of me knows that. But there's another part that knows this isn't the time for me to have a baby."

She walked to a window where three red geraniums stood in clay pots. She pressed her finger into the damp soil. If she had followed Steven's plan, it would be over now.

"Would there be a clinic near here, Annie?" she asked, consciously trying to keep her voice steady and low.

"Not in Ireland, love," Annie said sadly. "You've come to the one place on earth where there are no abortions."

Nora felt her eyes begin to burn. And then she laughed at herself. "How stupid of me," she said. But she hadn't come here for an abortion, she thought. She had come here to get away from the appointment back home. She had come here to decide what to do next. Or maybe she hadn't come here to decide anything. Maybe she had come here just so—

"A woman can go to the north," Annie told her before she could complete that thought. "You can find help in the north."

NORA WANDERED OUTSIDE, telling Annie that she needed some fresh air. She walked along the cobblestone streets to the town square, where she sat at the base of a statue and leaned her head back against the cool granite. She could hear the sound of a pennywhistle, shrill and solitary. When she looked up she saw that there were stars above her.

All the way to Ireland and now this, she thought. She could deal with Ireland on her own, without Steven, but Northern Ireland was something different. Twenty years ago Steven had wanted to travel to the north, but Nora had refused; it was too dangerous, she claimed, to take the children there. But in reality, Nora had been thinking of her own welfare as well. She'd had an image in her mind then that suddenly returned to her, the picture of men in black hoods dragging her by her hair, then throwing her into the back of a beat-up van.

WHEN NORA WENT BACK INSIDE, Annie was putting coal into the kitchen stove. She took Nora's hands and held them a moment. Then she walked across the room and came back with a pencil and a pad of paper.

She wrote down the name of a doctor. And then the name of the town in Northern Ireland. *Omagh.*

Chapter Ten

In the morning Annie drove her down the hill to the train station. Nora thanked her for her kindness and tried to explain herself. She wasn't sure what she would decide to do about the baby. A part of her believed that only when she was actually sitting inside the doctor's office, waiting her turn, would she be able to decide. Maybe it would be the way it was for all of us who step to the edge of a tall building and look down in order to convince ourselves that we don't want to jump.

SHE CAUGHT THE 8:05 TRAIN to Dublin and the 9:35 train to Belfast. The car she sat in was filled with mothers and children. And soccer fans reading tabloid newspapers. Twin boys sat across the aisle from her. "Can we have our sweeties now, Mum? *When,* Mum?"

Belfast was a city she had always been vaguely afraid of. SECURITY TIGHTENED was stamped in blue letters on the metal wall of the train car, just above the seat where a little red-haired boy was pestering his mother. "Are we sleeping on this train, Mum?" he asked.

"No, we're sleeping at Granny's."

Children know nothing, Nora thought. They just trust the big people around them because they have no choice.

"Look, Mummy, the cows, the cows! And look, the little baby ones are trying to get the water out of their mummies!"

"Milk, love. Not water. Milk."

This made Nora think of her own children when they were small. How confused they were at times. Sara had such a difficult time with maps. For the longest time she thought that Massachusetts was the name of the town she lived in. Then somehow she figured it out. But on her own, the way children do with so many complex matters. They accept gracefully what they cannot understand, more gracefully than adults, and bide their time until they gradually come to their own comprehension. And parents applaud each small accomplishment, never really seeing that each small accomplishment is a small step away, into their own world. This is how they leave us behind, measure by measure. Almost imperceptibly they make their way from our world into the larger world. Before long Nora's children were in middle school and were drawing maps for school projects on large sheets of construction paper on the kitchen table. She remembered Sara's map of Italy, and the way she had proclaimed that one day she was going to live in Italy—"Right here, on the toe of the boot." How determined Sara was when she said this. Children tell you all kinds of things as they are growing up. I'm going to join the circus someday, Mommy. I'm going to be a fireman when I grow up, Mommy. Like all parents, Nora had listened and sometimes not listened to her children, and that day, when Sara said she was going to go to Italy, Nora stopped and looked at her daughter, and it was as if she were seeing the first glimpse of what kind of woman her daughter would become.

FINALLY NORA COULDN'T TAKE IT any longer and she walked the length of the train, eleven cars, until she found a place to sit where there were no small children. She folded her raincoat for a pillow and rested her head against the window.

WHEN SHE OPENED HER EYES AGAIN, what she saw out the window set her heart pounding. Soldiers wearing camouflage uniforms and carrying black rifles were walking through a pasture. They looked so improbable in the pastoral setting that Nora found herself considering the possibility that she was hallucinating, or that she had come upon the filming of a movie. The soldiers were spread apart, carrying the guns across their chests, resting on their crossed arms in the benign way a schoolgirl carries her books. But when she looked closely she could see that each soldier had his finger on the trigger. They wore black berets and black boots. Some of them looked no older than college boys. Everyone in Nora's car had turned to the windows to watch them, and her first impulse was to take off her diamond engagement ring and diamond earrings. Then, when she had hidden the jewelry in her shoe, she felt embarrassed and silly, the true Ugly American protecting her material possessions.

She had an hour in Belfast before the first bus left for Omagh, and though her impulse was to stay in the station where she felt safe, she walked outside by herself.

More babies in prams and strollers or in their mother's arms. Babies in every direction she turned. On one corner there was a young mother breast-feeding a baby and begging for money. She held a sign that said simply: ABANDONED. Nora gave her a five-pound Irish note.

"Have you got any sterling?" the mother asked.

"Sterling?"

"British money," she said sternly. "We can't use Irish money here."

Nora wondered how many more things she was going to screw up on this trip, and if she was slipping into early senility brought on by too many years of dependency. *If only my life had fallen apart when I was still capable of doing things on my own.*

"All I have is Irish money," Nora said.

The woman put the bill in her pocket and looked away.

On her way back to the station Nora noticed a green tower rising fifty or sixty feet into the air. There was a barbed-wire fence around the top and what appeared to be a television camera. As she watched she could see the camera revolving slowly.

During the hour bus ride to Omagh she saw more towers set along the landscape. Finally she mustered the courage to ask the man beside her about them. "Army," he said harshly. "The Brits."

IT WAS JUST BEFORE NOON when she arrived in Omagh, the small city appearing suddenly at the bottom of a river valley after the bus had climbed a succession of steep hillsides like a boat riding ocean swells.

As the bus pulled into the station Nora's vision blurred. When she stood up she felt as if she were going to pass out, so she sat back down and waited until all the other passengers had left the bus. She tried to stand up again, but her legs went limp beneath her.

Finally the driver stuck his head back inside and asked if she was okay. *What am I afraid of?* she asked herself. The awful guilt was already mounting inside her like snow falling on a window ledge.

She thought once more about sin. Maybe she wouldn't be here if she had spent more time in church. Steven was opposed, but when they were making plans to go to Ireland Nora told him that she was going to take the children to church there. She was determined.

The first Sunday morning she was up early polishing Sara's little patent leather shoes just like her own mother had polished hers. She had them dressed and fed when Steven caught up with her in the kitchen. "You're really going through with this, aren't you?" he said. "A good Catholic girl." He came up behind her and said she hadn't zipped her dress up all the way. "Here, let me fix it for you."

He pulled the zipper down. He kissed the back of her neck. He knew how to touch her so that her resistance evaporated. He stayed behind her, pressed against her while he steered her into a closet and closed the door behind them. "I really want to take the children to church," she told him.

"But you want me to make love to you," he whispered. He was right, and this was not the first time she had been undermined by her desire for him. "Here," he said to her, dropping down to his knees. He opened the closet door a little for some light so she would see him undressing her. So pleased with himself, Nora could tell. "If the church finds out what you've done when you should have been at mass, you'll be excommunicated."

SUDDENLY THE DRIVER had her hand and was leading her off the bus. He sat her down inside the station. She could hear his voice, but not the words he was saying. She tried to force herself to read a sign taped to the window across from her:

IRELAND'S NUMBER 1 KELTIC ROCK!
THE SQUEELIN' PIGS
EDDIE'S BAR

The driver offered to walk her wherever she was going. At first she thanked him and declined. "But can you tell me where High Street is?" she asked.

"I'm going there myself," he said with a smile.

It was only a short walk. He carried her suitcases and talked the whole way about Boston, where he had gone as a young man. As they passed the shop windows Nora kept her head down so she wouldn't see her reflection in the glass. She was thinking that the phrase was wrong; this wasn't a *choice,* this was what a woman went through when she had no other choice.

The town center was crowded with shoppers. The bus driver told her that this was the traditional weekend in August when parents took their children shopping for back-to-school clothing.

It dawned on her then that if she allowed the bus driver to walk her all the way, he might be able to tell by the look of the place why she was going there. So when they came upon a coffee shop she told him she was going to sit inside for a while and have a cup of tea.

"I'd like to join you," he said, "but I have to get back."

She took a seat at the front window facing the street. The tea was served in china cups. At the table to her right an elderly man was eating a piece of lemon pie with whipped cream. He turned along with her and took note of a soldier in uniform two tables away whose cup rattled in its saucer when he touched it.

She closed her eyes and bowed her head. This was when she remembered where she had seen the cheerleader before. After Christmas the publishing company had held a public reading for some of its authors at the Hanzel Library on Boston Common. She had been one of the poets reading that night. Nora couldn't remember the nature of her poetry, but on the way home Steven had spoken of her as a rising star in the literary world, a writer whose early manuscript he had edited. He had given her his standard advice to all young artists—"Take off your beret and put on your hard hat." And apparently she had taken his advice. Nora remembered Steven's telling her how serious she was about her work. She had pushed him to be hard on her work, insisting that her work was all that she had in the world.

Not any longer, Nora thought. Now you have my husband.

A waitress wearing white stockings walked past her to the soldier's table. Nora caught his English accent when he apologized to her for spilling coffee on the table. His polished black boots held her reflection. Nora turned slightly in her chair. She heard the soldier's knees crack when he rose to his feet. She watched him go outside. The moment the screen door shut behind him, he tapped his shirt pocket with his right hand, the same smoker's gesture she had seen her father and her husband make during the years they'd smoked cigarettes and then long after they had quit. Nora took the notebook from her coat pocket and placed it on the table. She looked down at the silver shamrock and traced her finger around its border. When she opened it to the first lined page her mind went blank. She felt discouraged. Maybe she was just too tired to write anything. When she looked up through the window she saw the soldier standing on the sidewalk, watching people moving past him in the crowded town square. He turned to the side and Nora saw that the color had drained from his face.

It was half past twelve when she paid the cashier and walked back outside.

At the Bank of Ireland on the corner of Market Street and Dublin Road she changed five hundred dollars in traveler's checks into British currency.

Outside on the busy sidewalks she began checking the numbers of buildings as she walked up Market Street to where it turned into High Street. Northwest Bookmaker, Willy Duffy, Proprietor. Ulster Cancer Society. OxFam. Handifone. Strule Mortgage Center. McAlee Travel.

Number 819 was a narrow three-story brick building with three windows facing the street on each floor. Tall green grass was growing from the four chimney pots on the black slate roof. There was an iron railing, painted bright blue, leading up the five granite steps from the sidewalk.

There was a brass doorknob in the center of a black door. When Nora turned it, the door swung open.

A nurse with pale green eyes and a pleasant smile sat at a desk in the front room on the dark-blue-carpeted floor. There was a baby grand piano pushed in front of a side window and five straight-backed chairs against the walls, painted white, each with a red velvet cushion. All were empty. Nora began walking to the chair nearest her. There was a sense coming upon her that she was a young girl again on a summer night in her father's seaside house, getting into bed with sand on the soles of her feet. When she heard the nurse's voice it seemed to be crossing a great distance to reach her.

"I'm sorry," Nora said, "I think I just need to sit down here."

The nurse stood up and walked around her wooden desk. She sat beside Nora with a clipboard and several sheets of unlined paper on her lap. "The doctor will be free shortly," she said pleasantly.

Free, Nora thought. She considered lying, not giving her real name on the form. But when she tried to think of another name, nothing came to her. She caught the nurse looking at her three times. *It must be the suitcases,* Nora decided. *I must look like I've run away.*

"I haven't really made up my mind. I'm sorry," Nora said.

The nurse waited until Nora raised her eyes and looked at her. Then she nodded her head slowly. "You've come a long way?" she asked.

"I flew over last night. No, the night before."

"From America."

"Yes. I was here twenty years ago. A long time. Not here, but in the south."

"Where?"

"In County Wicklow."

"Ah, Wicklow. Lovely there, isn't it?"

Nora saw a silver cross on a chain sitting in the hollow of the nurse's throat. She wanted to ask her if she would come in with her, through the door behind her desk to wherever the doctor was. When she was a child, in the dentist's chair, she had always tried to make believe that she was somewhere else.

"I was supposed to make this trip with my husband," she said, and she must have looked away from the nurse when she said this, because she was surprised when the nurse touched her arm.

"I'll go and have a word with the doctor," she said. "He'll be glad to speak with you."

Nora watched her turn and walk away. She saw the heels of her shoes sink into the blue carpet.

A moment passed. Nora was about to walk back to the desk where she had left her suitcases and move them next to the coatrack when she heard the high voice of someone yelling in the street.

It seemed to take her a long time to walk across the blue carpet. She had just taken her place at the front windows when she heard a woman screaming in the street, "Don't take my baby! Don't take my baby!"

It sent the fear of God through Nora, and even when she saw the woman running up the street, she thought the screams were coming from behind the nurse's station, inside a room where she imagined a mother was lying on a table.

"Don't take my baby!" the woman screamed again. And this time Nora could see a soldier in uniform running up the hill just ahead of the woman, with a baby in his arms.

Why isn't someone helping her? Nora thought. And when the soldier came into view again, having passed behind a parked car, she realized that this was the same soldier who had left the coffee shop and stood gazing into the crowded town center.

Without realizing what she was doing, Nora ran out onto the front steps. When she yelled to the soldier to stop, he and the woman glanced back at her for half a second. Nora was turning back to ask the nurse for help, when suddenly the building shook with a deafening boom of thunder, a horrible sound that seemed to rise from the earth beneath her feet with such force that Nora was thrown back into the foyer, onto the floor, just as the windows in the door exploded in a blast of black smoke and shattered glass and the nurse was thrown on top of her as if she had fallen from the dark sky. And then there was only silence.

Chapter Eleven

Here is the moment when time runs into itself. When the straight line between past and future is broken and there is only the now. What was in front of Nora now—the nurse lying on her side with blood running from her mouth— maybe this is the story of our world at the end of the twentieth century. A time when the warning is meant even for us, a warning that we cannot stay forever in our soft, protected lives.

Her first thought, seeing the nurse, was to find Sara and Jake, to make sure they were all right.

It made no sense, of course.

In the next instant she *knew* that it made no sense, and she began to force her mind to comprehend what had happened.

Less than three feet from where she lay on the floor, a large cement beam had fallen from the ceiling, one end now leaning on the leg of the tipped-over chair with its red velvet cushion sprinkled with plaster dust. The other end had crushed the lower part of the nurse's face. Part of a bone had pierced the skin just below and to the right of her lips.

Somewhere in Nora's mind another thought began racing around in a tight circle, the thought of the madman who had once bombed the abortion clinic in Massachusetts. For some reason she couldn't stop herself from trying to understand the large question of how he could have crossed the ocean with a bomb and found *this place,* until she focused on the small question of why there were broken pieces of porcelain in the pool of blood next to the nurse's lips. She stared at them until she saw that they were pieces of her teeth.

A MOMENT LATER Nora was on her feet, wandering down the corridor beyond the nurse's desk, peering into the empty rooms. In the first room a white paper hospital gown hung over the back of a black chair. In the next a jacket lay in the center of the floor, its empty sleeves spread out so that it was in the shape of a cross.

When she walked back through the reception room and saw that the nurse was still lying the way she had left her, Nora began calling for help, the shrill sound of her own voice waking a new fear inside her, the fear that everything she had ever been, or done, or wanted, would now be unrecognizable to her.

She walked through the open door into the gray soot that had joined sky and earth. She walked outside and down the front steps, past the blue iron railing, then stumbled onto the street, where voices were softly wailing, crying for help through the dark smoke. Gradually people appeared before her, their clothes shredded and their faces blackened, walking as if they had been roused from deep sleep, coming toward her out of the smoke, one by one, with something like a child's wonder in their eyes. They took the small, uncertain steps of children too, with their eyes fixed upon the distance as if someone were calling to them.

A police siren started suddenly. And then an ambulance swerved onto the sidewalk, its headlights sweeping across

Nora's shins, burrowing through the smoky fog. When its front tire rolled over a small child in a yellow shirt, lying face up beside an overturned trash barrel, Nora made the sign of the cross. She began to ask God if He had done this to stop her from ending the life of the baby inside her. This, she began to believe, was her fault. All of this because of something no larger than a grain of rice.

Blame this on me.

NOT FAR FROM her a young girl in a nurse's uniform was panic-stricken, down on her knees, trying to administer CPR to a store mannequin that had been blown into the street by the blast. In a doorway lay the top half of a man with a tweed cap on his head. He was smiling, though his bottom half was gone. *This is my fault. All of this.* And the people set on fire who were screaming. And the blood everywhere. *I am to blame.*

How would she ever cook a meal again, or talk to a friend on the telephone? She sensed that there were no normal things left now. Dishes to be washed in the kitchen sink. The morning smell of coffee. Her life, which had been as uncomplicated as a child's drawing, would never be returned to her.

As she walked on, she heard herself asking God to take away the bodies. A man whose face was charred black was crying for someone named Fiona. *Please, God, get him to a hospital. Please, God, take care of them. And make all of this go away.*

WHEN SHE CAME UPON A PRIEST, kneeling by a mailbox, she dropped to her knees and sat down beside him because she had noticed the fine crease in his trousers. She reached out her right hand, touching him just above his ankle, the tips of her fingers tracing the crease in a slow, even motion while her mind struggled to recall a world she once understood, a world where a man took the time to have his pants cleaned and pressed. She could hear him speaking just above a whisper, his voice gently rising and falling as if carried on the wind. She saw then that there was a woman with beautiful long red hair lying across a storm drain beside him. When the smoke lifted, the woman's arm appeared, the skin as white as paper. The arm was draped across the throat of a lifeless child whose dress was ripped open down the front. Between the woman's legs lay two perfectly formed infants. They were naked, their eyes closed and their knees drawn up to their chests as if they were sleeping peacefully. Nora crawled behind the priest to get closer. Close enough to see that the babies were shining, and the hair on their heads was matted, as if they had been drenched by a hose.

The priest turned to Nora just as she saw that the infants were still connected by their umbilical cords to the red-haired woman. "I am to blame," she told him. By now she knew this, and she laid her head down upon the pavement, her cheek resting on a button cut in the shape of a pearl.

FOR A LONG TIME, even after the soldiers began running past her and the fire engines arrived in the town center with their sirens blaring, she didn't move.

Chapter Twelve

Everything now belonged to the landscape of a fever dream. Doors had closed against what was real to her. Her children's voices. The white flannel suits her father wore to work. Her husband's cuff links in the scallop shell on the scarred oak bureau. Time had taken on the weight of an undertow.

She awakened, lying on a green velvet couch. No memory of leaving the street or falling asleep. There were words in her head. Just behind her eyes she could see the letters in bold black print. The words of a prayer. *Dear God, show me what it is . . .*

Words that broke apart before they could complete whole sentences . . . *why do these things happen . . . give me the strength to . . . let me do something to help.*

A soldier in his uniform of dark blue wool slacks and a matching cable sweater was standing beside her. On his head a black beret with its red pom-pom like something a child would bring down from a trunk in the attic. It was enough to make the black rifle resting across his arms appear harmless as a toy.

She saw his lips moving before she actually heard his words. "Are you all right there?"

She began speaking to him but at the same time wondering

how long it would take her words to reach him, when she heard him answering her question.

"You're in the Royal Arms Hotel," he said. "You're safe here."

The chandelier hanging from the ceiling was reflected in miniature in the polished toes of his black boots.

Safe, she said to herself. *Safe, when so many others are broken?*

THE SOLDIER LEFT and then returned with a cup of tea on a silver tray with a glass cream pitcher and a matching bowl of sugar cubes. How long this had taken him, Nora didn't know. Couldn't even guess.

He told her that it was only going to be a few minutes longer before she was called.

What did this mean? "Someone is calling me? Is it my husband?"

"No, ma'am," he said. "It's the interview." He told her this without expression, and so she couldn't measure its meaning. Or what it meant when his eyes skipped past her face to the blackened windows and then back, as if he were trying to remind himself of something.

"Drink your tea now."

Of course. In the mirror surface of the red tea, one eye, part of her cheek and nose. Features of a woman who once drove a daughter into Boston to buy her first pair of ballet shoes. Pink leather. Pink ribbons. Traffic backed up on a bridge. A cement truck in front of them, its yellow barrel turning slowly. Plum-colored light in the sky. Dusk. The feeling that her life was being fulfilled.

TWO MEN ARRIVED to interview her. Their tweed coats nearly matching, or matching, Nora was trying to decide.

Given the dirt in the air, the soot on her arms, she was wondering how they could be so clean.

All she could say to them was, "I have to go home now."

"Yes, of course. Yes, of course. Yes, of course."

This much she heard. And then a question from the man with white hair. "You're on holiday from the States?"

What came blowing into the front of her mind like something torn loose in a gale wind was the sudden suspicion that these men were searching for the woman who had been sitting in the abortionist's clinic, the woman responsible for the explosion that ripped the street apart.

"Holiday?" she said. "Yes, my first holiday without my husband and children." A sentence that had taken all her comprehension to compose.

The men nodded their heads knowingly. "A terrible shame," one of them was saying. The other was lighting his pipe when Nora remembered that her suitcases were back in the clinic, where they would expose her lie.

The man with the white hair leaned forward then, folding his hands in the shape of a tent and resting his chin upon its peak. She saw the points of his elbows press into his thighs. "We are trying to discern what happened here."

"Yes."

"Anything that anyone might be able to tell us . . ."

"Yes, I see."

"And of course we'll help you return home as soon as possible."

He had read her mind. It was the only place she wanted to go. Home. She would fix breakfast in bed for Steven and his girlfriend. If they asked her, she would roll up the carpets in the living room so they could dance together. She would take photographs of them on the beach. She would bake them a peach pie with crumbs on top. Anything at all.

The cheerleader. She remembered this! That life in pieces behind her was a life she could recognize. The pieces she could measure, and fit together to construct a new life. Not perfect, perhaps, but at least far from here. Clean clothes. The teakettle whistling on the stove. Store mannequins dressed and in shop windows rather than lying in the street. A life she could learn to live in.

"But shouldn't we be outside, helping?" she asked suddenly. The question rushing out of her, from somewhere.

"Everyone has been helped," the white-haired man said as he looked into her eyes. "This needn't take long. We'll have you on your way soon enough. Where is it, then, that you're going?"

Another question she didn't know the answer to. She was lost momentarily, watching the man with the pipe. He had a pen in his right hand and a notebook in his left, and he was poised to write down her answer.

"I'm on vacation," she said, trying to make her voice sound hopeful so that it led in the opposite direction of her suitcases.

"And when did you decide to come to Omagh?"

"Oh, I'm not sure," she told him.

"You made a reservation?"

"I don't understand."

"For accommodations? A B and B? Or in the hotel here?"

Suddenly both men were looking into her eyes, waiting. The man with the pipe glanced down at the blank page of his notebook. She watched his expression changing slightly, his patience wearing thin, she thought, and this made her wonder if there was a right and a wrong answer to the question, and if the wrong answer might lead her to another room and more questions that would draw the secret reason for this journey out into the open.

She tried to speak with authority, a few clear sentences that might send these men away so she could go retrieve her suitcases and find a way out of this town. She remembered Annie back in the south, and the heavy taste of the beer she drank in the pub and the train ride this morning that took her from there to here.

"I've been staying with people in the south," she said plainly.

The man with the pipe wrote this down in his notebook. "You have your passport with you?" he asked.

"Yes," she said, and eagerly took it from the pocket of her jacket and handed it to him.

He read it carefully, turning the square pages from front to back, and then from back to front.

"You passed through customs on August fourteenth," he said as he made a note of this. "Yesterday, then?"

"Yes, yesterday."

"So you were staying with people in the south yesterday."

"Yes, I was."

"I see. You stayed just the one night and then you left?"

She was losing her way again. This time in the tangle of his questions. She began to feel small and to want Steven next to her. Women learn to forget these things. She knows this. Or at least to reach some accommodation. She will take him back on whatever terms he offers her. She will stand in front of him in the hooker's clothes. She will keep them on until they wear out, until the seams tear.

The white-haired man spoke again. "Why don't we do this

tomorrow," he said. "Why don't you get a room here, at the hotel, for the night, and we'll continue in the morning. Ten o'clock? Would ten be okay with you, ma'am?"

"Fine, thank you, yes." And she was careful to look into the eyes of both men and to nod her head with what she hoped would look like self-assurance.

Both men stood up simultaneously. Nora waited for them to leave and when they didn't, she realized that they were waiting for her.

She got to her feet. She thanked them, and when she began walking toward the door she heard one of them calling to her. "Ma'am?"

She stopped at the far end of the Oriental carpet and turned around. "Yes?"

"You'll want to register at the desk," the man with the notebook said, sweeping his hand in that direction.

It took Nora a few seconds. "Of course," she said then. This was a part she could play, the confused woman. "I'm sorry. I must be . . . well, I don't know, but I'm terribly sorry."

They smiled at her. "Yes, of course, a terrible ordeal."

She was aware of them standing behind her while she filled out the guest registration card. But sometime before the clerk handed her the key to room 412, apologizing that it had to be a room in back above the kitchen because the explosion had broken the windows in all of the front rooms, the men left.

Before she climbed the stairs to her room she stayed in the lobby, sitting on the velvet couch, waiting for the strength to walk back to the clinic for her suitcases. The questioning had shaken the dazed feeling from her mind and she was once again aware of time passing, and of people moving around her.

Just as she was about to stand up, she heard someone begin

to cry. At the front desk the young man who checked her in was down on his knees, while another man and a woman held both his hands. Tears were streaming down his cheeks. The plaintive sound of his crying seemed to Nora to be coming from far away, from an agony more fierce than anything she had ever known. The young man was about the same age as her son, and she had to fight the impulse to walk behind the desk and embrace him in his sorrow.

She waited until the woman had taken him into another room, then Nora stopped at the desk to leave her key before she went out. "Will he be all right?" she asked the clerk who had taken the young man's place. In the moment before he answered, she began to pray that he was not the husband of the mother with the beautiful red hair.

"He lost a brother," the clerk said. "The authorities are just beginning to notify families."

Nora thought to ask this: "How many were killed?"

"They don't know yet. But hundreds of people have been taken to hospital."

"I'm sorry."

"Sorry, yes, exactly," he said with deep conviction in his voice. "I'm sorry you couldn't come visit our city in better times."

Chapter Thirteen

The street was silent now.

Soldiers had closed off the demolished two-block section of the town square with steel fences that looked like bicycle racks. The groaning engines of the heavy equipment digging through the wreckage for bodies had stopped, and a procession of mourners was passing without a sound, laying bouquets of flowers at the steel barriers. The mourners would stop for a while, looking at the destruction, and then move on thoughtfully with such slowness that their footsteps made no sound.

As Nora watched, rain began to fall and a small noise overtook the street like a rising chorus as the raindrops ticked against the waxed-paper wrappers on the bouquets of flowers.

She fell into line, moving slowly with the others and reading the little cards beneath the waxed paper, each a handwritten note and below it, a signature. God's grace heal us, from Nicole. Let His light shine on us again, from the McDougal family. May the lost rest in peace, from Boots, the Chemist. No words can adequately express our grief, from Ed Winters Photography. To our lovely fallen neighbors, from OxFam. We will remember you always, from Instep Sports shop. How many seas must a white dove sail before she sleeps in the sand, from the Bandlow Family. To two unborn children whose lives were suddenly stolen from them, from John and Evelyn. In this bouquet there were two teddy bears wrapped in waxed paper as well.

When Nora reached the end of the barricade she discovered that the line of mourners continued on from there, up High Street to the Dromagh Bridge across the Strule River, where there were hundreds more bouquets and candles burning in tin pie plates. One note had been left by a school classmate: Don't forget to tell our joke to everyone in heaven—What did one cow say when the other cow mooed? Funny, I was just about to say the same thing.

As the rain grew more steady and began to extinguish the candles, people stopped and poured the rainwater out of the pie plates and relit them. This small act, relighting the candles in the rain, against the darkness, struck Nora. She stood off to the side of the procession and watched as it happened again and again. Bearing witness to these people as they lit candles in the rain did more than anything else to make her feel the loss of this town and the brutal clarity of what had been destroyed and would never be returned to the people here. And because the mourners silently accepted her into their ranks, because they were accusing her of nothing, she began to understand that she was not to blame for what had happened.

AT THE CORNER OF HIGH STREET and the Dublin road two armored personnel carriers were parked beneath a streetlamp. CONFIDENTIAL TELEPHONE: 0800 666 999 emblazoned in white block letters on their roofs. As Nora watched, the rear door opened slightly on one of the vehicles and a

British soldier peered out. She could see three soldiers sitting in back drinking something from white Styrofoam cups. Taking their tea break? It was only then that she noticed more soldiers standing in groups of three at each intersection of the road. They were wearing green camouflage jackets over the navy blue sweaters, and their collars were turned up against the cold rain. She could see the wariness in their eyes as they watched the townspeople passing on the sidewalk; any one of them might be their enemy. How frightened they must be, stationed in a country where the people hated them, knowing they were not welcome, and perhaps feeling that, in some way, their presence was responsible for each death. She thought of her son, and how she used to tell Steven that she would never let him be taken off to war, that she would hide him in the trunk of her car and drive him to Canada if it came to that in order to prevent the army from finding him.

SHE STAYED OUT on the street a long time, following along in the procession of mourners, up the hill a little ways where High Street turned into Market. On the doors of the shops that had not been damaged, identical small printed signs hung: CLOSED AS A MARK OF RESPECT. In Waterston's Department Store, there was an additional sign that said, OUR PRAYERS ARE WITH THE FAMILIES OF OUR THREE MURDERED EMPLOYEES.

Suddenly there was shouting ahead. The mourners had stopped and circled a lamppost where a British flag was hanging. A young woman stood in the center of the circle, her eyes bright with rage as she cursed the flag. Then an elderly man knelt down on the sidewalk so the young woman could stand on his back. She climbed the lamppost and when she reached the flag she tore it down and threw it into the street. A woman wearing a plastic trash bag for a raincoat turned to Nora and looked straight into her eyes. "As a mark of respect," she said bitterly. Then she turned away, raised her arm into the air, and shook her fist. "Bastards!" she cried out. She was looking up the hill when she said this, and Nora followed her eyes to where a tower rose into the sky. On the top, bright searchlights were revolving slowly, casting long shafts of white light across the houses, shops, and streets in that part of the city.

She walked on toward the tower, the street in front of her going from darkness to light, darkness to light, to the pattern of the turning searchlights. When she reached the barbed-wire fence, the light was bright enough for her to read the posted sign: HER MAJESTY'S ROYAL ULSTER COMMAND. FORTIETH REGIMENT, OMAGH CITY, COUNTY OMAGH.

There was a section of the barbed-wire fence that could be rolled away for vehicles to enter. Two sentries were posted there with German shepherd dogs. Farther back inside the base were more personnel carriers, trucks and Jeeps. And two long, low-slung buildings that looked like soldiers' barracks. The barbed-wire fence, the dogs with wire cages around their mouths, the searchlight, all of this cast an impression of unreality. Nora's only point of reference was an old television series she had watched occasionally as a teenager, *Hogan's Heroes*. And thinking of that farce made her feel ashamed.

Just across the street from the army base and farther up the hill was a church, and when Nora turned to face it, she was drawn to the steeple, covered with slate shingles right up to its peak, where there was a magnificent Celtic cross. She wondered vaguely if the steeple was higher than the green army tower, and she looked back and forth between the two, trying to decide.

She stared at the church for a long time, and then, when the searchlight swept across its dark granite side, she noticed a figure standing at a small door below a gabled roof. It took several passes of the searchlight before she could tell that the man was dressed all in black but for the white band of his collar.

WHEN SHE CAME UP TO HIM and told him that she had been beside him earlier, in the street, he became very nervous, shifting his weight from foot to foot as if he were trying to find a new way to stand. "Yes," he said to her, "I remember."

He was trying to light a cigarette, but his hands were shaking too badly to keep the flame steady. After several tries, he took the cigarette from between his lips and held it in one hand down at his side. With the other hand he drummed his thigh.

Something about him, his vulnerability perhaps, made Nora feel calm in his presence. Calm for the first time since she had left America. And she began to tell him that he had comforted her in the street. "It was your trousers," she said with a smile, "the way they had been ironed so carefully. I don't know. I mean, I know it sounds silly."

He put the cigarette back between his lips, tried and failed once more to light it. "Well," he said.

"She had such beautiful red hair," Nora said to him, smiling hopefully for him again.

He nodded slowly.

"Did you know her?" Nora asked.

"Avril Monaghan," he said, and when he spoke her name Nora saw a spasm pass through him so that his shoulders trembled.

"I'm sorry," she said.

This time when he put the cigarette between his lips, Nora

took the matches from his hand. "Here," she said, lighting a match and holding it until the cigarette was lit. She watched him inhale deeply. He seemed to hold his breath too long. The smoke rushed from his lips and his shoulders shook when he coughed.

"I haven't smoked since I was a boy," he told her through his coughing. Then he apologized.

"May I?" Nora asked as she reached for his hand. She took a drag from the cigarette herself and began coughing along with him. "I quit in college," she told him.

They passed the cigarette back and forth, and this opened a passageway between them. He told Nora that he had presided over Avril Monaghan's wedding and had christened her child.

"The little girl?" Nora asked.

"Yes."

"She died?"

"Yes."

"And the two infants?"

"Two weeks before their due date," he said, bowing his head and making the sign of the cross. "Avril Monaghan arrives in God's kingdom with her hands full. Three little ones to care for."

Just as he said this, the searchlight struck his face and Nora saw that there was dried blood on his cheek. He noticed her looking at him, and he slowly raised his hands and showed her the blood on his palms as well. "I don't want to wash it off," he told her. "When I do, I will begin to forget. And I don't want to ever forget."

Sometime while they stood together the rain stopped, and the priest asked her name and told her that he didn't want to forget her either.

"You have children?" he asked.

"Yes," she said. "Two."

"Then you will understand why I prayed in the street that Avril would die with her three daughters. She was leaving her husband, Ross, behind, but I wanted her to be with her children in God's kingdom."

Nora waited a moment while a silence fell between them. "You believe there is a kingdom?"

He raised his head a little and shrugged his shoulders. "It's something I must believe," he told her.

"Must?" Nora said.

He looked into her eyes. "Must," he said. "I think sometimes that faith is nothing more than defiance. In the face of all the evidence against believing, I believe anyway. I defy the evidence."

She told him that she had never thought of faith as defiance. But maybe this was how she had chosen to believe in her marriage to Steven. Maybe her faith in their marriage had been nothing more than defying what she knew was true.

She felt free to ask the priest then if he believed that God would hold her in contempt or judge her guilty for leaving her husband after he betrayed her.

He thought a moment, then said, "Till death do us part. I've seen enough life to know that there are many kinds of death. The death of respect. The death of passion. The death of honesty."

Nora waited, then thanked him.

"I saw something in the street here today," she told him. "I saw a soldier—"

He raised his hand to stop her. He looked into her eyes. "Whatever it was that you saw, if you tell me about it, I may be bound to repeat it. I mean if I am ever questioned, whatever you tell me I will have to tell the authorities. Unless you tell me in your confession."

"It won't matter if you repeat it," she said to him.

"You're certain?" he asked.

"I can't see why."

"All right, then. If you want to tell me."

She explained what she had seen. The soldier running away from the town center with a woman's baby in his arms. The mother running behind him, screaming.

The priest looked into her eyes with a puzzled expression. "Up the hill, was it? Up High Street?"

"Yes."

"You're certain?"

"I am."

"The warning said the bomb was at the top of the hill, at the courthouse," he said, as if he were reminding himself of this fact. "Everyone was sent into the center of town. How could he have known?"

The priest looked off into the darkness, and Nora waited for the searchlight to sweep over them again.

"Have you told anyone else?" he asked her suddenly.

"No," she said. "I was . . . two men questioned me in the hotel, but I didn't tell them. I was too confused to remember."

"Well," he said.

In the end, she told him everything, beginning with her drive to the summer house in Maine. She found it easy to make her confession and to ask him what she should do.

"We're all lost, Nora," he said. "We're like sparrows who have lost their way. But there is a strength in you, I can feel it."

He bowed his head for a moment and she told him that she

would never forget this day, and that she was always going to remember the people lighting candles in the rain because it seemed to be a sign for her. "Always in my life," she said, "I expected someone else to light my darkness for me."

He nodded thoughtfully. "After what happened here today on these streets," he said, "these sad streets, go and live, Nora. Spread your light across the world, and live."

Chapter Fourteen

By the time she reached the clinic Nora had already decided that all she wanted from her suitcases was the notebook with the silver shamrock on its cover that she had bought when she landed in Dublin. She had her money and her passport in the pocket of her dark green oilcloth jacket, and everything in her suitcases belonged to another life. Her life before the bomb exploded. Leaving behind the suitcases could be dismissed as a purely symbolic act, she knew, but it was also an act of commemorating what had happened in this small part of the world today by declaring, if only to herself, that her life would never again be the same. She would return home in the morning and begin the rest of her life with new clothes.

From the sidewalk she could see a light on in the front room of the clinic. Well, maybe she would forget the notebook as well. But this seemed cowardly to her, not to go inside for fear of meeting whoever might be there.

THE SUITCASES WERE IN THE FRONT ROOM where she had left them, coated in black soot. Someone had cleaned up the broken bits of concrete and lined the chairs back up against the wall. Even straightened the magazines on the little cherry table. There was just a faint stain on the rug; it might be only dirt from someone's shoe, not the nurse's blood.

Nora was on her knees, taking the notebook from one suitcase, when someone came up behind her and said, "Can I help you with something?"

He looked to be in his sixties, a man with a pleasant face and gray hair combed straight back. He raised his eyebrows and smiled at her.

"Are you the doctor?" she asked.

"Yes."

He smiled again, and Nora smiled back. "A friend left these here this morning," she said. An easy lie to tell him.

"Let me help you," he said, reaching toward her.

She looked at his fine hands, unwrinkled, like a young boy's, and for an instant she thought that she was going to begin to cry. "I packed too many things," she told him, exposing her lie, and then laughing nervously. "I always do whenever I travel. I tell myself that this time I'm only going to bring what I absolutely need, but then . . ."

"Most people do the same."

She could tell that he was nervous for her.

"Are you on holiday with your friend?" he asked kindly.

She wanted to answer right away rather than be implicated by the silence. But suddenly she lacked the commitment to take another step deeper into her lie.

"Actually," she confessed, "I'm not going to need any of this. I wonder if there's a place where I . . . maybe I could donate them. There must be someone who could use them. It's just clothing, nothing spectacular, but there are some nice things."

He nodded his head. "Any of the churches, I should think, ma'am."

"Yes," she said, "and can you tell me . . . see, I've been afraid to ask, doctor, but the receptionist who was in this room with me when the bomb exploded, I tried to find someone in the street to tend to her, and I wonder—"

"Kelly?" he said. "Her jaw was fractured and she has a concussion, but I've seen her in hospital and she's doing well."

He smiled once more.

"Oh, that's good," Nora said. "I'm so relieved."

"Others were not so . . . so fortunate."

There was an awkward silence, then he broke it by asking if she was all right.

"I wasn't hurt," she said. Then in his eyes she saw that this wasn't what he meant by his question. She looked down at the silver shamrock on her notebook and then up at his face. "Yes, I'm all right. I'm going to be all right. I'm going home now and I'll be all right."

SHE WALKED DOWN Market Street in the opposite direction until she came to Saint Matthew's Church. Just as she set her suitcases on the granite step outside the red double doors, she heard thunder in the distance.

On her way back to the hotel she paused once and turned back and saw that the church was bathed in moonlight. The rain stopping. The moonlight. Maybe it was because she was at the end of the strangest day in her life that she took these to be signs that she was safe now, she could lie down and sleep, and awaken to a new morning in a world where her husband's betrayal would seem only a small thing to endure.

Chapter Fifteen

In her room at the hotel she stood before the mirror. Her face was pale, and there were the small lines at both corners of her mouth that were always pronounced when she didn't get enough sleep. She ran her fingers through her hair, thinking she really had to do something with it. Maybe let it grow long enough to tie it up in a single braid the way she had always worn it when she was younger. She recalled her mother's braiding it for her when she was a girl, sitting her on the stool in the kitchen, her feet barely reaching the floor. She recalled braiding Sara's hair for her, and the pleasure it brought her. She often thought that this was one of the best things about having a daughter, even after those mornings of rushing through it to make the school bus, and the troubled years of Sara's adolescence when she accused Nora of not braiding it properly. By then Nora's own hair was half as thick as it had been before she had her babies. "Your mother gave her lovely hair to you," Steven had once told Sara. A compliment. Nora took this as a compliment. *This is the man I will go home to,* she told herself now. *A man who once loved my hair.*

SHE PUSHED THE BLUE CHAIR with the tall back up to the window. She stared down at the notebook until a few sentences came into her head: *Today I saw a British soldier stealing a woman's baby.*

She stopped writing and closed her eyes. A picture came into her mind of Steven and Sara and Jake sitting in the living room of her house, listening to her tell the story of this day. She was holding the notebook and reading to them, and each word drew them back together as a family, carrying them farther beyond the point of betrayal that had taken her across the ocean by herself, into a region of time where there was no longer a trace of the trouble that had descended upon them. Where it would seem as if nothing bad had ever happened.

Maybe this is within my power.

Maybe this was how people endured sorrow and misfortune, by giving away their memory to a blessed amnesia.

She opened her eyes and took in the room around her. The pale yellow walls, the burgundy carpet, the white linen curtains, one with an unraveling hem. *This is where I am,* she told herself. *And in the morning I will take a shower and dress in these same clothes and walk to the bus station and ride a bus to Dublin. And then another bus to the airport.*

She closed her eyes and tried to picture herself walking down the stairs into the lobby of the hotel in the morning. Paying the desk clerk. The long flight home over the same ocean she had just crossed. It was all fine until she imagined herself opening the door to her house, stepping into a room as empty as this room. Worse than this room. An empty room filled with loneliness. This thought had a certain weight that she could feel pulling down her arms and legs.

SHE CLOSED THE NOTEBOOK and placed it on the floor beneath the chair. She turned the chair so that she could look out the window, down into the parking lot. Soon she was sleeping, dreaming of the army tower and its searchlights. In her dream she was trying to get away from the white glare. Then she awoke and found the parking lot lit up like a stage. It took her a while to get her bearings and to interpret what was happening. A long white truck with the letters CNN on it was parked just below her window, and in the floodlights a man in a dark suit stood before a television camera, speaking into a microphone. Just beyond him, a woman also dressed in black stood before another set of bright lights. From the window Nora could see the letters BBC on the camera.

She pushed up the window and knelt down to listen. The man before the CNN camera was speaking into a microphone, telling the world about the devastation of the bomb. The number of people admitted to area hospitals. How the army had sealed off all thirteen roads where they crossed the border into the Republic. A moment later the lights went out and a man was led to stand beside the reporter. They spoke briefly, then stared into the camera as the lights went on again. "This is Mr. William McNaughton," the reporter said, reading from his notes. "He knows the family of one of the victims, a little girl just three years old. Can you tell us how you feel tonight, sir?"

The camera rolled closer to him. It took him a few seconds to begin speaking. "My neighbor," he said. "My neighbor's wee child lost both her feet. Twenty years from now when everyone has forgot what happened in Omagh, who will marry a woman with no feet?"

Until now, what happened today had felt deeply personal to Nora. She hadn't considered the possibility that the events would be transformed into a narrative, a story that the media would turn into a worldwide drama. The fact that it would be recounted in America between advertisements for denture cream and cures for athlete's foot filled Nora with a deep sense of loss that she knew she would never be able to explain if anyone asked her to. This, after what she had seen in the street today, felt to her like an obscenity.

She watched the man bow his head as the camera moved in closer to him. She was still watching him when a truck roared into the parking lot and screeched to a stop. Soldiers armed with rifles spilled out the back of the truck and raced past the cameras and floodlights toward the rear entrance of the hotel. She watched the last of the soldiers disappear, then walked to the door of her room and leaned against it, listening. Below her she heard voices in the stairway and the sound of heavy footsteps.

WHEN THE BRITISH SOLDIERS reached her door they had the night clerk with them. He had untucked his shirt to make a kind of basket with his shirttails in which he was carrying the keys to every room in the hotel. Nora heard them before they knocked. "Sorry, miss," he said when she opened the door. "The soldiers are checking every room now, miss. I'm very sorry."

Standing behind him were the white-haired gentleman and his colleague with the unlit pipe between his teeth. He still had the notebook in his hand.

"Oh, yes," she heard one of them say. "She's the American on holiday."

Then there were two soldiers stepping past her into the room, and she was looking at the white-haired man, waiting for him to call the soldiers back, to tell them that this wasn't necessary. "Sorry to impose," he said. He looked to one of the soldiers and pointed to the bed. The soldier responded by dropping to the floor and looking underneath it.

"I'm alone in your country," Nora said.

The white-haired man looked right into her eyes and held the glance long enough for her to feel her knees begin to tremble and the blood rush to her head. By then the soldiers had checked the closet and the tiny bathroom. "We'll be talking in the morning," he said with a smile. He made a kind of bow before he nodded again to the soldiers. He was already walking away from her, going to the next door, when he stopped and turned back. "Traveling alone as you are," he said to her, "I'd bolt the door."

WHO WOULD EVER blame her for wanting to be back in her own house, her own world, where she could step out of the shower and find some comfort in the plain, simple act of looking around a room she recognized, the white wicker laundry basket beneath the window, the linen curtains held by sashes on little brass hooks, the silver-handled hairbrush, the thick white towels folded neatly on the shelf. Until today she had never imagined how quickly the familiar could be lost in moments where nothing made sense.

AS THE NIGHT WENT ON and Nora was unable to sleep, she was overcome by paralyzing self-pity. It left her breathless, on the verge of hyperventilating. She made herself sit on the end of the bed, breathing slowly with her head bowed to her knees, concentrating on each sound that reached her through the silent night. A car's motor turning in the distance. Occasionally a piece of glass falling to the street like the last note bleeding from a music box. What calmed her eventually was the sense that she was sharing the emptiness of this night with strangers. The families of those who were killed or wounded in the street. Along with her they were waiting for the night to pass. She pictured them sitting at kitchen tables with their heads down, stopping halfway up flights of stairs as if someone were calling to them, bending over their shoes. The effort it took just to move.

OUTSIDE, the parking lot was dark again, the television crews having packed up their equipment like rock bands at the end of a concert. Nora knelt at the window. She felt the dampness of the countryside. Her knees began to ache. *I am a pregnant woman,* she thought. She had taken care of herself, her health was good. In many respects she didn't feel any different from the way she'd felt in her twenties. But it took nothing more than the stiffness in her knees to remind her that this was only an illusion.

Chapter Sixteen

Past midnight the sky above her shook with the thunder of helicopters. They swept low, their searchlights driving deep into the darkness. Nora drew open the curtains. She leaned her back against the wall to evade a long blade of light that crossed the floor, the bed, the wall, before vanishing. Along her spine she felt the plaster trembling, the room around her shifting, trying to settle itself. This is the truth that the night held for her: Always the siren's cry had been for someone else, someone whose life was less celebrated than her own. The families on the wrong side of town, the hallways of their apartments smelling like fried food when her Junior League Thanksgiving drive sent her there with boxes of groceries. The women parked outside the Laundromat with cigarettes between their painted lips. Until now, a world seemed to separate her from them. Their lives without prospects. Without hope. Waiting only for the next disappointment, the next thing that would break. Now she felt herself among them. Her own life precarious, shaken off its underpinnings like the walls of the hotel. This trip had already taught her something. That there was no longer any safe place in the world. The world itself is in pieces.

. . .

IN THE MORNING she would reverse her steps and return home. This is what she was telling herself in the falling silence, just after the helicopters lifted away and just before she heard the knocking at her door. The knocking, and then one word spoken barely above a whisper. *Please.* A single syllable as solemn as a prayer.

Maybe she was only imagining this. She could feel her heart begin to race. Something had been knocked down inside her by the thundering helicopters, or the searchlight skating across the room, or the sound outside her door that she was already pretending not to have heard. She pressed herself against the plaster wall, felt its dampness on the back of her head, and at her elbows. She was telling herself not to move, not to make a sound, that if she kept her body pressed flat against the wall she would glide unnoticed down a corridor that would lead her safely out of this country where she didn't belong.

But beneath her door the hall light was darkened in two places, unless she was only imagining the outline of someone's shoes. While she was squinting, trying to bring the darkened shapes into sharper focus and telling herself that no one would be looking for her in the middle of the night in a room that had no claim on her or her past or on any of the things she had ever desired in this world, she could not remember if she had taken the advice of the white-haired man and drawn the bolt into the lock. And she could not decide if there was time to cross the room and check the lock, how long it would take her to pull herself away from the wall, how many steps to the door and back, and if she could make it back before she knew for certain.

Finally she moved. Halfway across the floor when a board creaked beneath her left foot and the world didn't blow up again, she felt able to breathe. *It was nothing. Nothing at all.* She could see that the bolt was not drawn. *Not locked, how stupid of me.* But since there was no danger, no threat of any kind, she was free to spend a second or two admonishing herself not just for failing to lock the door but for being spooked by nothing, the way she had been as a child when the branches of the poplar tree would dance on her bedroom window. What was it her mother used to say when she would call for her in the night? "Nobody's here, Nora. Nobody but us chickens."

Something to smile about. And she was smiling. Her fingers were on the iron bolt, and a trace of a smile was still on her lips when the knocking started again. This time more hurried. More urgent. And the word, *please,* more insistent now.

The clerk, she thought. *The nice young man from the desk whose brother was killed.*

She touched her hair before she opened the door, pushing it into place, catching herself, a foolish gesture, a habit begun in the first days of sixth grade when she noticed there were boys in the world looking at her, judging her.

When she swung the door open, she saw the priest, and the strangest thing—he had a rolled-up carpet over one shoulder and the carpet reeked of whiskey.

He was thanking her and stumbling forward under the weight of the carpet, and the smell of whiskey was washing through the room when Nora saw that it was a man he was carrying. A man with only one shoe. The other foot was bare and white as milk. Nora was looking at the foot when she began trying to think back to the last normal thing she had done before all of this began. Before she found out she was pregnant. Before she saw the cheerleader. Before she bought the plane tickets.

"Thank you," the priest said as he laid the body on her bed.

The bed barely made a sound. It was as if the man were weightless. Nora's first thought was that he was malnourished. Perhaps someone living on the streets, barely alive, whose destiny had been left to the kindness of the church.

The last normal thing . . . , she thought again.

"Can we turn on a light?" the priest asked.

Until this moment she hadn't been aware that there was no light on, that she had been standing in darkness.

The priest was breathing heavily. He was trying to catch his breath when he asked her if she would close the curtains before she put a light on.

"Yes, of course," she heard herself reply.

The switch to the overhead light was by the door. She was walking toward it when she heard the priest telling her that he was sorry to intrude this way. With the light on, she turned around and saw him shielding his eyes with his hand.

"It's very bright. I'm sorry," she told him.

"No, it's all right, don't apologize. Come here, please."

She took a place by his side, looking down at the drunk man. His blue lips were parted slightly. He had a beard that was wet and matted, as if he had been lying in a puddle on the street. Why did it take her so long to notice that his blue-black trousers and sweater were a soldier's uniform? She had been concentrating instead on the hairs on his wrists, how some had dried and were standing up straight.

A young Abe Lincoln. Yes, the resemblance was there, though this face was fuller. She was trying to decide if the face was younger than hers when the priest thanked her. "This is the only hotel in town, and I knew that if I could find you, you would help. Tell me, please, do you know who he is?"

For a few seconds Nora thought that the priest must have

been the one drinking whiskey to ask such a strange question. But this was before she realized that he had brought to her room the soldier she had seen running up the hill with the baby in his arms.

"Yes," she told the priest.

"Someone found him on the riverbank and came to me for help. When I saw he was a soldier I remembered what you told me."

"Found him in the river?" Nora said, just as she remembered that the last normal thing she had done before any of this began was to buy a roll of stamps at the post office.

"I can't help him—not here, at least," the priest said to her. "I need you to take him. I have a car. Drive him away from here as fast as you can." Now he turned to look into her eyes. "There's a hotel in Enniskillen. You'll be safe there. The Wayside Hotel. A man named John Ferguson is waiting there. Are you listening to me?"

Then she saw that his hands were shaking. From the whiskey? There must be something, she thought, something she could say to him to make him change his mind.

"I don't understand, Father." She was trying to believe that in the next moment the young priest would apologize again for intruding and lift the soldier off the bed and carry him back outside, into the night, away from her.

"I'm going home in the morning," she told him. She was trying to smile at him when she said this, to reassure him. "The men who spoke with me are going to arrange for my plane ticket to be changed. They said—"

"There's no time," he interrupted her.

In his eyes she saw his desperation. He glanced at the soldier, then took her by the wrist and led her into the bathroom.

He had closed the door behind them when she began her confession. "I came here for an abortion, Father. It's not like me, not at all, because I loved being a mother, and no one ever loved babies more than I, but you see, my marriage is over."

Here is where he cut her off as gently as possible, just as she could hear her voice climbing toward some level of hysteria. "This isn't about *you*," he told her. "That man is being hunted by people who will kill him for what he did in the street today. For what *you* saw him do. He was lying under the Dromagh Bridge. Maybe he was running for his life. Maybe he jumped off to kill himself. I need you to drive him away from here. Stay with him until I figure out what to do."

With this, he turned his back on her and walked out of the bathroom.

SHE WAS STANDING beside the bed when he began undressing the soldier. "Get his sweater," he said to her. Their eyes met for an instant, and then she moved to help him.

She could feel the man's breath on her arm when she pulled the sweater over his head. Then the white T-shirt. His arms were heavy, the muscles like thick ropes. Around his neck a silver chain with a Saint Christopher's medallion. Mixed in with the black hairs on his chest were two patches of white. When her hand brushed across his heart, a deep sigh rushed from his lips and he moaned with pain. "I'm sorry," she said to him, to his closed eyes.

"I think his ribs are broken," the priest told her. "And maybe his ankle."

They had stripped him to his undershorts. His legs were bowed slightly at the knees, like a schoolboy's. She was trying not to look at him, trying to keep her eyes on the broken crystal of his wristwatch, the numbers magnified by drops of river water.

The priest took off his own dark coat, his shirt and trousers. Though it was summer, he wore long underwear beneath his pants, and Nora was thinking that she would remember this, this small detail, for the rest of her life.

Together they dressed the soldier in the priest's clothing. "I'll need a day, maybe two," he told her.

"I'm a housewife," Nora said to him as she was sliding the white collar around the soldier's throat. "I'm just a housewife."

He raised his voice at her. "In this country there is no such thing."

A silence, and then she said, "Maybe this isn't the soldier I saw in the street today."

He was walking to the window, putting on the soldier's wet shirt, when she lied to him, telling him that she couldn't be certain.

"Hand me his pants," he said to her.

He was wringing water from them when something fell to the floor from one pocket. A small black book, soaking wet. The priest picked it up and handed it to her. When she took it she saw that his plan was to make her an accomplice, to draw her deeper into this mystery with each small act he asked her to perform.

THEY CARRIED HIM like a rag doll, down the back stairs, out through the dark kitchen, which smelled faintly of onions. He moaned when they laid him down on the backseat of the car, and again when she bent his legs to close the door.

"Straight along this road out of town," the priest told her.

"Then you'll see a sign for Route 13. From that sign it's just two hours to Enniskillen."

He was holding her by her elbows and looking into her eyes. "Do you understand? Are you listening?"

"Yes."

"And when he comes around, tell him that the mother and baby are safe. Tell him I've taken care of them. Do you understand?"

"Yes," she said, though she understood nothing.

"All right, then," he said. "Just twenty-four hours, Nora. This time tomorrow I'll have a safe way home for you."

SHE WAS BEHIND THE WHEEL, pulling out into the street when he came running after her, pounding his fist against the back window of the car until she stopped.

"Wrong side," he said. "Drive on the other side of the road."

Chapter Seventeen

As she drove away she was thinking of the scene in *Romeo and Juliet* where the priest conspires with Juliet to deceive her family. The professor who had taught her Shakespeare in college had a beard like the soldier's. He always came to the lecture hall with a battered leather satchel.

"When I get home," she heard herself say, as if her passenger could hear her, "I'm going to paint the trellis in the front garden. And I've ordered bulbs to plant along both sides of the brick walkway."

It helped, talking to him this way. It made him less of a stranger, or more of one. And it allowed part of her consciousness to stray far beyond the place and the time that held her. She felt as though she were standing barefoot in the snow with a long way to walk. It came to her that life wasn't linear at all, but merely a collection of moments. The illusion of a straight line was no more accurate than the illusion that the earth was flat.

Soon she was talking a blue streak. "Years ago I was in Ireland, in the south, not the north. I wasn't supposed to be in the north this time, it was just by accident that I was in Omagh today. *Today.* God, it seems like weeks ago . . . like I've been here for weeks. I have to get home. Tomorrow I'll be flying home, and you'll be in this hotel if I can get us there in one piece, driving on the wrong side."

The sound of her voice calmed her a little, made her feel that she was following something familiar and real through the night.

"I didn't realize until this afternoon that I've always lived somewhere between my son and daughter and my husband. In the spaces between them, if you know what I mean? So I would change, you see? I would always be changing to fit into whatever space there was to fill. Depending upon how they were relating to one another. This is what a mother does, I think. I mean, the changes are subtle and so there is the illusion that you never change at all, that you're just at home all the time being yourself while the people you send out into the world each day do all the changing. But I had to learn to fill the silence, to bridge the distance between my children and their father. His distance was part of his allure when the children were small. They couldn't wait to see him come home at the end of the day. He always beeped the car for them when he turned into the driveway. And they were always so excited to see him. He was gone so much of the time, he had the allure of royalty when he returned. The conquering hero. You know?"

She paused. The trees on both sides of the road were bending low in a strong wind.

"I don't have any courage," she said. "Not an ounce. Some of us are braver than others. I've always been afraid . . . Why were you taking the woman's baby?"

SHE DROVE on an empty road. The world seemed to fall away to nothing beyond the reach of the car's headlights. The crosswind kept blowing in sudden gusts. Every so often the car would rock from side to side on its wheels, and she would glance in the rearview mirror to see if he had moved at all on the backseat. Each time there was just the shape of him, and it was impossible for her to see him running up the street again with the baby in his arms. The last thing she saw before the explosion. And earlier, in the coffee shop. The way his hands shook, rattling the cup in its china saucer. This is what broke into her consciousness now and returned silence to the interior of the car. There was something in his shaking hand that Nora was trying to understand.

THE ROAD NARROWED and grew more steep. In a small village there was a traffic light that turned to red ahead of her. She brought the car to a stop, and before she could turn her head to look at the shops along the sidewalk, a car pulled up behind her, very close to her. In the mirror she could make out two dark figures in the front seat. It sent a chill through her heart, the sight of them, and the thought that they might be following her.

But why would they be following her? Who would be looking for this soldier? Why had the priest told her that the soldier could be killed for what he had done in the street?

None of it made sense to her.

When the light turned to green she lifted her foot off the clutch too quickly and the car jumped forward and stalled.

"I haven't driven a standard in so many years," she said. When she turned the key, the engine wouldn't catch. She glanced in the mirror again. She turned the key harder, grinding the starter, pumping the accelerator. When nothing happened, she rolled down her window and waved the car around her. Very slowly it pulled to her left as if it would pass. But then it came to a stop beside her. For a moment she kept her eyes straight ahead, pretending it wasn't there.

The person on the passenger's side called to her. She turned and saw a woman in a bandanna. She leaned toward her and asked if she needed help.

"It's okay," Nora called to her.

"Hold the accelerator right down on the floor for a minute," she told her.

It was only after the car had driven away that Nora was aware she had been holding her breath. She watched the red taillights bleeding onto the dark, wet road.

SHE DROVE FOR MAYBE another forty-five minutes before she turned on the radio to help her stay awake and caught a police report in mid-sentence—"searching for anyone who may have seen a red Vauxhall sedan on Market Street in Omagh between the hours of half past eight and half past nine. Local gardai have posted the telephone number, which will be operating twenty-four hours a day. Seven, seven. Aught, nine, six, seven, nine, four, one."

As soon as the voice stopped, Nora heard the wind whistling. She tried to roll the window up tighter, but the whistling was still there. And this distracted her. Maybe she had taken her eyes from the road for a second too long, because suddenly the red taillights were out in front of her again, maybe half a mile ahead. In the next moment she could see the taillights of three more cars farther on. They had stopped and there was something in the shape of a cross standing in the road, rising high above the cars, with bright searchlights glaring down from its arms.

"All this trouble to find you?" she was saying to the soldier before she was even aware of the thought entering her mind. There wasn't time to try to figure out what he was guilty of. There wasn't time to decide anything or to question the forces in her life that had carried her here. There was only the time it took her to shut off her lights and turn off the car, to get out and open the trunk and search quickly for something to conceal him. Her fingers were on the spare tire when she felt the rain on her neck and turned slightly, to see headlights in the distance, behind her, climbing up the steep hill. The spare tire, and beside it a cardboard box and some kind of hammer and a tin can. And a fishing rod. And then, as the headlights were drawing closer, a damp blanket and a coat.

There was just enough time for her to cover him.

"A WET NIGHT," a man in a black cape said to her when she reached the spotlights and rolled down her window. And this she would think about the rest of the night—how he did not seem official enough to be a policeman or a soldier, though he might have been in uniform beneath the oilcloth cape. He shone his flashlight through the car, then asked her for the keys to the trunk.

"I'll have to shut off the motor," she said.

She saw the lid of the trunk folding back over the rear window. A fishing rod. A hammer. A tin can. A spare tire. Nothing there to implicate her.

"It's a narrow road," he said to her when he handed her back the keys. "Treacherous on a night like this."

"I'll be careful."

When he turned away she could see that there was something wrong with one of his ears. Along the top, a piece of his ear in the shape of a V was missing.

He seemed to be waiting for something. Perhaps for her to ask what he was looking for. And though she knew that if he was searching for the soldier it would be wise for her to ask this question innocently, she said nothing and simply drove off.

Chapter Eighteen

John Ferguson was asleep at the front desk, his head down on a calendar. An ashtray filled with cigarette butts was next to the telephone beside him. He awoke the moment Nora walked across the wood floor.

"I've been expecting you," he said, taking her hand in both of his. The outline of his watchband was ironed across his cheek. The fly on his trousers was unzipped and there was a gravy stain on his white shirt.

A man beyond vanity. She liked him instantly, and for the first time since the explosion she didn't feel as if the earth were going to give way beneath her in the next moment. While he still held her hand, Nora asked him to tell her everything he knew. "I don't even know why I'm here," she said.

He patted the back of her hand. "You're chilled," he said. "I'll put on some tea. There's electric heat in your room."

There was a small loading dock behind the hotel, off the kitchen, and they laid the soldier on a wheeled pallet, then took him up in the freight elevator to the fourth floor. Nora saw him open his eyes briefly when the elevator began to ascend.

The room overlooked the town center, and before she drew the curtains closed, Nora took note of a tall statue on a square of grass with benches and a bubbling fountain.

It was a newly decorated room, she could tell, with cranberry-colored wall-to-wall carpet, pale green tiles in the bath, a queen-size bed, and a small fireplace with a copper barrel filled with kindling and blocks of peat. After they laid the soldier on the bed, John told her that the hotel was empty. He'd had fifteen reservations for tonight, but after the bombing they all canceled.

"It's a hard time to be a businessman," he said without losing his diffident smile. "I could give you a room of your own if you'd like?" He made an effort to straighten his necktie. Each time he looked at Nora he raised his eyebrows a little as if to apologize.

They stood next to each other at the foot of the bed. Nora noticed that the soldier wore no rings.

"I should probably stay with him," she said.

"Yes, of course."

"The hard part will be getting him to the bathroom."

"Ring down whenever you need me so I can help. Right now I'll go and get us some tea."

She followed him out into the corridor. "Please," she said, "why would someone want to harm that man?"

He took her hand again, a fatherly gesture.

She asked, "Whose child was he stealing? And how—"

"Wait," he said. "When Father Conlon returns, he'll be able to sort it out for you."

Nora was in a deep sleep, sitting on the floor with her head against the bed, when he returned with a tray of food.

"Oh, you shouldn't have gone to so much trouble, John."

He seemed pleased that she had remembered his name, and he told her that it was no trouble at all.

"When Father Conlon gets here, he'll sort out the whole

affair for us, and there'll be no more troubles for you," he said while he arranged the tray on the bed next to the soldier's feet. On a pale yellow plate beneath a silver room service lid there were pork chops, peas, and three kinds of potatoes. Baked, boiled, and mashed.

"I hope the gravy is warm enough," he said.

To her surprise she ate everything. Each time she looked up from the tray, John was smiling at her.

"It's very good," she told him.

"I bet you're a good cook yourself."

"What can you tell me, Mr.—"

"John," he said sheepishly. He averted his eyes.

"I'm sorry. John. Did the priest tell you what happened in Omagh?"

"Well, now," he said, "in the morning I will have a doctor come look at his ankle."

"John. Did the priest tell you what happened?"

"Oh, it's been on all the news, ma'am. Terrible. His ribs too. I think there's something wrong with his ribs."

"Someone found him in the river and went to the priest for help."

"Father Conlon just said you were coming and I was to call him once you arrived safely. I called. I left word."

"And what happens now?"

"In the morning Father will sort it all out," he said again.

"I saw this man running up the street, John." She saw him cast his eyes on the floor. He seemed to be looking for a place to hide from what she was trying to tell him.

"It doesn't make any sense," Nora said. "He'd stolen her baby, I guess? Why would a soldier do that?"

"Maybe he's married to her, and they were squabbling? I don't know. I don't know anything."

"It doesn't make sense," she said again.

"There's quite a lot that doesn't make sense in this country."

"I suppose. But I need to know what this means. And why the priest would think that someone now would want to kill the soldier for what he did."

He just nodded his head and looked away. She couldn't stop herself from laying down the sentences again. "I'm sorry. John. I saw this soldier stealing a woman's baby, and then a few hours later he jumps off a bridge, either to get away from someone, or to kill himself. I'm going home as soon as the priest comes—"

"Today?" he asked with what she thought was sadness in his voice.

"Yes. I have to get back to my . . . my family."

Their eyes met, and Nora saw the question he was too polite to ask: *What are you doing in this country without your husband?*

"Let me take another look at his ankle, then," he said. "Which one is it?"

When he took off the sock they could see the swelling.

Ten minutes later, after John had said good night and gone back down to the kitchen with the dirty dishes, Nora sat on the bed beside the soldier, listening to his labored breathing, each breath carrying her farther from home and memory, across the silent borders of time and understanding. Home was somewhere behind her, beyond the whiskey scent of this man beside her, and she could feel its gravity pulling her toward all that was safe and known and predictable. While sleep rose through her, she was trying to get to the center of her feelings. To something that would be the same when she awoke in the morning. *I stayed in Northern Ireland to care for a man who stole a baby . . . I went home because I had my own life to put back together . . . I stayed because I knew that what had been safe at home was empty now, and because I also believed that I might learn something.*

Chapter Nineteen

In the morning the first cars passing on the street woke her. The soldier's eyes were still closed, and he hadn't moved at all in the night. From where she was lying on the floor beneath the window, she could see the little black book Father Conlon had given her. It was sitting on the bedside table, a few inches from his left shoulder. When she took it in her hand she could feel that it had dried a little during the night and some of the stiffness had returned to the pages, though she could still smell the river in it. She opened it to the last page. This was something she had done all her life, something that always drove Steven crazy, reading the last page of a book, like entering a house through the basement, discovering the place backward.

On the last page the soldier had written: "15 August. Katherine Foley. Drumore."

She read the name several times. In her narrow understanding of how the world worked, this would be the name of the woman whose child he had taken. She would be his lover, or wife. They would be in the midst of a divorce, or in the aftermath of one. He would have been denied visiting privileges by a judge.

She looked over at him. His face was buried in the pillow. If

Nora was right, then his heart had been broken. The separation from his child had led to a desperate act.

15 August. Katherine Foley. Drumore.

A date. The day of the bombing. A name. A town perhaps. All that bound Nora to him was the date. The bombing. If she hadn't seen him in the street, and then told the priest what she had seen, he never would have brought the soldier to her room. This was all she knew.

She read the words carefully, again and again. The letters, printed and large. How would she describe them? Not elegant. Not hurried. Resolute? Yes. And turning through the book she found more names, long columns of names. Only names.

So what did this mean?

She sat in the morning light, trying to feel her way through the mystery of this man. Perhaps he hadn't jumped in the river to kill himself. There are far better ways to kill oneself, aren't there? Perhaps he was running away from someone, hiding from someone. And what had become of the child?

"Yes," she said out loud. To finally come upon this question brought her a small satisfaction. She hadn't been thinking clearly or she would have asked this question before any others.

She knelt beside the bed. She told herself that she would ask him, just come right out and ask him about this later.

His watch was turned against his thigh. She had no idea what time it was, or when *later* would be. After the priest returned? Just before she left to return home? She leaned on one elbow and stared at his face. His perfectly shaped lips. His long eyelashes. She wanted to know his history. How did he get here beside her?

How had she gotten here?

To answer this question herself, she would say she took the first step toward him just twenty-four hours ago. But then it crossed her mind that perhaps she had been moving in this direction, crossing the space between his life and hers, from the beginning of her time. What if life is this way? A deep secret that never fully reveals itself to us. Like the man beside her smelling of whiskey and a river.

LET SOMEONE ELSE figure out the mystery, I'm going home.

With these words in her mind, Nora stood at the bus station in Enniskillen. Parked at the terminal with its motor running was a bus to Dublin and at the front door of the bus, a thin girl in skintight black knit pants and a tank top.

"This bus goes to Dublin?" Nora asked her.

The girl nodded and looked away. It was a small thing, a careless incivility, but it cut her.

"Doesn't anyone actually *speak* in this country? When someone asks you a question, a spoken answer is appropriate."

Now the girl looked at her as if she ought to be taken away and made to scrub floors for the rest of her life.

Nora could see inside the tinted windows to the rows of blue seats, which looked so comfortable that she wanted nothing more than to sit there and lay her head back and take a long, long ride. The blue seats seemed capable of carrying her back to a normal life, and she began to think of home again, of Bow Road, where she had lived for twenty-three years never guessing that a day like the past day was ahead of her, waiting for her to walk into it. Bow Road, when it was carpeted with autumn leaves. And when the snowplows woke her in the night. Bob and Judy Waldner wrapping cornstalks around their lamppost for Halloween. Sheila and John Earle stringing white lights on their cedar trees at Christmas. The patterns of a normal life. *A normal life,* she said to herself. And isn't one of the requirements of this life to keep hidden the other life that stands beyond the edge of the reality that we embrace? The life where buildings and streets are blown to bits, and men fall into rivers?

"I'm sorry," Nora said to the skinny girl. "Are you going to Dublin?"

"I'm leavin' this stinkin' place," she said. "I'm not dyin' in this place like everyone else is." She walked to the door of the bus and began banging the flat of her hand against it again and again until the driver ran out of the terminal with a cup of coffee steaming in his hand. He called to her that he wasn't leaving for twenty minutes.

"Fuck you, you massive big fool!" the girl hollered back.

INSIDE, NORA STOOD at the ticket window counting out her money. Fourteen thousand dollars in a bank draft from the Empire Savings and Loan in Winchester, Massachusetts. Sixteen hundred and fifty dollars in American Express traveler's checks. Two hundred and twenty-seven pounds sterling, and forty-eight pounds, forty pence Irish.

Enough money to begin a new life.

The woman behind the ticket counter wore eyeglasses that were taped at the bridge. She finished straightening her cash drawer and then looked up at Nora and asked how she could help her. Nora was so relieved to hear her voice that it took her a moment to respond.

"The bus to Dublin?"

The woman glanced at the clock. "Leaves at half seven."

"I'd like a ticket."

"One?"

"Yes, just one."

"Return?"

"Return?"

"Will you be coming back?"

"Oh, no, just to Dublin, just one way."

It cost nine pounds, seventy. Picking up her change, the cold heaviness of the coins in her palm, Nora began to think again that none of this was real. None of it had happened. No bomb. No cheerleader. No soldier lying in a priest's clothes. No diary with a woman's name. This was 1998 and she was an American. An American woman. An American housewife and mother, an American college graduate. An American dreamer and homeowner and member of the Junior League. She asked herself where she had gone wrong, and if it was possible for a person to cross over a line and never be allowed back? Or maybe we cross borders of time and leave people behind.

Outside with her ticket in her hand, she saw the skinny girl leaning against the closed glass door of the Dublin bus. She could see her underwear outlined beneath her tight pants. Nora smiled. She had never worn pants that tight, even when she was young and would have looked as sexy in them as this girl. She began to wonder why she hadn't ever dared to wear such tight pants. What had she been afraid of all her life? And what had she been afraid of when she went to Victoria's Secret to buy the hooker's clothes that she had hoped would make Steven interested in making love to her enough times for her to get pregnant? She had a difficult time bringing the black lingerie up to the counter, though the cashier, a woman half her age, a girl really, had examined it and taken off the alarm clip and folded it in tissue paper with complete nonchalance, as if Nora were buying an angel with gauze wings for the top of a Christmas tree.

She tried to follow these thoughts to a logical conclusion, but each idea led nowhere and all she wanted was to take a seat on the bus and to close her eyes.

SHE WAS WALKING ACROSS the street to a little shop, thinking she would buy a newspaper to take back home with her. *I stood right there. I was in the hotel right there,* she could imagine herself saying to her friends.

But why did you go there alone? they would ask. And so far she didn't have any idea what she would say to that. She paused to see if some answer might fall into her mind. But all that came to her was another question: What did it matter what people might ask? Why had this always mattered to her? Why had she always believed that the way people regarded her and her life was important?

She considered this as she stood looking down into the glass refrigerator where there were rows of cardboard containers of milk, each with a red heart stamped on its label. Was there some part of her that had always feared being banished from a respectable life? Was this what had sent her rushing into Steven's arms after her parents' divorce? Was this the part of her that worried about the *appearance* of her life?

She remembered then what she had been thinking last night, her last thought before she fell asleep. That there was something she might learn here in this country. She watched some school-age children charge through the open door and run straight to the candy counter. Maybe she could learn here, in this country, what it was like to no longer care what others thought of her.

What would it be like to let go of those cares and just be herself? Wouldn't it be a relief after forty-two years of trying to measure up to someone else's appraisal? Maybe she would have been better off wearing skintight pants and walking past people without saying a word. Separate from the world. Disdainful of it. Not needing its approval. Not running from its storms.

There had been only one storm in her life until now. And rather than face that storm, she had turned away and run into Steven's arms. *Yes, I'll marry you so I won't have to be on my own in this world.*

Maybe now she should stand up and not run. Maybe we have only so many times to stand up in our lives, and if we always run instead, then we live our lives without ever knowing who we are on this earth.

With this last thought she walked out of the store and away from the bus station.

Chapter Twenty

On her way back to the hotel she stopped in the town square, where the statue stood just below the windows of her room on the fourth floor, the lovely statue of a soldier, carved from rose granite. His head was bowed, resting on his hands, which were folded over the stock of his rifle. The rifle was upside down, its barrel pressed against the toe of one boot. His eyes were closed, and though Nora could see the plain weariness in him, in the slumped shoulders and the bend in his knees, what rose above this weariness was the profound sense of being safe. This is what she saw, and felt. Here was someone who had returned from a long journey that had taught him the blessedness of the simple act of resting. He appeared to be so extraordinarily grateful for the chance to put his head down. Maybe grateful for having arrived at a place where he no longer needed to be vigilant. A place where he could be himself.

For a long time Nora stood just below his left elbow, bowing her head and feeling her body sway slightly. She had a sense of it now, a sense that she had been nowhere in her life, that she was blind and narrow-minded and ignorant; she would die without even knowing the names of the constellations in the night sky or how a radio works.

JUST WHEN SHE WAS ABOUT to return to the hotel, farmers begin arriving in town, unfolding little tables in the market where they would sell their vegetables and meat. She watched them and their families setting up their wooden stands in the green, around the statue. One family had a car with no rear seat; instead, shelves had been built in the back of the car and they were lined with pies.

In another car a teenage girl had refused to get out and help her younger siblings set up racks of woolen sweaters and scarves that the parents were arranging with great care. The girl had a bored, superior look on her face, and she had turned away from the green to watch cars pass along the main street.

Maybe she was sixteen. One of the girls who, in another time, might have crossed the ocean by ship to become a nanny in America because that was the only chance she would have at something more than an ordinary life. Nora could see in her eyes that she wasn't going anywhere she didn't want to go. No one was going to make her get out of the car. She had that look. She was biding her time. Waiting to make her move. Nothing was going to stop her. Nora could see this. She was made of steel. She knew better than Nora how to get what she wanted in this world. She already knew more about life and sex than Nora knew. It was not an easy thing to admit. But watching her was a revelation.

Maybe this girl and these families will become a part of my new life. Maybe I will rent a flat in Enniskillen and fill my kitchen with things that these farmers have grown in their fields.

THE PRIEST WAS IN THE LOBBY talking with John Ferguson when she returned to the hotel. She could see through the frosted-glass doors that the room was empty but for them.

Father Conlon walked toward her and wrapped his arms around her. It was the embrace of a father, like stepping in out of the cold.

"Are you well, Nora?" he asked her.

She could smell tobacco on his breath. "I'm all right, yes. John has taken good care of me."

"I took some tea to your soldier," John said. "While you were out walking, I took him some tea."

"We're going to have a doctor look at him now," Father Conlon told her. "To be sure he can travel."

The priest took something from the inside pocket of his black coat and handed it to Nora.

Written on parish stationery, it was a letter to the Irish airline, Aer Lingus, instructing them to change the date of Nora's ticket.

"The Catholic Church still has a few privileges," he said with a shy smile. "You can fly from Dublin this afternoon."

"You must promise to come back someday," she heard John Ferguson say.

Nora recalled insisting to the priest that she had to get back home today, but now she felt ambivalent. The landscape of her life seemed changed now. The minute she walked into the airport in Boston, wasn't she going to wish she had stayed long enough to sit over dinner with these two men? Long enough to figure out the mystery of the soldier? Wasn't she going to wish that she had not come running home?

THE THREE OF THEM took the elevator together. Even after they had turned the corner of the long hallway and were twenty feet from the room, she didn't notice that the door was partially open. Suddenly she felt both men beginning to run to the door and she ran after them without knowing why.

When she heard John Ferguson say, "Sweet Jesus," her first thought was that the soldier was dead. She stood at the doorway watching John untie the lamp cord from around the soldier's neck. The priest was untying the other end from the doorknob.

She heard herself asking why, while the blue in the soldier's face was turning to pink.

"Just in time," Father Conlon said.

"Why would you go and do a foolish thing like that?" John was saying to him. "After these good people have risked their lives for you? Bleeding Christ, man!"

The two men raised him by his armpits, so he was sitting up in bed. Nora looked into his eyes, taking note that they were a shade of blue she had never seen before. He was looking at her hands while she wondered if he would have succeeded pin killing himself if they hadn't interrupted him. The lamp cord tied around his neck and the doorknob. His feet pushing against the door?

Looking into his eyes, she had the feeling he could read her thoughts. She stepped past the two men and sat on the bed right next to him. A corner of the priest's collar was turned down. His eyes were cast to the floor and she could tell that he was ashamed to look at her. A part of her wanted to touch him, just to reach across the space between them and place her hand on his forehead. But in the next moment she stood up and walked away.

THE THREE OF THEM stood at the windows while the doctor examined the soldier's foot and ribs. He wore muddy boots and smelled of dirt and hay, more like a veterinarian than a physician. Father Conlon was explaining things to Nora, and even as she was nodding her head, assuring him that she understood, she didn't really hear him. Finally she turned her back to the soldier. "Tell me again, please," she said.

It took a while for her to comprehend. "Many things that happen in this country are difficult to grasp," John told her. To make her feel better, she knew. To make her feel like they didn't think she was just a woman who understood nothing more about the world than how to shop and prepare a meal.

She didn't quite believe Father Conlon when he told her that someone had changed the bomb warning and sent people straight to their death. This made no sense to her.

"Whose bomb?" she asked.

"The IRA's," he said just above a whisper.

She wished that he would raise his voice, speak more emphatically, more convincingly.

"I would like to meet the people behind this," she said sternly, surprising herself.

John Ferguson and the priest looked at each other in silence.

"Who changed the warning?" she asked.

"Not the British government," Father Conlon told her. "Not directly. But an intelligence unit. Renegades."

"Why?"

"To create an atrocity so terrible that the Irish people would demand that the IRA decommission their weapons. If they're right, if it works, then the war is over."

"They'll be exonerated by history," John said. "In this country, Nora, that's better than being right."

She watched him take some money from his pocket and press it into the doctor's hand before he tipped his cap and left.

Then the three of them walked out into the corridor, leaving the soldier on the bed, the door to the room open.

They told Nora that they believed a plan had been set in motion the morning of the bomb when the warning was called in, and that the soldier must have found out at the last minute.

"He could only save the mother and her child—there wasn't enough time," the priest said. "And once he did that, he was a dead man."

Nora figured out the rest of it before the priest was finished explaining. Of course the people responsible for the plan would now have to kill the soldier to silence him, to make certain the world never learned the truth.

"And the mother," the priest said.

"But you have the mother, you told me that you had her," Nora said.

The priest nodded his head unconvincingly and said that his *people* did. "Yes, the mother is well."

"And there's me," Nora said. The moment she said this, both men began staring at their feet.

"I saw him save the mother, so I have to be killed as well."

After a long silence, the priest told her hurriedly that there were people who would help them. "I only need some time. A little time. If you decide to stay and help."

"But the letter? The letter that you wrote to the airlines? Don't you want me to go home?"

He didn't respond to this.

It was unfair and purely crazy that at this moment she should think about her husband, but suddenly he came into her mind. He was waiting for her to return home so he could tell her that she was the one who pulled away first. She was a great mother, but somewhere along the line she had forgotten how to be a wife.

She glanced through the doorway. The soldier's eyes were

open. He was staring at the ceiling, perhaps trying to hear what they were saying.

Is it my fault? Am I the one who pulled away first?

"I'll get you to the airport," Father Conlon said to her. His voice seemed to be coming from far off. From the other side of the world.

"I'm not going home," she said.

Both men raised their heads and looked straight into her eyes. "The danger—" the priest began.

"You're in danger as well," Nora said, interrupting him. "I placed you in danger."

She waited, then watched him blink his eyes. Maybe she was waiting for him to deny this, to make things easier for her.

"So what can I do now?" she asked.

The priest looked at John, then back at her. "You won't be safe here. It won't be safe keeping him in one place. I may have been followed here. Or you may have been last night."

This part Nora thought he might be exaggerating. The fear of being harmed for what she had simply witnessed was not real to her. "Keep running, then? For how long?" she asked.

"I'm not certain. A few days, probably. Just until the other side can make arrangements."

"The other side?"

"Yes," he told her. "The IRA."

"The IRA?" she said.

He leaned close to her and whispered, "It will be upon you to keep that man alive. You understand this, Nora? To do whatever it takes to keep him alive."

Chapter Twenty-one

Maybe she knew that there were days ahead when she would need a reason to get up in the morning, and this was part of the reason why she was staying with the soldier. This would be proof that she was once a valued person. If her son and daughter blamed her for the destruction of her marriage, if the *world* accused her of being the one who had set the destruction into motion, then she would have this to fall back on, this reason to get dressed and begin a new day. *Here is a man who risked his life to save a mother and child, and I am helping him stay alive.*

NORA WAS DRYING OUT the pages of the black book with the hair dryer from the bathroom. She was sitting on the end of the bed while the soldier lay on his back, staring up at the ceiling. *A voice,* she had been thinking. I need a voice for this, a way to reach him. This was something you learn raising teenagers, the importance of drawing them out of themselves, into the open.

At noon John Ferguson came to the room with more food. "Oh, John," she said when she met him at the door. "I don't think I've ever been treated this well. You'll spoil me."

They sat at the window talking for a while. "I remembered

how green everything was here," she told him. "After twenty years it was something I thought I had only made up."

She asked him if he had any children. "Oh, yes," he said. "I have five grandchildren now."

"Grandchildren? You don't look old enough."

"I got an early start," he said with a grin. "I live for my grandchildren. Every Christmas I make snow for them."

"You make snow?"

"I do. It's my grand moment each year. We build a snowman in the garden. I'm the center of attention."

"That's something, John," she told him, touching his arm with her hand. Her own story was expanding with each passing hour. "I'll always have to tell people that in Northern Ireland I met a man who made snow."

That afternoon, waiting for Father Conlon to call, Nora discovered the soldier's name written inside the front cover of the book. Private James Oliver Blackburn.

She said his name out loud, "Private James Oliver Blackburn. I'm going to read you these names that you wrote . . . Patrick Rooney. John McQuinn. Kevin Conley. Melissa Conley. Edmund Mahoney."

He was staring at her when she looked up from the page. *A voice,* she thought again. Something to stop the silence.

"I'd say by the date that you've been a soldier here for nineteen years. Would that be about right?"

She read the date of his first entry again. "July 7, 1979."

"I think it was the tenth of July that same year when my mother went into the hospital." She watched him as he closed his eyes. It was too much like the way Steven used to tune her out, as if she were simply beneath his notice. She stood over him, looking down. "What I don't like, James Oliver

Blackburn—and I hate it, believe me I hate it—is that people do all kinds of despicable things every day of the week, all their lives. Horrible things that destroy other people's lives, and they just go on living in splendor anyway. And here I am, I do the first crazy thing I've ever done, and I'm going to be punished for it?"

She told him they were going to walk together whether he liked it or not.

"You can make this hard or easy," she said. "It's really up to you."

He didn't like it, but soon he was walking. He leaned his left side against her right side. Her right arm was around his waist. They walked to the window and back, and then to the window again. He seemed to her to be about the same size as her son. "Ask me something," she said. "Ask me any question you'd like. My life is a great ocean of fascinating stories and if you're lucky I may share some of them with you. My father was a cigar maker from Havana. My second husband was a duke. I'm not kidding. He was also a champion ballroom dancer."

A smile, she was thinking. She would get him to smile the way she used to get her daughter to smile at breakfast on those dark, cold winter mornings when she didn't want to go to school. Calling her Miss Caboose. *Come on, Miss Caboose, drink your juice.* And then when her mother was in pieces after her father left her, making her smile, not giving up until she had made her smile.

It went on like this for half an hour, her talking, their walking. When she helped him sit back down on the bed she asked another question: "What do you believe in?"

She saw a faint light in his eye, a trace of recognition, and she tried not to seem surprised, not to scare him away. "No more small talk," she said. She moved the stuffed chair closer to the bed and leaned forward toward him. "I'll tell you what I believe," she began. "I believe that people should remain true to one another, no matter what. If you promise to love someone until the end, then you should forsake all others. How do you like that?"

He closed his eyes for half a second.

"And there's more. I also believe that no one has the right to give up, to take their own life. No matter how bad things are. And no one has the right to become hard and mean and cold either. We all owe the world more than that. And besides, James Blackburn, anyone can be happy when things are going well."

WHEN JOHN FERGUSON came to their room again he had dye to color the soldier's hair and a small round carrying case with a strap, like her mother's old hatboxes for traveling. He set this on the floor at the foot of their bed and then stepped away from it.

"I'll drive you to the bus at quarter till five," he announced. "Father Conlon is to call me with the name of a place in Warrenpoint. Is everything all right, then?"

"The bus?" Nora said.

"By now it's safer than a car. I've got clothes for you both."

The idea was to make them look like American tourists. They would carry three matching suitcases, one of these being the round hatbox with the strap. And two bags of golf clubs. When they arrived at Warrenpoint they could dispose of them.

It won't do any good. Nora could see this written on John Ferguson's plain face. He was busying himself in order to drive away his doubts.

"Tell me," she said, "will they find us no matter where we go?"

A silence like that between the final note of a symphony and the audience's applause followed her last words. He looked toward the door as if he had heard something outside in the hallway. This set Nora's heart racing again. "The mother," she said. "I'm worried about her as well."

Katherine Foley, the name James Blackburn had written in his book. She understood now; when he saved her life, he also condemned her.

"But Father Conlon has taken care of her," she said, only to reassure herself.

"Yes, they're safe now, remember?" John said. "You don't need to worry about them anymore."

John turned and looked at the soldier. She saw the light draining from his eyes.

Chapter Twenty-two

L ater Nora dyed the soldier's hair jet-black. He sat in a chair with his head bowed over the sink. She wore the plastic gloves that came with the dye. The back of his neck was tanned. She used a razor and scissors to cut the light brown hairs. Then she shaved off his beard as well. He was becoming someone else right in front of her. And the strange part was that this new person seemed vaguely familiar to her, as if she had known him in another life. Or in a dream.

"I want you to tell me everything," she said as she tipped his head back. "Everything that I need to know so I can see what we're up against."

She thought that maybe he wouldn't speak because he didn't want her to know how long the odds were against them.

But she kept speaking to him, her voice being the only thing that could move time. Move time so that what had happened in the streets of Omagh would begin to fall away behind them.

She told him eagerly about the roadblock they had passed through last night. "I don't think they suspected me," she said. But the country was a labyrinth and she couldn't be sure of anything.

She could tell that he was waiting for her to leave him alone. She started to walk to the door. Then she stopped and told him that she was supposed to be interviewed this morning by the two men at the hotel in Omagh. This made him close his eyes for a moment.

"Yes," she said to him. "So you see, they'll be after me as well. Which means I need your help as much as you need mine. We're in this together."

It took her a bit of time to find the courage to speak the rest of it. "So, what happened here this morning when I was gone can't happen again. I need to know that I can leave you alone and you won't try to do something stupid. There isn't going to be any more of that. Not on my watch, or it'll be on my conscience. And I'm the kind of person who will suffer every day for the remainder of my life if you do such a stupid thing. Do you understand what I'm saying?"

Like a child being scolded, he stared past her.

"Because I'm pregnant, you see? So there's another woman and child in this world that you have to look out for now."

Make him look into your eyes.

She reached to his face and turned his head until her eyes found his. "And don't tell me that we're not going to make it, because we are. Do I sound like your mother?"

SHE LEFT HIM ALONE in the bathroom to take a shower. By the time he had finished, Nora had opened the hatbox and found a gun inside. A pistol with two metal clips of bullets. When she saw what was inside, she carefully set the box down on the floor as if she were afraid it might explode in her hands.

She was staring down at it when he walked to her side, limping across the room, steadying himself on the back of a chair, then the bureau. The look on his face was a mixture of fear and bewilderment, and it took away her desire to say anything. *Maybe we can both just drift away in silence.*

But then, as she was watching him, he picked up the gun and the clips and put them in the pockets of his coat.

THERE WAS NOTHING TO DO but wait for word from John about which bus to take out of town. He had told them that it would be a later bus now, they would travel in darkness. This is a problem in Northern Ireland in August when it doesn't get dark until ten o'clock.

THE SOLDIER HAD BEEN STANDING at the window for more than an hour, looking up and down the street. Nora lay on the bed, drifting across the space between sleep and waking, wanting to let go. But each time she closed her eyes, a reel of film like a silent movie began to turn in her mind and she was walking out into the street after the bomb, black soot rising into the air like a curtain.

Once when she opened her eyes, the soldier was looking at her.

She felt a flash of heat across her forehead and with it, a peculiar sense of herself; for the first time in her life she could see that she had been an actor. How many times had she just been herself, without trying for some effect, some particular way to speak or to walk across a room that would make someone love her better or desire her more, or at the very least believe in her essential goodness? She wondered again if this was how it would always be, or if she might finally become a woman who did not care so much about how others saw her. Or if not caring meant giving up in some way.

She wasn't ready to give up. Instead she kept trying to reach him. "Let me tell you why I was in Omagh," she said. "I was in the clinic, waiting my turn. I was there for an abortion."

She watched him turn his head slowly, as if her words had brushed across his cheek.

"Most of the hard things that happen to people, they don't deserve," she said.

He looked at her again, and she wondered if he was waiting for her to explain.

"Maybe this was all meant to be. Maybe there's some purpose in my being here. It's possible, you know? Could you believe in such a thing?" A part of her wanted to draw close to him, to feel his breath on her face.

"The priest told me that we're all just little sparrows. I think I believe that. What do we know? We can't even look up at the sky and know how far it goes. Maybe I've always known how small I am, and that's why I've accepted so much without questioning it. I never tried to change anything."

She told him that she wasn't sure what she would have changed, given the chance. And this was the truth; she wasn't yet sure what she would have changed, or even if she would have changed anything. Maybe she wouldn't even have changed finding Steven with his cheerleader. Maybe she was glad that the years of living with Steven like two people bundled up in winter coats and scarves inside a freezing-cold house, each of them in separate worlds, was behind her now.

One last thing to tell him. "I think that for a long time I've been waiting to wake up. I've been telling myself, *You'll have to wake up someday.* And when I walked out into the street, after the explosion, I wondered if most of the world has been asleep for too long like I have. You get wrapped up in your little life, and the time goes faster than anyone could ever imagine, and there you are, lost in your own life. I'm not making any sense. I'm sorry about that."

Chapter Twenty-three

A change in plans. There are soldiers posted at the bus station in town, and John heard that they were also at every major stop across the counties. So he will drive them to a small bus stop somewhere along the route outside Enniskillen. And they are not going to Warrenpoint after all, not right now. Instead they will be heading north to the North Channel of the Irish Sea.

DARKNESS HAD COME when they made their way out of town. By the time they waited for the bus at the side of the road outside the village of Trillick there was only the pale light of the moon to show Nora the soldier's trembling hand, which rested beside her on his knee. "The bus should be along in five minutes," John Ferguson was saying, but she wasn't listening to the words. She was lost in her concentration. His hand was faintly shaking as if from some tremor running through his bones. His fingers opened slightly, then closed again into a tight fist, and then opened. There was a kind of rhythm to this, the clenching and unclenching, and she wondered if he was trying to ride away from his pain on this rhythm, to escape his interior. Perhaps it was a way for him to return to the world of motion and meaning. And what about herself, she wondered next. Was she trembling, too? Was there some visible sign of her own estrangement from the world? Was some part of her already adapting to the emptiness in her life, like a room in which a pane of glass is missing, the paint cracking in the sudden cold, everything blown flat by the wind.

Without deciding anything, she took his hand in hers, enclosing his fingers so that the tremor ran across her palm. This was enough to make him turn his head slowly toward her. She felt his glance like light falling across the side of her face, the space between them closing like the skin over a wound.

In the dark they boarded the Ulster bus with DUNGANNON on the destination banner above the windshield. Their suit-cases and golf clubs were in the compartment below their feet. He was dressed in olive-green corduroy pants, a blue cable-knit sweater over a white T-shirt. And a Dallas Cowboys hat that John Ferguson took from his lost-and-found box at the hotel. The gun and clips of bullets were in the pockets of the black raincoat that was folded on his lap. She was wearing blue jeans and a white Irish sweater over a white blouse. They rode along in silence. She was watching him as he leaned his head back and looked out at the passing dark fields. *Maybe we only think we understand our lives,* she thought. *Maybe what we don't know defines us.*

A newspaper lay on the empty seat across the aisle from them. A colored photograph of Market Street in Omagh, moments after the blast. Below, an artist's sketch of the red Vauxhall sedan that the police were looking for.

There were half a dozen other passengers on the bus. Nora was looking at them, thinking of the lyrics from an old song by Simon and Garfunkel—*She said the man in the gabardine suit was a spy. I said "Be careful his bowtie is really a camera."*

A web of dreams, this is what her life felt like to her now. Closing her eyes, she could still see her children when they were babies, with feet small enough to wash in a teacup. Opening her eyes, here, beside her, was a young Abe Lincoln dragged out of a river. And sailing past the bus windows, a lovely country inhabited by murderers.

THEY RODE TO THE BORDER of County Antrim and got off where John Ferguson had told them to, in a small village called Maghera. From there they took a taxi to Portrush, pulling up to the sidewalk in front of a small hotel called the Ashmore. It was a vacation town on the Irish Sea, with little booths along the sidewalks selling cotton candy and postcards.

"I'd like to take a walk," Nora told the man who was leading them up the stairs to their room.

"Perhaps," he said. "We'll have to be very careful, though."

He owned the hotel and ran it with his sister. He explained that he and Father Conlon grew up together. They played football for the same parish.

The soldier was in front of them, climbing the stairs slowly, pulling himself up by the wooden railing.

WHEN THEY WERE ALONE in their room, the soldier disappeared into sleep and Nora stood at the window, telling herself that she had to stop thinking she was responsible for other people's sadness. Down in the street two men wearing winter gloves were unloading barrels of beer from a truck. A few people were out walking. A young woman was selling candy apples. Two elderly men on a bench were talking. About what,

Nora wondered. Maybe just talking about life, their lives, how far the orbit of their lives had swung, the mysteries that swept them here. Old age coming upon them like mist over the sea. There is the lovely sea, the same yet always different. We trust it enough to fall asleep in its presence, then, while we are sleeping, the mist rides the sea to shore, to claim us. We awake and find ourselves cold.

The last thing Nora saw from the window was a Ferris wheel lit up against the black sky.

IT WAS A LONG, empty night, sleeping and waking in a chair with a dusty gold slipcover. In the gray light of morning, she remembered that she had left her notebook behind in the hotel in Omagh. They had it by now, of course, the men who were returning to interview her. *Today I saw a soldier running up the hill with a baby in his arms.*

The one sentence she had written in the notebook—what would it cost her? She considered telling the soldier of this, asking him what it would cost. But then she decided against it.

WHEN SHE FELT THE LONGING for home coming over her again, she put on her coat and went downstairs, leaving the soldier asleep in the bed. The sister and brother were waiting in the foyer, trying to look as if they had other things to do, pretending they were busy and that there were other guests to tend to in a hotel in a country at war, a country without tourists.

When they both asked her if she would like breakfast, she didn't have the heart to turn them down.

They spread out a banquet before her, everything swimming in grease, so that when she leaned over her ham she saw her reflection. They gave her the privacy of the empty room, but she could hear them just beyond the open door, talking softly while she ate the stewed tomatoes. The ham and bacon and fried potatoes. The granola with strawberries. The heavy brown bread that had the weight of a book in her hand. She ate as if she were preparing for a long journey on foot. Or for a hard day's work, like a longshoreman.

When she was finished she told the brother that she was going to take a walk and that she would be back in an hour.

Out on the street she began telling herself to see everything, and to remember it all, and to return here someday, after years had passed and she finally knew the purpose of these strange days.

The sun broke through the gray sky with a brilliant light, and suddenly Ireland was there in every detail. The miniature truck delivering fresh milk in glass bottles. Down each side street identical houses, pastel-colored, joined at their shoulders, each rooftop a little higher than the one before it, like steps climbing the hill. At one corner a group of schoolgirls in their blue jackets and gray skirts. The first day back at school, Nora heard someone say. They were just being girls. One, a tall, curvy blonde, years ahead of the other girls, was wearing a skirt two inches shorter than the others'. She stood off a ways, showing them her secret, pulling her skirt down and then up, down to get past the nuns, Nora guessed, and up when she was safely out of the schoolyard. A plain-faced girl was watching the blonde longingly. *That's me,* Nora thought. Plain and average, never more than average, always listening to someone else's story, like a nurse far beyond the front line of the battle, learning the truth secondhand.

Until now. *Now I have a story of my own to tell.*

UP AHEAD THERE WAS a mother with two strapping sons. She was tiny and they were huge, with great hulking shoulders. The top of her head barely rose above her sons' elbows. Nora couldn't keep from smiling. The thought of this mother cooking them sausage and making their beds. These two boys towering over her and yet taking orders from her as if she were a tiny field general. She will march them to church against their will. She will see that they change their underwear. These bodies as large as bureaus, with hands that could break her bones. Odd to think how they were once folded inside her, deep inside her. Even when they have grown to be men with children of their own, they will have the memory of their mother's voice calling them home for supper.

For the longest time Nora watched them, following them for four blocks. The mother walked just slightly ahead of her sons. She stopped to look at a washing machine in a store window, and again at an arrangement of flowers. Both times the boys stopped too, shuffling their feet, looking off into the distance, patiently biding their time until she resumed. Nora thought of the secrets they kept from their mother. The secret world of girlfriends and sex that had drawn a line between her and Jake when he was around sixteen years old. Sex. She had always been far too modest to ask him the things she was dying to know. The whole time she was raising him, she was conscious of trying to teach him to be a gentle person so that one day he would be gentle with the girls and women who trusted him to place his hands on them. But it was a subject they never discussed. Not that it was a wall between them that would have required a hard climb; it was just a simple line that either of them might have stepped across. She would have liked to ask him if physical touch made him feel a sense of his own worthiness, as it had her when she was first touched.

SHE WALKED ON THROUGH the streets a little farther, surrounded now by babies in prams, their mothers taking advantage of the bright, warm sun. Could she have come to any other place on earth where there were so many beautiful babies?

And the little children. Those slightly older, already trained to take the younger ones by the hand. To scold them when they needed it, to wipe the dirt off their cheeks, and to bribe them with sweets when nothing else worked.

An elderly woman with gold shoes pedaled past her on a bicycle. At the bakery there were hot cross buns in the window. In the butcher shop a red-faced man was tying on his white apron.

Chapter Twenty-four

Darkness had fallen and she was reading beside a small lamp with deep blue mountains sketched on its shade. Some of the names in the soldier's book had letters missing. They were incomplete, like washed-out roads. *Maybe this is how we remember our lives,* Nora thought. At the end, looking back, just fragments, a collection of moments.

She set his diary aside. He hadn't touched the food she brought upstairs for him. It was cold on a yellow plate. Two pork chops smothered in thick gravy. Boiled potatoes. Bread and butter. He was lying with his back to her, but she could tell by his breathing that he was awake. Perhaps his eyes were open. Perhaps he was waiting for her to convince him that he must not give up. She considered this, considered the effort it would take to persuade him to eat. And in the end she could not force him. Eating is an assent to live.

She acknowledged that she was beginning to give up on him.

Suddenly it began to rain, and they discovered together that there was a tin roof above their room when the rain became a joyous riot of sound, like buttons poured from a jar. It was enough to make him roll onto his back and look up at the ceiling.

That's better, she thought. And then she put the plate of food on her lap and began cutting the pork chops into small pieces.

She raised the fork to his lips. His eyes turned to hers. She nodded her head once. The shower of buttons seemed to have moved them nearer to one another by filling the space between them. He breathed deeply, a grimace at the pain in his ribs, then took the fork from her hand.

"Good," she said, placing the plate on his thighs. Then, rather than stare at him, she went back to his journal, but could only look at the page, listening beneath the rain for the small sounds of his not giving up.

"It's no use," she said. "I'm like my grandmother, I talk too much. So you eat, and I'll talk. I'll tell you about my grandmother. When I knew her, of course, she was just an old woman who sat in a chair, but she'd had a life. She was very tiny. When she was a little girl the circus came to New York City and there was a display of Tom Thumb's house. You probably don't know about Tom Thumb. He was a midget, a rather celebrated one. The circus offered a silver dollar to anyone who could walk through the front door without hitting her head. The idea was that if you were old enough to know how to walk, you would be too big. But my grandmother won the silver dollar."

She paused when lightning flashed at the window.

"I didn't learn her story until her funeral when I sat at a table with two of her oldest friends. She never married when she was a girl. When she was forty years old, working as a maid on Long Island in a mansion, a boy came to visit the family and somehow he and my grandmother ended up as lovers. He was her first lover, apparently. She thought she would never see him again, but he came back. And he hung around and they spent more time together, and in the end he asked her to marry him. She refused and begged him to leave her alone. She was twenty years older than him, and she told him it would never work. She told him he would grow tired of her and leave her for a younger girl. But he kept at her, he wouldn't give up, he'd had everything he ever wanted in his life. And he got her for his wife. Of course he wanted children, a family, and my grandmother was now forty-one years old. And still a terribly small woman. Whenever she found a store that had her shoe size, she would buy every pair they had. So she carried a baby to full term, all nine months, and it was stillborn. Every feature perfectly formed, right down to the half-moons on each fingernail. But no heart beating.

"And she gets pregnant again, and the same thing happens. Two babies carried full term, only to be delivered dead. By the time my mother came along, her husband had fallen in love with a woman his own age."

Nora had never told this story to anyone before. Not even her husband or children. Why did she tell the soldier? she wondered as she watched him taking small bites of the boiled potatoes. Because she had read from his diary? Because they had been through the end of the world together?

She didn't know, and might never know.

And then she figured it out. "I never told anyone this story before because I was always afraid it might happen to me. I mean, my husband leaving me. And now I've told *you*, James Oliver Blackburn."

AGAIN THE FEELING of being in a fever dream came over her. There was the knock at their door and the terror in the soldier's eyes, and the buttons still pouring on the tin roof, and she couldn't bring herself to move toward the door. Not until the knocking had gone on a long time.

And then they wanted her to come out into the hallway and to close the door behind her. The brother and sister who owned the hotel. They both looked as terrified as the soldier. The sister took Nora's hand in hers before she told her. "John Ferguson called," she said. "There's still no word from Father Conlon. He was supposed to be here this morning. We've been trying to reach him all day."

By the looks on their faces, this was the worst news. Nora couldn't quite fit the pieces together until the brother told her that she would have to leave with the soldier.

"But why?"

"Understand, please, ma'am, if there's been some trouble, then we could be next here. It's for your own safety, ma'am."

"It's the truth, ma'am," the sister said.

Nora looked at both of them and knew at once that there was no room for discussion. "What time is it?"

"Almost seven," the sister said.

"Will we be able to get a bus?"

"I'll drive you," the brother said.

"Where now?"

"John Ferguson gave me the name of a place in Ballykelly."

"How does he know?" Nora asked.

The brother looked at his sister, then back at Nora. "It's best for me not to say, ma'am."

Nora was losing her patience. "If anything has happened to the priest, it will be my fault. I need to know."

"Please," the brother said. "John Ferguson will meet you tomorrow in Ballykelly. We must hurry now."

THEIR ROOM AT THE LAMBERT HOTEL in Ballykelly had
twin beds under peach-colored blankets and a wooden boat
model standing on the mantel above a stone fireplace. In the
morning she awoke to find him holding it in his hands, admir-
ing it.

She watched him and pretended to be sleeping. He left
shortly, and when he hadn't returned an hour later, Nora
decided to go out and look for him.

ON HER WAY THROUGH TOWN she came to a divided road,
like a boulevard, where she saw a sign for a convent, with an
arrow pointing up a side street.

When she was standing before the small blue door in the
stone wall she told herself that she had walked here only out of
curiosity. But then she knocked.

Soon a nun opened the door. She was young, not much older
than Nora's daughter.

"I know someone who is in trouble," Nora said. "He needs a
place to hide. He's done nothing wrong."

The nun looked at her and then past her to the street where
a truck was grinding its gears to climb the hill.

The nun smiled and said, "You mean like in the movie *The
Sound of Music*? I'm afraid that was only a picture, dear. I'm
sure we wouldn't be permitted to hide anyone here."

Nora heard a radio playing something by Neil Diamond.
"I'm sorry," she told the nun.

"No need to be sorry."

Her voice was pleasant, maybe too pleasant. Like the voice
of an adult reading a bedtime story to a child. It made Nora
feel as if she had lost her place in the world.

Across the street from where she stood, four teenage boys
with spiked hair were taking turns kicking a trash can. They
wore matching Nike sneakers and sunglasses and looked as if
they were ready to take on the world. On the back of one boy's
black T-shirt there was a picture in violet of a man playing a
guitar behind a column of silk-screened words:

BIRTH

SCHOOL

METALLICA

DEATH

She had walked for a long time with no sign of James Blackburn when she saw a lake in the distance, a flash of bright light
through the trees, and then the green outline of its shore
beyond a brick farmhouse. She wondered if anyone would
object to her cutting through the fields of potatoes. Before she
could decide, a tractor appeared from behind a barn and made
its way toward her, pulling a flat wagon behind it. Her first
instinct was to look for a place to hide, but it was already too
late for that, and she saw that a woman was at the wheel of the
tractor and a girl maybe twenty years old with a black dog
rode on the wagon in back. When they stopped, Nora asked
permission to cross their fields to reach the lake.

"Mommy'll drive you," the younger woman exclaimed.

All the way to the lake the black dog kept his head on
Nora's lap. She was thinking how this must have been a common scene in America at one time, mother and daughter
spending their days together working on a farm. She remembered the two pregnant women in the YWCA pool that night,
modern in every way, speaking of the rush of time. Instead of
the self-absorbed lives we live, instead of spending so much
time analyzing everything and dissecting things, maybe we

were meant to do hard, physical work every day, to wear out our bodies and die before we were old enough to be a burden on anyone.

They talked a little while when they reached the lake. The daughter was going to be married in the spring. "Then she'll take her babies to the market every week to show them off to her girlfriends," the mother said. "Just like I did."

"Oh, Ma," the daughter complained, blushing.

As everyone else had, they asked Nora if she was on holiday. It was easier for her to tell them that she was. "My first time on my own in many years," she said.

"Ah, good for you," the mother exclaimed.

When Nora was alone she undressed to her bra and panties behind a tree, wondering how many lies she was going to have to tell while she was in this country. Then she made herself run into the water as she had that night on Cape Cod. After the first shock of the cold, she felt herself relax and fall into the rhythm of her strokes. She swam out far, until she could see the whole village above the hill. A church at either end, each with a pointed steeple piercing the sky.

She wished that Sara were here, swimming with her, and that tonight they could sit somewhere talking about all the things Nora had always wanted to ask her. Like her father, Sara held things back, kept her distance from the world. She made you work to get close to her. But *here*, Nora thought, *in this place*, it would be easier to talk of the important things.

She reached a part of the lake where the water was suddenly much colder. She could feel the muscles in her legs begin to cramp. She knew that she would turn back soon, and swim to shore, but for a few moments she let the cold water enclose her. She took a deep breath and let herself drop through the shadows. Above, the darkness closed over her. She kept her arms flat against her sides and let her weight pull her down deeper. Who would find her, who would ever find her here? How easy to slip from this earth the way the people on the streets of Omagh had.

She needed one reason to put her arms out to her sides to slow her descent and pull herself to the surface, one reason other than fear. She waited for some answer, dropping deeper and feeling her lungs begin to ache. Isn't this what she had wanted to do that night on the airplane when the endless dark ocean lay below her? Wouldn't this be the best thing to do?

SHE WALKED ALONE, back across the potato fields toward the village. The sun was shining brightly by the time she reached the church. She decided to sit in the cemetery, drying her hair. She didn't want to go back to the hotel room and hide from the world.

She walked inside the stone wall that surrounded the graves. She found a place to lie down in the grass. For a long time, maybe an hour, the sky was clear and the warmth of the sun entered her.

WHEN SHE RAISED HER HEAD and leaned back on her elbows a breeze carried the faint trace of a peat fire burning in someone's cottage. How well she remembered this smell from her winter in Wicklow. The cold was always at their door. Steven used to walk five miles to Rathdrum to buy a thirty-pound sack of peat, then hike back to the cottage with it on his shoulders like a laborer. She would hear him coming and open the door for him and help open the sack. They could keep only the one room warm, and they slept there with the babies. They never used that room to make love. Instead she opened her arms to him in the kitchen. On the stairs. They made love every day, sometimes during the babies' morning nap, and again after they'd put the babies down for the night. In the empty years that followed, Steven had used the memory of this against her. "You're the one who's changed, not me."

For a long time he was right. She couldn't explain exactly why she no longer desired him this way, but each time he reminded her of it, she desired him less. Maybe it was just the natural progression of a marriage. They'd become friends, or something else. Enemies, perhaps.

THE MAIN STREET was only five small shops. No cars passed her, only tractors, their tires flinging mud and manure behind them. There was a food store where you could also buy a rocking horse and mail letters. Three pubs and two beauty salons. One with a gold-framed blue ribbon in its front window saying the shop came in second in Northern Ireland's beauty salon contest. A little farther down the street was the shop with a red ribbon for winning.

She came upon the village's tiny school made of stone that the weather had blackened. Standing in front of its red door, she thought the school looked forlorn and forgotten. The same was true inside the pub. Three narrow windows let in so little light that it was perpetual night inside. There was a television in one corner, and the only people inside the pub—the woman behind the bar and a man who held a blue handkerchief to his nose—were watching intently. Some kind of British soap opera. The actors looked as if they were from a different century from the man and the woman in the pub watching them. When a pretty waitress on the television show told one of her customers in an upscale restaurant that he was free to date whomever he wished but she wasn't going to wait around for him to decide who it was he wanted, the man with the handkerchief said to the woman behind the bar, "Well, she's left him in the lurch, aye, Mary?"

"She has," Mary responded.

Nora smiled to herself.

After a little while, a man and four grown boys entered from a rear door. They smelled of manure as they passed through the pub into a room behind the bar. Soon the woman tending bar left, replaced by a younger woman who looked exactly like her.

"She's left him in the lurch today," the man with the handkerchief said to her, as he had to the older woman.

"That's so you'll watch again tomorrow," she said wisely.

"And I will!" he exclaimed.

Nora could hear a baby crying in the room behind the bar. Probably this girl's baby, awakened by her father and brothers returning from the fields for their midday meal, which the girl's mother was now preparing.

Why be sad about this? Nora asked herself. *Why?*

Because she smelled cabbage cooking? Because the linoleum floor was filthy and the arms of her chair were sticky and because the montage of snapshots arranged in the frame above her showed brides and grooms in this room smiling as if they had inherited the earth?

Who could be happy here? Nora wondered. The girl filling in for her mother behind the bar, day after day, seeing her whole life ahead of her inside these little nailed-together rooms?

"Oh, Harold, look, the sun's come out," Nora heard her say. "Throw open the door, Harold."

When he did this, the air that swept inside smelled of clover.

"Lovely," the girl said.

NORA LEFT SOON. The sky was a pale shade of pink. There was music coming from a shop across the street. She stood at the corner for a long time, thinking about the woman in the pub who would stand behind the bar all day tomorrow and the day after, watching the soap opera with her solitary customer, relinquishing her place there to her daughter when it was time to cook the midday meal for her husband and sons when they came in from the fields.

Soon Nora knew what it was that had made her so sad. Twenty years ago she was content in the simple life in Ireland. All day long on the floor in front of the peat fire with her children. A walk down the road was a journey worth embracing. Not going anywhere, not expecting anything at the other end, just a walk. But now she wondered if she could ever be content again with so little. There are times in life when the love we possess is enough. When we do not ask for anything more, when what we have is plenty for us. But once we pass that time, is there ever any going back?

SHE FOUND THAT HE WASN'T in the room. He had left the door unlocked, and the small television on the bureau was turned on. She saw her coat on the chair where she had left it.

She heard the voices of children outside, and when she walked to the window she saw two boys on a soccer field kicking a ball around. He was sitting on a bench beside the field, watching. He had his sleeves rolled up. When the boys turned toward him several times, Nora realized that he was giving them instructions. She tried to open the window to hear his voice, but it had been painted shut.

Just as she was thinking that she would go outside and join him on the field, a small orange car pulled off the street onto the grass alongside the field. It didn't come to a stop in the grass, instead it moved slowly the length of the field. Nora could just make out the dark shape of the driver. It was the way the car was rolling slowly along the side of the soccer field that made her skin go cold. Without another thought she pushed on the window again. She pushed harder and then called his name in the empty room. The car was still rolling. She banged on the glass, but he was too far away to hear. When the car stopped, she thought of breaking the window and shouting at him.

The driver of the car got out, closed the door, and stood looking around for a few seconds. He turned, and when she saw that it was John Ferguson she felt a great relief that caused her to wonder what she had been afraid of to begin with. What harm would come to the soldier in broad daylight on a soccer field? She watched John Ferguson walking toward the bench where the soldier had now turned to face him. All of this, she thought, all of the running and hiding and worrying had been nothing more than the unjustified fear of Father Conlon, a priest who had seen the worst of people and had reacted the way anyone might, by becoming suspicious of everyone.

The sound she heard at that moment, a cracking sound that she thought might be the window frame breaking because she had pushed too hard on the window, caused both John Ferguson and the soldier to drop to the ground while she was watching them. It wasn't until another car appeared, this one with the passenger's side door open, that she knew something had gone wrong. A gunshot, she thought. Then the car sped away.

By the time she had gone down the stairs into the lobby of the hotel, there were two chambermaids in white uniforms standing in the front room, looking out one of the wide windows.

"Don't go out there!" one of them yelled at her as she opened the front door.

She kept going anyway, and she didn't look back or even think of what might happen to her.

THE SOLDIER SAT in the backseat of the orange car, breathing his breath into the mouth of Ferguson. Nora was driving with her foot down hard on the accelerator. She heard herself say that she didn't know where she was going. She turned right and then right again, losing all sense of direction. And then she drove in silence, listening to the soldier breathing steadily and cursing. At some point she knew that this man who made snow for his grandchildren at Christmas was dead.

Chapter Twenty-five

After almost an hour of driving around in circles, Nora pulled to the side of the road in a dirt and gravel parking lot beside a brick building whose roof was half gone. She got out of the car and walked behind the building. Near a pile of old railroad beams she knelt down, thinking she was going to throw up. *Let him drive away without me,* she thought. *Let me stay here.* Her mind crossed back over the years to her first mornings with Steven just after they were married. He used to do push-ups on the floor in the morning, and she would be half asleep, counting by the number of times his Saint Christopher medallion struck the wood floor of their bedroom.

When she looked up, James was standing at the corner of the building. She looked at him. "All this because you saved a woman and her child?" she said. "What kind of people would do this?"

He took a step toward her. "Don't," she said. "Just give me a minute by myself."

HE DROVE FROM THERE. Nora sat beside him, leaning her head against the door. For more than an hour he drove in circles until he was satisfied that no one was following them. Soon after they had crossed into County Down he spoke to her for the first time. "He came to tell me something," he said. "I have to find out what it was."

She looked at him. "They meant to kill *you,* didn't they?"

"No," he said. "If they'd meant to kill me, they would have."

AS THE CAR MOVED into the night, she felt as if she were hovering above her body, looking down at herself and the soldier and the dead man in the backseat. They stopped at a house set by itself in a broad rolling meadow.

"We'll be safe here," he told her as he drove the car into a barn behind the house. They stepped out onto the planked floor, into air smelling of hay and manure, and then walked to the main house.

He knocked on the back door. Soon a light came on and a woman with cropped hair and thick red lipstick walked toward the door. She pulled aside a curtain and looked out the glass panel at them. Seconds passed, and she didn't move to unlock the door.

"Theresa," James said to her, "open the door for us."

She just stood there, staring at them until James called her name a second time. Then she unlocked the door, turned and walked away before they entered. She was halfway across the room when James called to her again, "Theresa, tell Colin I'm here."

When she turned back, Nora could see the heat in her eyes. "Bringing your troubles to our door again, Captain?" she sneered.

"Just get Colin," James said. "Please."

She left them standing there and turned off the overhead light on her way out so that they were standing in darkness.

As soon as they were alone he said to Nora, "You asked me what I believe in. I believe the truth is only the way things can be made to *seem* and to *sound*. That's all."

His voice was calm. He told her that he was sorry for everything that had happened to her. He surprised her by taking her hand. In the darkness Nora could see only his shape dimly outlined by the pale blue pilot light on the gas stove. It crossed her mind that he might be right: Maybe what is true in this world is merely whatever one tries hardest to believe.

"They'll find us wherever we go," she said.

"No. We'll be safe here."

"They'll find us wherever we go," she said again. It came into her mind then, only briefly, but it was there, the thought that when she left the Maine house she should have tried to forget everything she'd seen there.

HE WAS GONE SOON, leaving with a tall man who had to duck his head in the doorways of his house and who smiled winsomely at her when he told her his name was Colin. He wore a white shirt and a narrow blue tie that was knotted precisely at his throat. Before he left, he marched ahead of Nora up to the third floor where he opened the door to a room that faced the barn behind the house. "You should rest well here," he said pleasantly.

Nora stood just behind him. "Can you tell me where you're going?" she asked him.

He stopped hurrying then, long enough to turn and face her. He lowered his eyes and turned his head slowly. "Theresa is in the kitchen. James and I will be back as soon as we can."

Nora listened to his footsteps as he descended the stairs. There was also the sound of the wind begging at the windows and below her, the dull banging of one of the barn doors. She tried to settle things in her mind, to place everything that had happened to her in an order that made sense. There was the moment she stood at the window of the Maine house watching Steven and the girl coming toward her on their bicycles. And now there was this moment, standing at the window, watching Colin and James back the tiny car out of the barn. Its trunk was sagging, and this made her stomach turn again.

ALONE IN THE ROOM, she found that nothing felt real to her when set against the sound of the wind at the windows. She was hovering in space again, high enough to see all of her past falling away far below her.

She listened to the wind racing across the roof, imagining that this wind might ride across the ocean and reach the house in Maine. Rattling the boathouse doors. Nothing stood between this field and that shore, and from the vast space a deep, perplexing loneliness took hold of her as the night air cooled the hard panes of window glass.

She sat on the end of the bed. She thought of the children and grandchildren in John Ferguson's family getting the news that he was dead. Catholics praying for his soul. Maybe waiting the rest of their lives to learn what had happened to him.

She pictured the priest lighting a candle in the back of the church for him.

WHEN SHE WENT DOWNSTAIRS she found Theresa in the kitchen cooking and she asked if there was something she could do to help.

"I'll manage," Theresa replied without looking at her.

The kitchen was meticulously arranged with open shelves

and cupboards with glass doors. There was a large black six-burner stove for cooking, and a blue enamel coal stove for heat.

"There must be something I can do to help," Nora said to her. "I need to do something."

"You've done plenty already," Theresa said bitterly. "In this whole godforsaken country, my door was the only door you could find?"

Beside the toaster in a square container were a few of those miniature plastic ears of corn you use to hold real ears of hot corn on the cob so you won't burn your fingers. On one side of the container someone had written in a black marker, "corn holders."

All right, Nora thought. *Drop it. Go back upstairs.*

But then she felt something coming to her. She imagined Theresa writing on the side of the Tupperware container, a woman tidying her kitchen.

"I didn't choose your door," Nora told her.

There was a second's pause. "Of course not," Theresa said. "You're just along for the ride. How could I forget?"

Using a knife with a wide blade, she was splitting chicken breasts on the stainless-steel counter.

"That's me all right," Nora said, "along for the ride my whole life. Just give me enough money to buy the groceries every week, a little extra for the kids at Christmas, maybe a family vacation every once in a while if you can find the time, and fuck me twice a month so I think you still care about me. I'll go along for the ride."

The two of them stared at one another then. A few seconds of silence passed. Then Theresa set her up with a wooden crate of carrots to peel. She told Nora that she had a meal to prepare for thirty people at the church fair in town.

Just the act of doing something as banal as peeling and cutting carrots made Nora feel grounded again in a reality that had abandoned her at the Maine house. Soon it was easier for her to speak her mind to Theresa.

"I'm here in your country because I ran away from home," she told her.

"You've got it backward," Theresa said. "People run away from *here* to America."

"You have a wonderful country. The people are very kind." Nora waited to see how Theresa would react to the irony in this.

She gave Nora a skeptical glance. "Well, don't be thinking there are heroes in this war, or that there's some kind of romance in it either. Both sides will rot in hell for what they've done, that's my opinion. There's only five percent of the people on both sides that want this fight. The rest of us just want to be left alone."

Nora watched her carry a cast-iron frying pan to the stove and light the burner under it. She could hear her muttering under her breath. And then once she had set the pan down, she started in again. "It's the people in your country who sent all the guns. You and the terrorists in the desert. You people think this is some kind of romantic struggle for freedom."

"I didn't send any guns to anyone, Theresa."

With the mention of her name, she looked up at Nora and studied her face carefully for a little while. The only sound in the kitchen was the blade of Nora's knife coming down on the counter.

Nora knew that she had been a pushover her whole life in tense moments like this, always taking the road of least resistance. Anything to avoid a confrontation. The few times when she wasn't able to escape a heated discussion, she had always been betrayed by a heart that beat too fast and left her breathless. But tonight she felt strong and calm.

"So," Theresa began as she turned her back to Nora and walked toward the double slate sinks, "have you gone and fallen in love with him?"

Now Nora felt her heart start to race. She made herself take a deep breath. "Fallen in love with James Blackburn?"

"Of course."

"I'm a married woman."

"You're an *American* woman."

"Meaning *what*?"

"Meaning nothing."

Theresa crossed the room, pushed open the swinging door to the dining room, and disappeared. Nora cut the carrots, looking up now and then at the shelves, reading the labels on the goods to distract herself. She was alone for a long time before Theresa returned.

"Are *you* in love with him?" Nora asked her.

"I was once," she replied. "Before I had lived long enough to understand certain things."

GRADUALLY THEY FOUND their way to some common ground. Theresa lit a blue candle on the kitchen counter. She opened a bottle of Burgundy with a corkscrew and took two long-stemmed glasses from one of the cupboards.

"None for me," Nora said.

"I'll drink alone then," she said. "It won't be the first time."

While she poured the wine she began talking about James. Her own father was an army officer. She met James at a formal dance on the base in Londonderry. "It was his first or second year in Ireland," she recounted. "He stopped my heart the first time I saw him."

"Do you know what happened in Omagh?" Nora asked her.

"A waste," she said angrily.

"I mean," Nora went on, "do you know why they're after him now?"

"Who's after him?" Theresa asked with such surprise that Nora could tell she knew nothing.

After Nora explained, Theresa said, "Never. Lies, that's all. Both sides lying through their teeth. In the first place, the British wouldn't do such a thing."

"If it's a lie, then why is he running?"

"I couldn't tell you, not in a million years. And I don't care, either."

She told Nora that her father was responsible for recruiting James into the Intelligence branch of the army.

"My father saw the promise in him. He once told me that it was James's innocence that most impressed him. Innocent men are more corruptible. They can be fed the official soup, and they'll keep swallowing it three meals a day."

"Your father was a cynical man," Nora said.

"A realist," Theresa said.

"Like you?"

"Like me."

Finally Nora told her that she had seen him save the life of the mother and child.

"Just before the bomb went off," she said. She watched Theresa carefully.

"So, how did he know?" Theresa asked.

"He must have found out just before."

Theresa looked at her and said nothing.

"What?" Nora asked her.

She shook her head. "You're trying to decide if he's a good man. That's it, isn't it? You want me to settle that for you. Well, find out for yourself. And don't tell me any more," she said, raising the glass of wine to her lips. "He owes me for all the nights I waited up for my husband to come back from somewhere, never knowing if he was dead or alive. Idealism can be deadly if you happen to be on the opposite side of it. If you see him again, ask him to tell you what happened long ago at a hotel called the Maison."

Nora went upstairs alone. It wasn't until she had closed the door and turned on the lamp by the bed that she remembered his diary was back in the hotel room in Ballykelly. First her notebook, and now his diary. It was as if she were unwittingly leaving a trail to be followed. She lay still for a long time trying to recall if she had seen the name Maison Hotel written in the diary.

Chapter Twenty-six

Long after Nora had gone to bed, she heard someone outside her door. She listened and waited, suddenly remembering eight or nine years ago when Steven asked her if she thought she might one day love him passionately again. At first she thought this was a rhetorical question that required no answer. But when he pushed her, she told him that there was a chance, if he began to take an interest in his family, to become more a part of their lives. A woman, she explained, observes her husband all day long, her desire for him building slowly, one glance at a time. He raised his voice at her then, insisting that love didn't work that way. Passionate love, he claimed, must always be unconditional, for it betrays all reason. That is where passion originates, it gathers its power in the rejection of reason. You either feel it or you don't feel it, he had told her. At the time she hadn't pressed him. But now she knew that he had never learned the difference between passion and lust.

When she opened the door she found James sitting on the floor, leaning against the wall. His eyes were closed and the gun was in his hand.

When he looked up at her he said he was sorry.

"For what?" she asked.

He didn't answer right away. Nora watched him for a moment, waiting for him to say something. For some reason she felt that it was within her power to call him back. "Tell me," she said.

"I have to go back to Omagh," he said. "I have to find the mother."

"Katherine Foley," she said.

"Yes."

"You don't have to worry about her," she said. "Remember, Father Conlon has her."

The wind was rattling the window in its frame, and cold air was blowing in. When she saw him shudder she went back into the room and took the blanket off the bed. He looked up when she draped the blanket around him. And then she sat on the floor beside him and began telling him the first thing that came to her mind. "I was always cold when I was a child," she said. "I think that I was four or five years old when my mother gave me a blue woolen blanket. She told me that it was one hundred percent wool. That struck me as being very special, *one hundred percent wool,* and I went around telling everyone that I had a one hundred percent wool blanket."

She laughed and then went on talking, filling the silence with her voice. "But I've always been cold," she said. She could tell that he was trying to listen to this, but couldn't.

"Something went wrong," he told her slowly.

"What?" she asked.

"I don't know," he said. "I should know, but I don't."

AT DAWN THE FOG and rain returned. He woke her when he sat down on the end of the bed. He had a cup of tea in each hand. While he spoke he traced a finger around the outline of the cup. "There'll be a logic to everything they do. Not a single move until they have me where they want me, and then the most illogical move one could imagine to end it."

Nora was watching his hand, how gently he touched the rim of the cup. "You'll be safe here," he said.

"While you go back to Omagh?"

"Yes."

"No," she said to him. "I'm going with you."

When he didn't oppose her she knew that he must have seen she wouldn't be dissuaded.

BEFORE THEY LEFT, he showed her how to use the gun. "I really don't want to know," she told him. But he went on speaking softly to her, showing her how to hold the pistol with two hands, how to disengage the safety, and ease the trigger back. They were standing before a full-length mirror, he was behind her, with his arms around her, his hands over hers on the gun the way Steven had tried to teach her to hit a golf ball before he'd given up. "We'll just bring it up without any hesitation, like this. There, right, that's it, now you have it."

She thought of how she had never been called upon to defend what she loved most in the world. She felt the weight of the pistol in her hands, the smooth, cold metal. She didn't know if she possessed any physical courage. Some people say that the world is growing more and more unsafe; a year ago when they had replaced the storm door on the house in Maine, the man at the hardware store advised Steven to consider a door with bars. He refused, arguing that the world was no more dangerous than it had always been, it only seemed this way because the media had no sense of history, of the barbarism and destruction that had dominated the past. Nora had wanted to believe him.

Looking in the mirror, holding a gun, she felt the same sense of disorientation that she had experienced when she first transformed herself for the junior high school prom with makeup, eye shadow, and a padded bra. And then when she stood in her wedding gown.

She saw him looking at her face in the mirror. "You may have to save our lives," he told her.

LATER, IN THE DARK KITCHEN, they ate some brown bread and apples, sitting across the table from each other. He began telling her of his childhood in England, and how he had once dreamed of studying gems. He loved geology as a boy, the order of the physical world. And numbers. "Numbers," he said. "The language of nature."

He raised her diamond ring to her lips. "Feel the cold in it? That's because diamonds conduct heat. You can feel it draining the heat from your lips."

He told her that in the world of nature there were inviolable laws, and consistent patterns, which he took comfort in as a child. The way that buds on certain flowers were arranged in the series 1,1,2,3,5,8,13,21,34. "Every third number is the sum of the two that precede it."

"Is that true?" she asked. "Or only something you made to *sound* true?" She was smiling when she said this, testing what he had said to her about truth. But he didn't notice. He went on telling her that he had joined the army believing he could bring order to this part of the world, ending the chaos and the fear.

She listened to him for a long time. Already, light seemed to be returning to the night sky.

"What did you say to her after you gave her baby back to her?" Nora asked him.

"I believe I can get safe passage for the mother and you," he told her instead of answering her question. "I might be able to bargain for this."

"Tell me what you said to her, James."

"I told her that I wouldn't let anything happen to her or her child."

THEY SPENT THE NEXT DAY talking and waiting. After he made two telephone calls he told Nora that he had an inside contact who was brokering a deal with the people who were after them. "I'll get you home, you needn't worry," he told her.

"I'm not worried," she said. "What happens to you in this deal?"

Again he didn't answer her. He told her that for a long time in his life he used to make himself return each year to the site of every IRA bombing. "I stood in the place where the bombs had gone off. It was like the way Catholics return to the Stations of the Cross."

Chapter Twenty-seven

They boarded a bus six miles out of town in the late afternoon. Soon after they got on, the bus stopped to pick up a farmer on the side of a narrow road enclosed by tall hedges on both sides. He was an old man with a creased face. He wore muddy black boots and a tweed suit large enough for two of him. The seat of his pants was an empty bag. On the bus he stood and talked to the driver for ten, fifteen miles until the bus stopped to let him off in a small village called Lisbellaw. Before he stepped down he turned to Nora and his eyes were lit up like a child's. "Doesn't the town look brilliant?" he exclaimed. "There'll be a wee bit of music in the pub tonight." He tipped his cap to her. She watched him stride down the sidewalk as the bus pulled away. He stopped outside the first shop he came to, taking off his cap and holding it against his side with one arm while he combed his hair in the window. For some reason this filled Nora with pleasure.

They passed a cemetery where an elderly couple were working with a hoe and rake, turning over the earth on a grave. A box of perennials was on the ground near the headstone, white and purple flowers. They were taking such care, their movements slow and thoughtful. In a country where people were killed indiscriminately, they might have been tending the grave of a child.

A little farther on Nora closed her eyes. This was the first time she thought about calling home. Not to ask for anything, but to reassure her children that she was all right.

When she opened her eyes she saw James looking out the window at a nun sitting in the sun with her black dress hiked up to her knees. He turned his head to keep her in sight until the bus was far ahead of her, and this made Nora believe that he was returning to the world by delicate degrees, laying claim to the physical landscape around him.

THEY BOTH SAW HIM at the same moment—the farmer with the muddy boots who had gotten off the bus thirty miles behind them was now up ahead, standing beside a tan car parked at the bus stop. James was already out of the seat and going down the aisle when a woman in a red coat pulled the overhead cord for the driver to stop. She passed by Nora, moving quickly to the front of the bus. When she put her hand in her pocket Nora yelled for James without thinking of the consequences. He turned, grabbed the woman by her arm and wrestled her to the floor. A few people began screaming. Nora saw that James had his foot on the woman's throat and his gun at the back of the driver's head.

"Don't stop," he told the driver.

He kept the woman in the red coat pinned to the floor beneath his foot until they had gone maybe ten miles and James was certain the farmer wasn't following them. Then he made her empty her pockets before he ordered the driver to stop and let her off. She took one step down before she turned and looked into Nora's eyes. She raised her chin, and drew her shoulders back. She raised her arm slowly and then pointed at her, saying nothing.

. . .

FIFTY MILES AHEAD James took the driver's cell phone before he and Nora got off. When the bus had driven away, they began walking through the woods. The sky was heavy with a summer storm. They walked for hours and were both soaked to their skin by the rain when they came upon a farm a few miles outside Omagh. They hid inside a barn filled with old rusted machinery, taking off their wet clothes and hanging them from a beam in the loft to dry.

Just as she had remembered Steven doing his push-ups, she suddenly recalled a small detail her mother had told her once about her tiny, brokenhearted grandmother. How, after her husband had left her for the younger girl, she kept herself alive by sewing for people. Sewing night and day, and toward the end of her life she splurged and bought herself a silver thimble, which she grew to cherish more than her wedding ring.

James was sitting by the barn doors keeping watch. She considered telling him what she had just realized. That she was the third in a line of wives left by their husbands.

He looked at her when she knelt down beside him. "As soon as it gets dark," he said.

She heard something beyond his words.

"What is it?" she asked him.

"I have to manage now on my own, Nora."

"Why?"

"You must know why," he said, looking away. "If they've already killed the mother and the priest . . ." He paused before going on. "There's a boat up north," he began slowly. "I might be able to keep them following me long enough for you to get there. You can get across to Scotland."

She tried to think, to find her way ahead of this. To find

the words that would bring all of this to an end. She looked outside across the flattened farmland, to the hills off in the distance.

"If they've already killed the mother and the priest, then you'll give up," she said to him.

She saw him turn away from her. He stood up and made that gesture again, tapping his shirt pocket for the pack of cigarettes that once had been there.

"No," she said angrily. "You look at me." She stood up next to him and waited until he had obliged her. She spoke each word slowly, without a trace of doubt or self-pity. "You can't give up, no matter what. And neither can I."

THERE WAS A STARLESS SKY and not a sound in the night. Across the valley there were a few lights on in the farmhouses. The city of Omagh to the north was buried in low-hanging fog.

They walked down a narrow road toward the village of Drumore. Again the hedges and thistles rose above their heads. A small house, dark at every window, appeared in a clearing. A bicycle was leaning against the picket fence in front. They took it and kept moving.

SHE RODE SIDESADDLE on the crossbar while he leaned over her, pedaling hard. She thought of Steven and his cheerleader arriving by bicycle. How many days ago? she wondered. She tried three times to count the days in her head, and then she gave up.

The night was quiet enough for them to hear cars coming ahead of them or behind long before their headlights appeared. Each time a car approached, they hid behind the roadside hedges until the car had passed. She was in this with him now, she could feel it. She was part of however this would end.

As they rode along she recalled the young priest's struggling to light his cigarette. His warning—*Anything you tell me about what happened here today, I may be forced to repeat.* Though she could not have known or even guessed the consequences, she was to blame for whatever might become of the priest now. *Blame my innocence,* she told herself bitterly. *Blame my sheltered life.*

They came to a steep hill that James couldn't climb. They walked side by side to the top with him leaning on the bicycle, pushing it with one hand on its leather seat. At the crest of the hill they climbed back onto the bicycle and coasted for a long way. Nora closed her eyes and felt the damp wind on her face. Her fingers were numb on the steel handlebar. The smell of coal smoke in the night sky was what she would remember years from now when all of this seemed even more unreal to her, like something someone had told her long ago, years before her old life vanished.

Chapter Twenty-eight

Drumore was a single main street. A butcher shop with empty stainless-steel pans in the window. A feed store with a wooden loading ramp at the side door. A grocery store, and a pub called McElroy's.

They walked the length of the street toward a lighted window. They were less than a hundred yards away when the sound of a car's motor came out of nowhere, behind them. Before Nora could turn to look, she felt his arm around her back, pulling her down. They lay in the wet grass, waiting for the car to pass. It came upon them going very fast, but then it slowed and Nora felt his arm tightening around her. She saw the automobile's red taillights reflected in the bicycle's chrome chain guard when the car came to a stop. When the passenger's door opened, a light went on in the car's interior and she saw a girl on her knees on the seat leaning next to the driver. The girl lingered a few seconds, then slid along the seat until she was out the door. " 'Bye, Johnny," she exclaimed in the determined whisper of a conspirator.

As the car drove off, James told Nora that they needed to ask directions to the mother's house.

NORA WAS SURPRISED how easily the lie fell from her lips. She stood with the bicycle, explaining to the girl how she and

Katherine Foley had met in Omagh just before the bomb went off. "I had to come and find her."

The girl told her pleasantly that her cottage was a mile from the village, just up the hill from a church. Nora thanked her and gestured to the lighted window. "Your mother's waiting up for you?" she said.

"No, my sister," the girl said. "Up with her baby. Katherine's probably up with hers as well. They say God counts the lights on in Ireland in the middle of the night to keep track of all the infants."

IT WAS A ONE-STORY COTTAGE with whitewashed walls and a steeply pitched roof whose eaves were no more than six feet off the ground. A postcard cottage, lacking only moonlight or a farmer in a crushed cloth cap, exactly like the cottage in Wicklow where Nora and Steven had lived. This made her stop and take a deep breath. She watched James moving ahead of her through the open meadow, stepping over sleeping sheep as if they were sacks of flour. He walked purposefully and quickly, as if someone inside the cottage were calling his name.

When she caught up with him and heard the sound of someone singing faintly she reached out her hand and touched his shoulder. He paused a moment. "See," Nora said. "She's all right, James."

The door was unlocked. She saw his hand on the latch, and when he pushed the door open the scent of burning coal rushed out.

The singing was on a radio that lay on the floor. It was the only thing left unbroken. Chairs and lamps, the glass from framed photographs. Nora heard him curse. She was staring at a box of disposable diapers scattered across the floor like bandages. She heard him going off by himself, down a narrow corridor. A crazy thought came to her—*How did the bomb reach this far?*

And with this question Nora saw that she had been drifting through time and space again. It had been happening to her this way since the bomb exploded. No, since she saw Steven and his cheerleader arriving at the summer house in Maine. What had happened since that moment seemed real to her at first, as it was happening, but then veered off somewhere, crossing the line of reason and carrying her away on the adrenaline of sorrow straight to the edge of the world, where she stood now, looking at everything around her through a mist of fear.

AND THEN SHE COULD hear him singing in the next room. Singing along with the radio. She turned on an overhead light and found him in the hallway, sitting on the floor, slumped against the wall. Singing with a lovely tenor voice, in a language she didn't understand or recognize. His eyes were open wide and his head was tipped back as if he were singing to heaven. He was slipping off the edge again, and this is what made her forget herself. She wouldn't allow him to give up. She would move both of them back from the precipice by the force of her will alone.

"We'll find her," Nora said to him. "We'll find her and her child, you'll see."

He was looking at the floor. She called his name. "James."

She made him stand up and walk outside with her. She took his hand. Off in the distance there were a few lights on in cottages and barns. The anonymous time of the night was ending, and the people were reclaiming their lives. She stood in front of him and placed her hands on his shoulders. "We can't stay here," she said. "We have to hurry now."

THIS TIME SHE PEDALED the bicycle. When they climbed a small hill she stood up on the pedals. She felt his back against her thighs. They were moving slowly, as if they were riding through drifting snow. She was weighing everything she didn't know about this man and couldn't know, against the only thing she was sure of: He had saved a woman and her child.

IN TIME THEY CAME to a church standing alone in the middle of a cemetery surrounded by a high stone wall. At the far corner of the cemetery they found a dilapidated shed with a rusted tin roof. Its door hung by only the top hinge, which was a strip of leather nailed to the frame.

Inside, Nora saw that it was an old potting shed with broken clay pots and straw on the floor. She was aware of James standing in the doorway and watching her as she made a place for them to lie down. In one corner of the shed a green vine was growing. She knelt down and felt its stiff leaves. Something abandoned and yet thriving. A metaphor for her that her husband would appreciate.

When she looked back at James, she saw that a large section of the night sky had cleared to a cobalt blue and there was a single white star above his head.

He thanked her. She was surprised to hear his voice. "Are you going to be all right?" she asked.

He bowed his head sheepishly. After a moment he said, "You'll have to go back."

"Back?"

"Into Omagh."

"Why?"

"They must have her—" he said. But he didn't finish.

She took a half step toward him and saw him match this by moving backward a half step of his own. He was self-conscious about this; she could tell by the way he looked away from her glance.

"If I had a way to get you back," he said, "back to your own people . . ."

She watched him raise one hand to his face and draw his thumb back and forth across his forehead.

My own people. "That's not up to you. I'm running *away* from my own people," she said. She heard her own voice rising. "I'm *here* now. And we're not going to talk about me going home. Here," she said, taking his hand.

They lay down together. "I made a little nest," she said. "Something I'm good at."

When she smiled at him he told her that his own mother used to tape photographs of dead relatives on her children's cribs when they were babies. "In the event we died in our sleep, she wanted us to have faces we could recognize where we were going."

"Heaven," she said. "When my daughter was three I had to tell her that her pet rabbit had died. When I found myself telling her that it had gone to heaven I knew that all of religion had been invented just to make death easier to take."

He looked straight into her eyes, drumming the fingers of his right hand against his thigh. "What do you believe in?" he asked her softly.

This took her by surprise, his soft, reasoned voice. "What did you say?"

"What do *you* believe in, Nora?"

"That's my question."

"All right."

She waited for him to look into her eyes again. "I believe that people have the right to know the truth."

"The truth?" he said.

"Yes, and it's more than the way things can be made to seem. I've always believed it was more than that."

Just before they fell asleep he told her about his mother and father. He was the youngest of ten children. Both his parents were artists before they died. Painters.

"I was born in Scotland, in a castle," he told her.

It could be the beginning of a fairy tale, she was thinking.

"During the First World War the castle was converted to a hospital. There were nearly thirty thousand men in England and Scotland whose faces had been disfigured by wounds. They were brought to the castle and they lived there while artists made them masks, perfect imitations of their faces before they went into battle."

"And your parents lived there?"

"Yes, after the second war, and again after Korea. I was born in the castle in 1955. My father passed away in 1960, but my mother was recommissioned after the Falklands. She returned to the castle. Then again in 1980, she went back once more. A month before she died she painted her one-thousandth mask. It was for a young man from Essex. An army paratrooper wounded in this country. I was with her in the last hours of her life. She told me she remembered every face. All one thousand masks that she had painted."

"I would have thought that she might have forbidden you to become a soldier," Nora said. "I mean, after all that she saw."

"Yes. But she loved soldiers. She told me that in order for

her to paint a perfect mask, a part of her had to fall in love with each boy. When the fighting in this country grew worse, there were more and more soldiers going from here to the castle. She had a colleague, another painter, who did masks for two boys from the same family. Fighting on opposite sides."

Chapter Twenty-nine

His plan. If his hands hadn't been shaking, and if she weren't in a country where people had been killing each other for hundreds of years, she might have simply refused to believe him when he told her that his only chance of rescuing the mother was to set a trap.

He told her that the men who had the mother were the men who questioned her after the bombing, the same men who came to her room with the soldiers and who told her they would speak with her again the next morning.

"They will keep her alive to try and get me," he said. He was standing in the doorway of the shed, gazing at the blackened granite crosses in the cemetery. A flock of birds landed on the church roof, several of them sliding down the wet slate shingles, fluttering and then settling their weight before tucking their wings beneath them.

He turned to look at her. She could feel him returning from another world. She waited a moment, then told him that she had lost his diary. "All those names," she said.

"They were the ones who were wounded. I always wrote down their names because no one remembers the wounded."

"You do."

"Yes. It's been my life," he said. "It's what I've done with my life."

He looked at her in a way that made him feel familiar to her.

"I wanted to remember," he said sadly.

"Remember?" she said. "Maybe you need to forget. I mean, people don't want to remember, they want to live. Just live. They want to work, they want to sit out on their porches, and walk their kids home from school. Didn't you ever want to just—"

She stopped. She noticed that he was standing with his head bowed and his hands clasped in front of him like an altar boy.

"Have you thought of killing me?" she asked him. "You could have killed the mother and me and the priest. You could have gotten rid of the witnesses. What's three more bodies in a country at war?"

He took her in his arms then. She laid her face against his ribs. "I swear to you, Nora."

"Don't swear to me. Don't bother."

"Please."

"Sometimes people need to forget. Those mothers who've lost sons, and the widows, what good does the remembering do them? The remembering of ancient grudges."

Somehow she had brought herself to the center of the confusion in her own heart, to the unanswered question.

"How did you know where the bomb was set to go off?" she asked. "Did you send people the wrong way?"

He gazed steadily into her eyes. "By the time I knew, it was too late," he said.

She believed this, perhaps because she wanted to. She saw the pain in his eyes. She told him that life required us to forget certain things. "A normal life, I mean. Didn't you ever want a normal life?"

"I don't remember," he said.

And this also seemed true to her. He was being honest; she could hear something in his voice, not sorrow but a sense of wonder.

THEN HE LAID OUT his plan for her. She would go into town, to the hotel. She would place a call.

"There's a number you can call to reach them. Call them from the hotel and tell them to meet you in the dining room."

"Then what, James?"

The sound of his name startled him. "No, no, I have to back up. Wait. You stayed the night in Omagh, the night they came to your room. Then in the morning you went to the church and I was there. I needed your help and so you went with me. To Donegal. Yes, a hotel there called the White Cross. That's where you'll take them tomorrow."

He grew more animated as the lie rose up between them. "You'll tell them they can have me but only after I've been given proof that you and the mother and her child have safe passage to America. Yes. Do you understand?"

"What about you?"

"And the priest," he said. "The priest too."

"And what about you?"

"I'll have a way out. Don't worry. The White Cross Hotel, two o'clock tomorrow. Now, here's the number to call."

She made him stop. "Maybe they won't believe that I went with you to Donegal."

He thought about this, drawing his thumb back and forth across his forehead again. After a few minutes he asked her what day it was.

"Wednesday."

"Wednesday. All right. That's it then. We would have

arrived in Donegal on Sunday. At five o'clock every Sunday in the summer the Jesuit monks from Saint Michael's sing in the village square. If the sun is too hot, or if it's raining, boys from the chapel choir stand behind them on the cobblestone wall, holding blue umbrellas above them. Remember this, and tell them you were there."

She told him that she would do the best she could. For a while neither of them spoke. Then he talked about his mother again. "I told her that I was going to give my life if I had to, to end the war here. It was a pledge I made to her. Stupid, I suppose."

"Why? Why would anyone think it stupid of you?"

"Setting out to do something grand with your life? You know, something on a large scale. I realize now that a great life is one lived modestly, for those who are depending on you."

She told him that she had never had big dreams for her children. "I wanted them to be happy living average lives. I wanted them to learn the difference between happiness and pleasure. To learn to find happiness in things that can't be taken from them. The ocean. Time with friends."

"Friends?" he said. "I've seen friends taken away. I've seen the end of happiness here."

"I suppose you have," she said. "I'm sorry you've had to see that."

He nodded his head thoughtfully. "Every time I've ever thought of having children of my own I've known that I would have to lie to them constantly. And to myself."

"About what?"

"I'd have to make myself believe that I could protect them in this world. Either that or go mad with fear."

"We all lie about that, James," she said.

HE INVITED HER to lie down and sleep for a few hours longer while he kept watch. It was the furthest thing from her mind, but she slept anyway. When she woke she found him still standing in the doorway. He had taken off his sweater and draped it over her. She was going over everything he had told her, and watching him, feeling that she would never see him again.

"Why did you stay?" he asked her. "Why haven't you gone home?"

It was a question she didn't expect to answer. But then she found herself telling him about her mother. "It was like walking on glass with her after my father left. I was pretending that everything would be all right even though she was drifting into space somewhere. The dark side of the moon is how I thought of it then. She became very fragile. Then there was her anniversary, what would have been their thirtieth anniversary. I was home with her. We had just sat down for dinner when she left the table and went upstairs. When she came back down she was all dressed up. She had painted her nails with this awful pink polish. She told me that she was getting ready for her date with my father. He was coming for her, she said. She was trying to dry her fingernails, walking around with her hands out like this, like a surgeon waiting for the gloves. She called me into the bathroom and she said, 'Nora, come pull down my pants for me so I can pee.'

"I guess that was when I knew that she would never be the same. And it was, well, for me, that was the end of whoever *I* was. Looking at her all dressed up, with her pink nails, I felt the fear that we all feel when our parents leave. You know, like the umbrella of immunity has been lifted from our heads. And we're next. She was all alone in the world. And I didn't want to end up that way. After that night I caught the first train that led to a safe life."

She stopped for a moment before she acknowledged that she might have turned the other way, she might have fled from the kind of married life that she had seen fall apart. "But I didn't," she said. "I didn't want any surprises after that. *Come pull my pants down so I can pee,*" she said again. "Funny, but I think that's why I haven't gone home."

She called to him, to come and lie down beside her. She put her head against him and they were still, as if asleep, and the dark night closed around them. This was the day of the month when her period normally began. It was a small thing, unnoticed by the world.

Chapter Thirty

She repeated the telephone number in her mind as she waited on the road for a ride back into Omagh. Cows were lumbering out into the fields in the rain, which was lighter now. Off a ways a farmer was riding a tractor with a child at his side, tucked under his arm to keep her dry. If she found the men at all, and if they allowed her to leave, she was to take a bus to Donegal, check in at the White Cross Hotel, a room with two beds. Hang the Do Not Disturb sign on the doorknob, then get a room at the Blue Finch Bed and Breakfast at the north end of the street and wait for him there.

It wouldn't work. She knew it wouldn't work. First of all, she had never been a good liar. You must believe a lie in order to tell it convincingly. This was what she was no good at. "Act confused," he said to her. "You have the right to be confused, they'll expect this. Remember the monks under the blue umbrellas. Remember the White Cross Hotel, two o'clock tomorrow. And if everything fails, if we are separated, we'll meet back here."

SHE GOT A RIDE from a bus driver on his way to work in a pale blue panel truck, telling him that she had been out taking a walk from Omagh into the countryside and had wandered too far. On the pocket of his blue suit coat the words "Ulster Bus" were embroidered in white thread. A newspaper lay on the seat between them. The front page was divided, a colored photograph of Market Street taken moments after the explosion on the top half of the fold and below, a photograph of a woman in a hospital bed, holding a newborn baby beneath the headline JOY IN THE MIDST OF SORROW.

He asked her if she was here on holiday and without missing a beat Nora began spinning an elaborate lie about how her daughter was coming here as an exchange student in the autumn and she had come in advance to look for accommodations. The words fell out of her mouth into sentences that were preposterous to her.

"We've had no troubles in Omagh before," the driver said. "No troubles at all. Enniskillen, Newry, Cookstown, Armagh, all around us there was trouble in the past, but never in Omagh."

It turned out that they both had daughters named Sara. Nora watched a smile come to his face when he spoke of how his Sara planned to attend college. With the sun coming up across the fields, burning through the fog and rain, and his sentences so full of hope, Nora closed her eyes and let his voice surround her.

"Where should I drop you, then?" he asked when they came upon the town.

"Where are you going?"

"Well, I go right to the station."

"That's fine," she said. It was then that she decided she would go first to the church to try to find Father Conlon.

ON MARKET STREET she watched three trucks unload maybe twenty men in jeans and sweatshirts, wearing carpenter's belts and carrying tools. Soon three more trucks arrived carrying hundreds of sheets of plywood. At the far end of the street a dozen soldiers in brown coveralls were erecting a high metal wall, painted dull green, exactly like the wall surrounding the army base.

Nora stood in front of the Bank of Ireland watching two men in goggles and hard hats using long wooden poles to knock out all the loose and cracked panes of glass in the buildings along the street. They moved from one building to the next while the carpenters waited. Then, when the windows were cleared, the carpenters nailed plywood to the openings. They worked methodically and in silence, without speaking to one another, as if talking would somehow dishonor the suffering that had transpired here. Some of the buildings had their fronts ripped off. *Like me,* Nora thought. *The front of my life torn off. The rest of me exposed for the world to see.*

SHE RECOGNIZED the priest's car parked in front of the church, the car that she had driven to Enniskillen the night of the bombing. The sight of it filled her with such hope that she was practically running when she entered the church. She saw a line of people waiting at the confessional booth and she took her place behind them.

"I THOUGHT YOU WERE DEAD," she whispered to Father Conlon.

"And I you," he told her. "Thank God."

"John Ferguson," she started to say.

"I know," he told her.

She told him everything she could think of. He was against her meeting the men at the hotel.

"It won't work, Nora," he said to her. "These men won't

stop. Even if he turns himself in, they won't stop there either. There must be no record of what happened, no one left alive. You, and I. The mother."

"You had her," she said.

"No," he said softly. "I was lying to you. I felt it might keep the soldier alive. That's all. I thought he would give up if he knew. I'm sorry, Nora."

"So they have her, then?"

"They must."

"Then all of this is worthless," Nora said. She could feel everything shutting down inside her.

Father Conlon told her of a woman in Londonderry who could get her through to the other side. "There's a pub called the Grindstone. She works behind the bar. A Scottish woman."

"I'm going to meet these men," Nora told him. "He would never turn himself over to the IRA. I know that much about him, Father."

In the end, he insisted that she give him a little time. "Half an hour," he said. "I'll be parked in the alley behind the hotel. If there's any trouble, tell them you have to use the bathroom, then make your way to the back alley."

"Yes," she heard herself say. She told him that she understood everything he had told her, though much of it was mixing in her mind with everything James Blackburn had told her.

"And where is the soldier now?" he asked plainly.

When she described the place, he said, "My God, Nora. That's Saint McCartin's Church. I buried Avril Monaghan and her babies there."

This took her breath away. She couldn't speak.

"Now, listen," he said. "I'll go there now and bring the soldier. He'll be in the car with me, Nora. And when you've finished, I'll take you both to Londonderry."

He paused. Nora heard someone coming in through the front doors of the church.

"Now let me say a prayer for you," the priest said. "A prayer for you, and for the child you're carrying."

Chapter Thirty-one

Inside the lobby of the Royal Arms Hotel there was the smell of bacon frying, and Nora was surprised to find the dining room filled with men in black raincoats. Some of them were drinking pints of beer with their breakfast. Eventually a woman in a yellow apron who was waiting on them brought Nora a pot of coffee and two raisin scones on a white plate.

"All these men?" Nora whispered to her.

"The burials," the woman said. "Undertakers and pall-bearers. So many people to bury."

SHE MADE THE CALL from the front desk. Then, while she was standing there, she dialed her number at home. It was four in the morning across the Atlantic. While the number was ringing she pictured Hank Waters on his silver bicycle, throwing newspapers onto the lawns on Bow Road. Finally the tape machine picked up and she heard her own voice saying she was sorry she wasn't home to take the call. She tried the Maine house and got her own voice there as well, though for a moment it sounded like a voice she had never heard before.

THE WAITRESS CAME BACK to her table. She had been to America once herself, to Boston, in fact. "Oh, you're from the north, so you cannot understand the people in this country," she said.

Nora was confused.

"In South America they understand. Am I saying it right—*South America*? Nashville. Alabama."

"Oh, you mean the *South*. The south of America."

"Yes. I have a sister who has traveled there many times. She's told me about the black people. Those are people who feel deeply, the way the Irish feel. In the north of your country the people are too cold, my sister told me. Too cold. Maybe it's the weather that has made them that way, I don't know. Isn't the weather terribly cold?"

Cold, Nora thought. The word Steven used to describe her.

THE MOMENT THEY WALKED into the dining room she was certain that this would not turn out the way the soldier had planned. The white-haired man was walking in front, looking around the room carefully. When his eyes moved toward her, she raised her hand.

They greeted her so warmly, with such open smiles, that she felt dizzy and chills began running along her spine. All her fears returned in a rush. The fear that she might say the wrong thing when they questioned her. The fear that they might pull out a gun and shoot her on the spot. The fear that they would lock her up so that she would never see James Blackburn again.

"The chocolate cheesecake here is gorgeous," the white-haired man said. He ordered three slices and a pot of tea. And then before Nora could speak, he placed a manila envelope on the table. Nora couldn't take her eyes off it for some reason. The other man lit the pipe that previously had only been clamped between his teeth. His tobacco filled the room with a magnificent cherry scent.

They didn't seem at all concerned about the meeting she had missed the day after the bombing. They made no mention of it, and this puzzled Nora.

"There's no way, I'm sure, that the British government can make adequate recompense for the ordeal you have suffered here, Mrs. Andrews," the white-haired man began.

"Certainly not," his partner added, speaking through curls of gray-blue smoke.

"But I do hope you'll allow us to be of service now."

"Service?" Nora heard herself say stupidly.

"You, no doubt, have a return airline ticket for a date that is no longer appropriate?" he said. And then he waited, picking lint from the sleeves of his sweater, until Nora figured out what he meant by this.

"Oh, yes. My return ticket to America. I think I fly back on the twenty-fifth."

"Yes, well, we'll certainly change that ticket for you, if you agree, of course, so you can return home at once."

"Any additional charge by the airline will be covered," the other man told her.

Both men were smiling at her now. Identical smiles, she thought, looking from one to the other.

And they were so kind to her that even when the white-haired man addressed her by her name, *Mrs. Andrews . . . Mrs. Andrews . . .* and she recalled that she had once checked into this hotel using a different name, it didn't worry her.

She watched the man pushing tobacco into the bowl of his pipe, tamping it down with his thumb. When she looked back at the white-haired man he was laying her notebook in front of her, open to the page where she had written about the soldier running from the mother with her baby in his arms.

"I believe you left this in your room," he said. "One of the maids found it."

Then, before she could reach across the table, he began to lay out black-and-white photographs on top of the notebook. It was difficult to make any sense of the first photograph, and Nora had to lean very close to it before she saw that it was a body without a head, sprawled across a mound of splintered boards. Then another of an elderly woman lying naked on her back, all of her skin blackened like burned toast.

She felt a sinking in her stomach.

He kept laying out more photographs, even as the cheese-cake arrived on blue flowered plates. Laying them out steadily, as if he were dealing cards. And then speaking to her as well. "This country has been engaged in a long and costly war, Mrs. Andrews. Costly to all sides. People speak of the Troubles as having lasted thirty years, but I can assure you this war spans far more time than that. Over the years individuals have tried, at times, to take matters into their own hands, not so much out of a desire for personal gain—that is seldom the impetus—but from an overwhelming desire to bring an end to the murder. Captain Blackburn has devoted his entire life to ending the fighting here. And with the peace process held hostage to one final demand—the demand that the IRA lay down their weapons, he took it upon himself to change the warning that was called in to our office two hours before the explosion on Saturday morning, the fifteenth of August. Then he used the chaos to escape. 'Desertion' would be the more precise word for it."

She watched him lean back in his chair, a satisfied look on

his face. "You took the mother," Nora said, though by now she was barely hanging on and she wanted only to close her eyes.

He didn't deny it. "For her own safety," he said. "We had her picked up."

"You destroyed her home."

"We were searching," he said.

"Searching?"

He nodded slowly. "We took the woman before Blackburn could get to her."

"He saved her life," Nora said. "Why would he harm her after he'd saved her life?"

"Because she knows too much. So do you. I don't mean to frighten you like this, but it *is* the truth."

He paused. Nora felt as though a hole, a deep hole, were opening beneath her chair. She was looking into his eyes when he went on. "You and the priest are the only others who know. We're protecting the priest, and we want to do what is best for you."

In her confusion Nora remembered the diapers scattered across the floor of Katherine Foley's cottage. She watched the man lean back in his chair. She was lost momentarily, thinking of the crease in the priest's trousers. And the last thing he said to her in the hotel the night he brought James Blackburn to her room. *Keep this man alive.* As if that were in her hands. And what else had he told her, when she went to the church after the bombing? *You have a strength in you, Nora. Go and live.*

And now he would be waiting in the alley behind the hotel, waiting with James in the car.

BY THE TIME she heard the man's voice again, she had nearly decided that James Blackburn had used her, sending her into town this morning in order to give himself time to get away, to disappear into the countryside before these men could find him.

"You will, won't you?" he asked her.

She had missed the question. "Will *what?*"

"You will let us take you to the airport straightaway."

He raised his eyebrows as he waited for her answer. She was trying to recall precisely the expression on James Blackburn's face when she first saw him in the coffee shop, staring out into the street. She had it now. And yes, it could very well have been the expression of a guilty man.

"Or if you insist on staying . . . ," he said.

"Yes," she told him. "I am staying. I'm not going home."

Now the man with the pipe leaned toward her.

"We can take care of the priest and the mother," he said. And then his voice slowed. "That leaves you. The only other person Captain Blackburn has to worry about. You see what we're saying."

What she wanted most was to leave this room, to find a place to lie down. Maybe wash her face.

"I have to use the bathroom," she said.

Both men nodded at her, and moved as if they were going to stand up and usher her out of the dining room.

"No, please, sit, it's okay," she told them. "I'll be right back."

Maybe the truth *isn't* anything more than the way things can be made to seem or to sound.

THE BATHROOM WAS one floor above the lobby. At the top of the stairs she paused at a window that looked out into the street. Some of the carpenters were scaling one of the bombed buildings on ropes.

Inside the bathroom she locked the door behind her and

stood before the mirror. She saw the exhaustion in her face, and the longer she stared at her reflection, the more difficult it was for her to recall how she had looked before this journey began. She pushed her hair behind her ears and recalled how she used to do this to her daughter's hair during the summer when her hair was always wet from swimming. Sara called it "my Maine hair."

This small journey into a memory of her daughter revitalized her, opening some channel in her mind so that she realized something in a sudden flash: The men downstairs had never questioned her about the mother when she told them she knew they had taken her. *How would she have known this? How could she have known this?*

So what did it mean? She stood at the mirror feeling the stillness of the room, and the building around her. What did any of this mean?

In the stillness, something was bearing down upon her. Or seeping into her consciousness. She turned in the direction of the door, wondering what it was, and then she smelled the scent of cherry tobacco. She moved very slowly to the door, and the nearer she came to it, the stronger the scent. Then she saw the knob turn. A half turn until the lock caught it. She stared at it to be sure. She tried to tell herself that he had followed her up the stairs just to make sure she was all right. He was waiting outside the bathroom door to smile at her and to reassure her again that everything would be all right in her life.

Even as she was backing away from the door and then walking to the window above the silver radiator at the far end of the bathroom, she was trying to bring into focus in her mind the houses along Bow Road, the rolled newspapers on the front lawns. She pictured the blinking red light of the security system at each front door.

She looked down at her hands on the window. She thought to flush a toilet to drown out the sound she would make getting the window open and climbing out.

It was a four-foot drop to a flat roof below. An iron fire-escape ladder, painted black, took her to the street in the alley.

Something told her not to run, not to draw attention to herself. She walked with her head down, until she smelled gasoline. She walked a little farther and the fumes burned her lungs. When she looked up she saw the priest's car in flames. Great bursts of red and orange and a curtain of black smoke obscured the end of the street. People had gathered on the corner and were watching, holding on to one another in the face of it.

In an instant she knew that she was alone for the first time in her life.

She took back streets out of town to the Dublin road, crossing the Dromagh Bridge, where she pictured James Blackburn in his soldier's uniform lying in the river.

THE WHOLE TIME she waited, the air smelled of burning gasoline, even after the black smoke had blown away. It took her almost an hour before she got a ride to Drumore. From the road she thought she saw him beyond the cemetery wall, standing in the doorway of the potting shed. But when she reached the shed there was no sign of him.

Chapter Thirty-two

She waited for hours, hidden in the hedges along the road. She was lying in the brambles, her cheek on the wet grass, overcome by the urge to pray. She had never believed that there was actually a God who listened to her prayers, but she had prayed hard at various times in her life. For a healthy baby during each pregnancy. That her mother would die quickly after she was diagnosed with liver cancer. Now when she closed her eyes she saw the images of the street in Omagh moments after the explosion. The young nurse panic-stricken, down on her knees, trying to administer CPR to the store mannequin lying in the street. The top half of a man with a tweed cap on his head. The woman with beautiful long red hair lying across a storm drain. At her side the lifeless child, and between her legs the two perfectly formed infants coated with jelly, their eyes tightly closed. Their grave, she knew now, was just a little ways from her in the church cemetery.

As hard as she tried, she couldn't ask God for anything for herself.

WITH DARKNESS she began walking. A farmer pulling a wagon piled high with manure took her as far as Cookstown, where she caught the last bus. There was only one other passenger, a man reading a book, sitting right behind the driver, whom he seemed to know. *She said the man in the gabardine suit was a spy* . . . Lyrics from that old song. She laid her head back and when she closed her eyes her mother was walking toward her with her hands out in front of her, trying to dry the pink nail polish. Maybe the course of our lives is set in a moment like that. All our courage suddenly gone. And the moment is sewn through the rest of the hours of our lives. We pay ransom to that moment, a certain price demanded again and again. This is the meaning of history.

HER FIRST VIEW of Londonderry from the rain-streaked bus window showed a city shimmering on a hillside above a wide river where barges swung from iron-chained mooring lines. She climbed a narrow street against a wet, bitter wind. She walked with her head down, leaning into the gale, along the promenade to a small bed and breakfast, a miniature Victorian house in a row of seven identical houses, three stories painted pale green with two gabled peaks. When she knocked, the door swung open on rusty hinges, and the wind took it from her hand and sent it crashing against the foyer wall. From where she stood she could see five closed doors, each looking as if it hadn't been opened in years. The wind rattled them in their frames until she leaned against the front door and pushed it closed. She called hello and pressed her face to each door, listening for the sound of footsteps.

SHE WAS SITTING ON a wicker couch in the foyer when a woman's voice called to her.

"Oh, God," Nora gasped, "where am I?"

It was not a woman but a girl, seventeen or eighteen, with

two long braids, black as ink, hanging down in front of her shoulders. "Derry City, ma'am," she said.

"Not Londonderry?"

" 'Tis, ma'am. The same city."

"And do you have a room?"

"I do."

While Nora filled out a registration card, the girl told her that she helped her parents run the B and B. They were in the south for a few days.

"And so you're alone here?"

"I am."

"And you don't mind?"

"No, I don't mind."

"And you're not afraid?"

"Not at all."

Nora smiled at her. "I was in Omagh."

"Oh, dear. So sad. Terrible, wasn't it?"

"I was in the street right after the bomb exploded."

Now the girl looked at her. Nora could see that she didn't want her to go on. "I'm just traveling now," she told her.

"Oh, yes. This is your first time in Derry, then?"

"I just got here, yes. I haven't seen anything."

"How many nights, then?"

"Excuse me?"

"How many nights will you want the room?"

"Oh. Well, I don't know. I mean, can I tell you tomorrow?"

"Sure."

These simple exchanges were a comfort to her. She began to feel that this part of her journey had been well planned to bring her to a place where she would be able to think clearly.

• • •

SHE WAS IN A SMALL ROOM on the third floor. A wooden
ironing board unfolded from one wall. A red chair with stuff-
ing like lamb's wool falling from a rip in one arm was pushed
up to the front windows. Kneeling in it and looking down the
street, Nora saw the river. Far off, ringing through the mist,
was a bell buoy that reminded her of the bay in Maine, a place
she always expected to keep in the center of her life. A bell she
had fallen asleep to as a child and as a grown woman.

On a table whose legs were held together with white twine,
there was a radio. When she turned it on, the BBC news was
being broadcast. War in some part of Africa. Accusations that
the Swiss government had facilitated the Nazi Party. Fighting
in Bosnia. She was beginning to see the world differently, to
feel more a part of it. Her old life had been about decorum and
veneer. A life of diplomacy. Like a passenger on a great ocean
liner, she had left the sanctuary of the upper staterooms and
was now close enough to the engine to feel its vibrations and
to smell its fire.

SHE TOOK A TAXI to the Grindstone Pub and stood inside
the door. There were a few couples in booths, and four men at
the bar and they all turned to look at her. When the bartender
turned out to be a man, she left and returned to her room.

She held the telephone in her hand twice that night, thinking she would call home, but both times she hung up. What
would she say? How would she begin to explain what she had
been through? Before she fell asleep she tried to picture her
father's face when he was young and she was a girl. To keep
from thinking of other things, she concentrated on this. She
remembered the winter night he taught her to skate, placing
her feet on top of his at first until she was ready to make her

own way across the ice. If he were here she would tell him that she had just lost two people she cared about. She could hear herself telling her father about them.

SHE AWOKE TO FIND that the mist and rain had blown off and the promenade and the river behind it were bathed in warm sunlight. Opening her eyes, she half expected to find that the soldier had slipped into her room in the night and was sleeping on the floor beside her. She thought of what the men had told her about him. She told herself that if he was guilty of killing all those people, it would have been better if she had never met him.

BEFORE NOON SHE WALKED outside and sat on a bench just up from a small beach directly across the street, watching the sky fill with the fine blue light of a summer day. Soon there were families arriving, the shouts of children running into the water. She tipped her head back and held her face in the sunlight. A little ways from where she sat, three small children were covering their father with sand. "Don't forget my feet," the father was telling them. "Don't forget my big toes."

She watched them for a long time, knowing that it would always be this way, she would always be reminded of the life she had had when her children were small and everything seemed right in the world.

She walked the promenade for two hours. A few sailboats were on the river, crossing the wind. She could tell the more competent sailors by the trim of their sails.

THIS TIME THERE WAS a woman tending bar at the Grind-stone Pub. A woman whose face was flushed and who had long silver hair. The whole time she carried on a conversation with the patrons at the bar, she moved along the length of it with a wet rag in her right hand, wiping its wood surface clean.

Nora walked up to the bar and stood beside the cash register at the far end of the room and waited for the woman to approach her.

"A friend told me you could help me find someone."

The woman narrowed her eyes and glared at her. "Your friend was wrong," she said, turning her back. When she started to walk away from her, Nora followed her. She felt as if something inside her was going to break into pieces. Suddenly she reached across the bar and grabbed the woman by her wrist.

"Now you listen to me," she said. "Two people I cared about were killed in front of my eyes yesterday. One of them knew you. I'll stay right here all day if I must, and then I'll follow you home."

The woman looked down at Nora's hand on her arm.

"Tomorrow I'll be here again," Nora said.

At last she nodded to one of the empty booths across the room and Nora let go of her wrist.

NORA SAT IN THE BOOTH and watched the woman wait on the men at the bar. Then she wiped her hands on the front of her dress as she walked to the telephone.

An hour passed before the woman came over to the booth. "Come back in two hours," she said.

Chapter Thirty-three

She walked in the sunlight to the top of the hill and stood before a handsome stone house with elegant floor-to-ceiling windows. Above the double front doors these words were carved into stone: STAR OF THE RIVER, PRAY FOR US.

She could see white-haired people sitting inside. Tiny paper sailboats were taped to the three windows in a room on the first floor. She imagined that this was a common room. There are circles in life, she told herself, and sometimes we see them clearly. You live to be very old and it is like being a child again. Like your first days in nursery school, cutting paper with blunt scissors.

There was something comforting about this for Nora, and she lingered for a long time just watching the people behind the windows. She had always tended to see life in its simplest geometric form, as a straight line that ran from beginning to end. Now she wondered if a life only began to make sense once it became a circle. Perhaps the straight line of her life had already begun to turn.

IN A BAKERY WITH CHAIRS and tables set against the front windows she bought a cup of tea and sat down. There was the scent of cinnamon in the air. A black iron cookstove. A ceiling fan with wooden blades turning slowly overhead. The humming of the refrigerator. The sight of everything neatly in its place made Nora think of the mother's cottage in Drumore. The broken picture frames and overturned tables. How would she ever be able to return there with her child? The thought of this mother down on her knees, searching through the broken glass, filled Nora with longing and disappointment. A persistent hollowness, a chill in her bones. An ache in her stomach. Where was the mother now? Held by strangers against her will, guilty of nothing.

I don't know anything, she thought.

When two young girls sat down at the table beside her and smiled at her, Nora began telling them about Omagh. She could see that they were not terribly interested. Even after she had described the red-haired mother lying in the street with her dead children, the two girls looked down at the menu they were sharing. For some reason she couldn't stop herself. "It was the saddest thing I have ever seen, or known about," she said.

One of the girls looked up at her. "Three little ones so close in age?" she said.

"Yes."

"Sounds like she was a Catholic, and it was a Catholic bomb that killed her, so you see, ma'am, it isn't nearly so sad."

Nora watched her as she pointed to something on the menu. Her elegant neck and thin fingers. Her hard, flat reaction. Showing no emotion. Maybe this is what a long struggle does to a person, deprives you of feeling. Nora looked at the smooth white skin of the girl's legs. Shapely, strong legs. A proud girl.

"Are you going to have a family someday?" Nora asked her.

"Oh, I suppose I will."

Nora felt the anger rising in her. "When you do," she said, "when you have a family of your own I want you to look back to this day, okay?"

Now the girl eyed her suspiciously. "What do you mean by that?" she asked.

"Think back to the American woman telling you about the bombing in Omagh. And remember yourself telling her that a *Catholic woman* being killed by a *Catholic bomb* was not terribly sad. And you will see how ignorant you were when you were a girl."

HER FACE STILL FELT HOT and her palms were sweating when she returned to the pub. She was just inside the door when the woman behind the bar put on a dull green raincoat exactly like Nora's. She walked to the door and gestured for Nora to follow her outside.

They walked three blocks down the street and then waited in silence. Nora felt the whole country in front of her. The ancient streets, the slate-shingled roofs, grass growing from each chimney. She watched a man unloading sacks of Queens New Potatoes from a small truck. He stacked four burlap sacks of potatoes on his rusty red trolley, then pushed them to the front door of a shop and kicked the door open with his foot. He repeated this three times with the same motions.

Nora was still watching him when something farther down the street caught her attention. An elderly man with a dog on a leash had stopped in the middle of the street and was looking up toward the sky, shielding his eyes from the sun. Above him in a window on the top floor of a brick building, Nora saw someone standing. The top half of the window had been pushed down rather than the bottom half pushed up. This struck her as odd. She looked back at the old man, then when her eyes returned to the window she saw that the person was aiming a rifle up the street. The old man raised his hand just as Nora raised hers. Then, in the next instant, the person at the window was flying through the open air, a shower of glass raining down behind him, and his rifle falling to the street just before he landed there on top of the dog, facedown with his arms out to his sides.

When the woman beside her saw what had happened, she leaned close to Nora and said, "Go somewhere. Anywhere but the pub. And don't follow me." Then she walked off quickly.

IF NORA STOOD THERE a long time, weeping and wiping her tears away, who would know why? Who would know that she was facing the piecing together of a nightmare, a slowly passing parade of faces that would inhabit her sleep for the rest of her life.

A crowd of people gathered quickly, and from this crowd a nun appeared, taking Nora's arm and leading her away. "You don't remember me?" she said. "In Ballykelly? I was in the convent there. You asked me if we could help you hide someone."

The Neil Diamond music playing. Yes, she remembered.

"What are you doing here?" Nora asked.

"Just come with me," she said.

"The man I wanted you to hide is dead," Nora told her. "You might have saved him."

"He's not dead," she said. "The priest was alone in the car."

With this Nora stopped. She pulled her arm free. "I'm not going anywhere with you," she said. And she turned and ran back to where the man had fallen.

. . .

BY NOW POLICE HAD BLOCKED OFF a square in the street with yellow rope. The body had not been moved. It was lying beneath a gray blanket beside three policemen who were standing with their arms crossed. Occasionally one of them glanced down at the body as if he expected it to stand up at any moment and walk away.

Nora pushed her way through the crowd until she was standing at the yellow rope. Her mind was trying to measure the dimensions of the body beneath the gray blanket. She felt herself slow down; some part of her was pulling her away. Wouldn't it be James Blackburn lying beneath the blanket? Wouldn't he have followed her here, watching her from the window above the street, protecting her from these people she had come here to meet?

Someone must have discovered him and pushed him from behind.

Leaning under the yellow rope, nearing the body, she felt like she was falling.

The sound of her heels on the street was the last thing she heard before the policeman with long sideburns raised his eyes to look at her when she said, "I want to know what happened to this man." She looked into his puzzled face, and when he didn't answer her she turned to the other two men—the one with the yellow-and-blue-striped tie like one of her husband's, and the other in shiny black leather boots with brass zippers on the side.

"One of you must know what happened. I saw him standing at the window."

THE FIRST MAN, the one with the Elvis sideburns, glanced at the other two with a certain look that Nora was still trying to interpret when he said to her, "We've taken care of things here. Why don't you go now, ma'am? There's nothing you can do here."

Why don't you go now? . . . Go home to your people . . . Go and live . . . Since she arrived in this country everyone had been telling her to leave. She had been given ample warning.

"I'm going to see who this is," she told him. And in the silence following this declaration, Nora searched the faces of all three men, trying to find something, some small indication that this was not the soldier lying beneath the blanket.

"I may know this man," she told them.

It took a nod from the man wearing the shiny boots. Nora was looking down at the dead man's hand when the blanket was pulled back. There was something odd about the hand, and it took her a moment to realize that the man's arm from the elbow down had been twisted in the wrong direction.

She didn't dare look at the face until after she had assured herself that this body was too wide across the hips to be James Blackburn.

She shook her head no. The man began to draw the blanket back over the face. She saw it then, matching this face to the face of the man who was stopping cars that night on the road outside Enniskillen. A V was cut from the top of his ear.

Another face for the nightmare. It was enough to practically stop her heart. She felt the blood pounding through her head and a dizziness coming over her.

Chapter Thirty-four

When she started to walk away she saw the nun waiting for her. "I have a ride for you," she said. Nora walked past her.

"Father Conlon wanted us to help you," the nun called to her.

She stopped then. Overhead, dark clouds were sweeping across the sky. The moment the sun disappeared, the street turned cold and damp as a basement. She didn't move, couldn't move. She saw two gray-haired women on the sidewalk looking at her. She had made her hands into fists, cutting off the circulation to the tips of her fingers, which were white now, as if they'd been frozen.

"We have to leave," the nun said to her.

THEY RODE IN THE BACKSEAT of a car driven by a man who was humming "The Star-Spangled Banner" in a low monotone. The nun asked him for something and he passed her a large envelope. Inside there were pages from old newspapers, which she handed to Nora to read. Each page was the story of another bombing. The moment she saw the newspaper photographs of the blackened skeletons of two buses lying on their sides, Nora had the sense that something spiritual or mystical had brought her to this moment in time. The newspaper article told how a bus carrying British soldiers had come to a stop at a place called the Narrow Water Keep. There was a truck filled with bales of hay parked there. It exploded at once and killed six soldiers. A second bomb was detonated moments after another bus of soldiers arrived to help the wounded. Someone on a hillside two hundred yards away had set off both explosions with a radio signal.

It was August 27, 1979. The eighteen soldiers killed marked the worst loss of life in a single IRA attack. On the same day, Lord Mountbatten, Queen Elizabeth II's cousin, and three others were killed by another IRA bomb on Mountbatten's yacht off the coast near Sligo.

Most of the soldiers killed in the explosion were eighteen and nineteen years old, on their first assignment in the British Army. The story told how the wounded boys called for their mothers.

This one detail made the horror seem real to Nora. She stared for a long time at a photograph of Prince Charles standing at an open grave before she noticed the two soldiers in uniform standing just to his right. One of them was James Blackburn. Nineteen years younger, but it was his face, his eyes, she was sure. She leaned over the photograph, trying to see what this picture could tell her about him. But instead, she found herself reaching back to her own life. August 1979. A summer day in Maine. Probably sailing the bay with Steven. Leaning a blue seat cushion against the varnished mast so Steven could take a nap in the sun while she sailed them to Hancock Point. His dark hair was against the blue seat cushion. The blue cushion against the orange-brown varnish of the mast. He was lying there when they first spoke about having a third child.

In each newspaper story there was a list of names. The dead. Never the wounded. As he had told her.

Soon they were passing the shipyards of Belfast, where enormous tankers under flags from Iceland and Holland were at rest in the black water, tied to the pier beneath tall cranes.

The water widened as they left the city behind them. The Irish Sea, Nora thought. For miles she kept her eyes on the water, thinking of the Maine house, the dock, and the small sailboat.

Eventually the sea fell away behind them and they were passing through small villages with manicured lawns and hedges to the northwest of Belfast. They were distinctly different in their appearance from the towns Nora had already seen, and it took a while for her to realize that they were *too* well manicured, as if they'd been clipped and scrubbed obsessively. And their immaculate appearance contrasted sharply with the signs that hung from flagpoles. A white-haired woman dressed as if she had just returned from the symphony was sweeping her front walkway with a broom beneath a banner that said KILL ALL IRA COWARDS.

THE TOWN OF COMBER turned out to be a village of only a thousand people, who had worked very long hours hanging banners on every street. THE ULSTER VOLUNTEER FORCE. ORANGE ORDER OF UNIONISTS. THE RED HAND COMMANDOS.

Across the main intersection another banner—LONG LIVE THE QUEEN. And at the next intersection, another with two coffins beneath the words: REMEMBER ENNISKILLEN! REMEMBER BALLYKELLY! NEVER SURRENDER!

· · ·

NORA FELT UNEASY. It was as if she had weathered a terrific storm and was now in the eye, a temporary calm that would lead to devastation once the back side of the storm closed around her.

They crossed train tracks and followed a side street that led them out of the village onto an open road. On the top of a hill, from out of nowhere, the heavy clipping sound of helicopters swept across the sky. It took her a few seconds to tell which direction they were coming from and by then the driver had already pulled the car off the road and out of sight.

THE PARKING LOT WAS EMPTY at the Maison Hotel. The driver stayed in the car with the motor running while the nun took Nora inside.

They passed through double glass doors into an empty lobby. The long mahogany counter looked newly varnished. There were fresh flowers in crystal vases on all the coffee tables. The burgundy carpeting smelled new and the matching burgundy couches looked as if they had never been sat on. The whole place gave the impression of a stage set waiting for the actors and the audience to arrive. "This way," the nun said, showing her to an interior door that led to a glass corridor that smelled like a greenhouse. "Most of the hotel has been rebuilt," the nun told her. "I thought you might want to know what happened here."

At the end of the glass corridor she showed her the big open room, which had been a dance floor when the IRA fire-bombed the hotel. The nun knelt down in the corner of the room and Nora thought she might be praying. But then she saw her touching part of the mopboard that was blackened by the fire.

"We went to a great deal of trouble making this bomb," she said. "Mixing in a special substance that made the flames stick to the victims. Water alone couldn't extinguish them."

She told her that it was snowing the night the hotel was bombed. "We were after your soldier. He sang here every Wednesday night. But that night the weather got in the way."

"Why are you telling me this?"

She didn't answer her. Some part of her must have known then what the soldier had concealed from her. Hadn't she known from the moment she saw his hand trembling in the coffee shop, the teacup rattling against the saucer?

LATER THEY WAITED OUTSIDE, behind the hotel where barrels of beer were piled against a brick wall in the shape of a pyramid. Nora said nothing when a milk truck arrived and the nun opened the front door for her. The door closed behind her. She looked straight ahead as they pulled away.

"I'm afraid it's the floor for you," the driver said.

Chapter Thirty-five

He pushed the seat back to make more room for her. She heard the glass milk bottles clinking as they drove along. They seemed to be climbing the side of a mountain, the truck pulling hard as the driver shifted gears. Outside the window of the truck, clouds were thickening.

"Tell me where you're taking me," Nora said.

"Just up ahead," he said, pointing down the road.

They stopped at a vegetable stand in a parking lot alongside a gas station. Maybe fifteen seconds later a sky-blue car pulled up alongside them. The driver rolled down his window and nodded. He had a dimple in his chin. He got out and ushered her from the milk truck to the seat beside him.

He drove her a few miles, then pulled to the side of the road where there was another car waiting, this one with a badly bent front bumper. When she looked carefully she saw that a man's leather belt was all that held it on. The chrome piece was in the shape of a crooked smile. The windows of this car were tinted so that it wasn't until she was inside that she saw the driver was wearing a black ski mask with only slits for the eyes.

He blindfolded her with a piece of cloth that smelled faintly of shoe polish and then ran tape over the cloth, around the back of her head.

"If it's too tight, tell me," he said.

She could tell by his movements that he had taken off the mask.

"Where are we going?" she asked.

"A lovely spot," he said.

Nora was trying to think clearly. From her memory came the television pictures of the terrorists in ski masks who had killed the Israeli Olympic athletes in Munich so long ago. She remembered sitting on the couch in the Maine house with her father, watching that atrocity unfold.

"Who are you?" she asked.

"Me?" he said, pausing as if to decide how to answer. "I'm just a hardworking man."

"Do you have children?" she asked.

"Five," he said. "That's why I have to work so hard."

She listened to him lighting a cigarette, then smelled the smoke. The idea came to her that if she could keep talking, nothing bad would happen.

"What time is it?" she asked.

"Just after five," he said. "The day is still young."

"I want to see my children again," she told him.

"Ah, you will, miss," he said. "You're in safe hands now. Don't worry about that."

THE SUN WAS STILL HIGH in the sky when Nora was placed in another car with a man who took off her blindfold and said, "Derry City. Back where you started."

He told her that he was a taxi driver. His photograph and license number hung from the glove compartment.

"Where are you taking me?" she asked.

He looked at his watch. "You've an appointment this evening. We have a bit of time to kill. Would you like to see our lovely city?"

"I already saw it," Nora said. "Appointment with whom?"

He acted as if he hadn't heard this question. He drove them a few blocks and parked along the side of the street in front of a large Marks and Spencer department store. On the sidewalk, standing beneath a streetlight just a few feet away was the first American family Nora had seen in Northern Ireland. Two teenage children, a son and a daughter, both wearing designer braces on their teeth. The father carrying a golfer's umbrella. The mother in a plain dress printed with whales. Nora wondered what had brought them here. They had the look of invulnerability. Unlike the citizens of this country. She wondered if this was how people regarded her when she was with her family. The perfect family. One boy, one girl.

The driver turned on the radio. An old, stupid American song, she recognized. "Wooly Bully," by Sam the Sham and the Pharaohs. "Could you turn that off?" Nora asked.

He did, with his apology.

Nora kept watching the American family. It took her a while to understand what it was that struck her about them. They never touched. Each of them moved within his or her own boundaries.

She heard a plane overhead and it made her think of going home.

"Listen," she said to the driver, "whatever this is all about, it's a mistake."

"Ah," he said sorrowfully, "I'm sure it will all be sorted out for you."

• • •

HE DROPPED HER IN A PARK where most of the grass was worn away. Some young boys were kicking around a soccer ball. An enormous cathedral stood at one end of the park. The other three sides were bordered by small flats, identical in shape and color.

A man wearing a black suit, a white shirt, and a dark tie, and carrying a schoolteacher's leather satchel came up to her. "Let's take a walk," he said, putting his arm around the small of her back.

He began speaking at once. "There are two hundred and sixty British soldiers stationed in Omagh. Saturday mornings most of them come into the center of town to do their shopping. Two hundred people were injured in the bombing. How many soldiers were among them?"

Nora felt his hand on her elbow. She could smell cigarette smoke on his breath, and some kind of aftershave lotion.

"I have no idea," she said.

"Not one," he told her. "We'll sit over there."

They stopped at a park bench directly in front of a simple granite pillar maybe ten feet high.

"The truth is, ma'am, you and your captain would have both been murdered by now if we hadn't been looking out for you."

Nora was trying not to look at his face. "I don't know what you're talking about," she said.

He accepted this with equanimity, lit a cigarette, and continued. "The Bogside mothers didn't have the money for an elaborate statue. They settled for this piece of granite. You've had a history lesson this past week, miss, but an incomplete one. That's the trouble with history, you always have to ask yourself what's been left out."

He pointed to the carved words at the base of the monument. He put on a pair of dark-framed glasses that made him look like an undertaker and began reading the names to her: "Patrick J. Doherty, aged 31 years. Gerard V. Donaghy, aged 17 years. John F. Duddy, aged 17 years."

Nora stopped him. "I've heard enough names," she said.

He looked at her and took off his glasses. With his eyes narrowed he said flatly, "I think I'll just finish. Now then. Hugh P. Gilmore, aged 17 years. Michael G. Kelly, aged 17 years. Michael M. McDaid, aged 20 years. Kevin G. McElhinney, aged 17 years. Bernard McGuigan, aged 41 years. James G. McKinney, aged 34 years. William A. McKinney, aged 27 years. William Nash, aged 19. James J. Wray, aged 22. John P. Young, aged 17. John Johnston, aged 59, who died later as a result of injuries received that day."

"Who were murdered by British paratroopers on Bloody Sunday, 30th January, 1972."

Nora watched him drop his cigarette on the ground and crush it with the heel of his shoe. "What were you doing in January of 1972?" he asked her.

January 1972. Sixteen years old. Her second year in high school. At the time, she had been younger than the names on this monument. Now, time that had stopped for them had made her old enough to be their mother.

"I'm very tired," she told him.

"I'm sorry," he said.

"Sorry?" she said in an accusing voice. "I've seen what your bombs do to people. I was in Omagh. I think you're cowards. You hate the British government, but you don't have the courage to fight it. Instead you kill children."

He had opened his leather satchel while Nora was speaking.

Now he took out a black-and-white photograph and placed it on her lap.

Nora recognized the bed-and-breakfast where she and James had spent one night. In the lower left-hand corner of the picture, a man sat alone in a car.

"British intelligence," he said. "If you can tolerate that oxymoron. They had a little surprise for you. Fifty-five rounds in a machine gun."

Seeing this photograph, evidence of the threat that brought James into her life, made her want him back.

He showed her another black-and-white photograph. "Here's another bloke who would be enjoying a whiskey tonight while your corpses were on a table at Scotland Yard."

"So, you killed all these people who were following us?"

He took the photographs from her lap and carefully put them back in his satchel.

"And the man who fell from the window? You've had quite a lot of practice killing people in this country. And I'm supposed to be pleased that you protected me."

"And your captain."

"He's not *my* captain."

"Well, I'm a romantic sort."

"You're a cold-blooded killer," she said.

"Only as cold as the enemy. Tell me, do you know your history?"

Nora said nothing.

"We had our nation back, you know, we had it in 1914. The Parliament in England voted to grant Ireland home rule. One country, free of England. But then the First World War began. Luck of the Irish."

The boys playing soccer ran within a few yards of the bench

where they were sitting. He waited until the last of them had run off again.

"My father grew up here in Bogside. When he got married he wasn't allowed to buy a house because he was Catholic. When you're back home in America maybe you'll go to the library someday and read about what happened here on Bloody Sunday."

"What makes you think I'll get home?"

"Oh, you'll get home. But first you're going to have to help me."

Just then the bells of the cathedral began ringing loudly.

When the sky was still again he said, "We need Captain Blackburn to help us. We need you to persuade him. We've got the mother and child."

He turned and looked directly into her eyes. "Have you not sorted it out?"

She said nothing, though it was all in her mind now, taking shape.

"Loyalists changed the warning in Omagh and sent those people to their death. We want the world to know. We want to stand Captain Blackburn on the steps of Stormont Castle, in front of the press."

"He won't do that," she told him.

"If he doesn't, we'll stop saving his life. And yours. We'll let the Brits bury you. On the other hand, if you help us bring this terrible truth to the world, we'll protect you both. We have associates in America who can give you a new identity, a safe place to live."

He paused, watching her. She felt the heat of his glance. He took her by the arm, gently, and said, "If you care about him, help us."

HE HAILED A TAXI for her, telling her that he would have people in Omagh the next day at the memorial service. "Bring your captain to the confessional where you met the priest."

When the taxi pulled up, he said that he hoped he would see her again. "Just so you know," he told her, "he couldn't have stopped what happened in Omagh. Once it had been set into motion, he couldn't have stopped it."

THE TAXI DROVE HER out of the city, south along the river. For the first time, she found herself talking to the baby. No longer a grain of rice, but a baby, its knees drawn up to its chin. You be the judge, she said in her mind. A good man does something terrible. You be the judge. You who are without sin.

Chapter Thirty-six

She was taken to a cottage in the countryside where the nun and three men with rifles sat at a table with her, eating sausages and biscuits by candlelight. When Nora got up to pee in the night she found the four of them playing Scrabble at the same table.

"You settle it for us, ma'am," one of the men called to her. "*Gaff.* G A F F. That's a real word, isn't it?"

IN THE MORNING they drove to Omagh. Half a mile outside the city she began to see the traffic and the crowd in the streets. They turned onto the Dublin road and crossed the Dromagh Bridge. The bombed-out area of Market Street was still hidden behind the towering green metal walls constructed by the British Army.

From the other side of the wall, all the way up High Street to the courthouse, people were standing shoulder to shoulder, so many that it was impossible to drive through.

They dropped her two blocks from there. "We'll be waiting for you in the church," the nun said to her.

When Nora turned onto Drury Street, she looked back and saw that they were driving away. She could make out the sounds of a band playing "Nearer, My God, to Thee." At the end of the street she saw that a stage had been erected on the steps of the courthouse and draped in black cloth. She had just reached the corner when she saw a priest stand up and walk to the microphones.

"We declare that evil will not triumph." He was an old man and his voice was shaking. "We reclaim our town and, together, we shall rebuild our lives, our faith."

When he led the crowd in the Twenty-third Psalm, Nora bowed her head and repeated the words, surprised that she could remember.

Then a young woman with an acoustic guitar climbed onto the black platform. She had curly blond hair and was dressed in black jeans and a black shirt.

She sang with a sweet, solemn voice. Simple words that set everyone crying. Twenty thousand people wiping away their tears. *You can have my heart if you don't mind broken things.*

Her words carried Nora away, back across her own history to the morning when she found the box Steven had hidden behind his shoe rack in their bedroom closet. A blue cardboard box from Filene's department store filled with small squares of white paper, like miniature boxes, each one carefully cut with scissors, all identical in size, maybe an inch across. She couldn't imagine what they could possibly be, or mean. When he told her that he had cut one each time he tried to make love to her and she turned away, she went back and counted. Down on her knees, his suits brushing her hair, the scent of him like a taste in her mouth. Seven hundred and eleven little squares. Tears running down her cheeks. This was part of the price she paid for losing who she was, for running in fear, for giving away the responsibility for her own life.

And Steven had paid a price as well. She knew this now.

• • •

AT THE END OF THE SERVICE Nora made her way through the crowd to the bus station.

A British soldier with an automatic rifle stood beside the ticket window. Nora found herself speaking to him. "It looks like it will rain again," she said.

"Hallelujah," he remarked without expression. "Worse than home. The bloody weather here is worse than home."

THE BUS DROPPED HER two miles from Saint McCartin's Church, on a narrow road with thick hedges on both sides. Above the hedges, across the open fields, she could see the steeple of the church, and she kept her eyes on it, following it as if it were a marker at sea.

Sometime along the way she began to tell herself that every person in this country who ever believed that the IRA had a right to drive the British out should be made to take this walk to the church along with everyone who ever believed that the British should have authority over this country. They should be made to walk this way through the Clogher valley down the ancient road through the deep green hills, past tin-roofed barns, grazing tan sheep, and cows with noses shining from the wet grass. The little calves ran in fear to their mothers' sides as Nora came upon them. As she walked she had a feeling that there was something in the world for her that she would finally reach.

INSIDE THE STONE WALLS of the churchyard she went first to the new grave instead of the potting shed.

It was the only grave she had ever seen that was not a rectangle. Too many coffins in one grave, it took a square to hold them. Maybe the men who had dug the grave made this decision on their own; to bury Avril Monaghan and her children in a large square would be more intimate than in the single long row of a rectangle. This way they could lie alongside each other. A square gash in the earth for Avril and the babies and her year-and-a-half-old daughter.

Kneeling in the dirt, Nora felt that she was now within something. An understanding, perhaps. Or a memory finally completed. She placed her hands in the soft dirt beside the little plastic statues of Mary and small bottles of holy water. She imagined the sorrow of the young husband during the funeral procession. Perhaps someone had given him one of the statues of Mary to hold while they lowered his wife and children into the grave.

Sitting there in such a safe and lovely place, Nora saw that these deaths were beyond all reason. Except perhaps to show us all that nowhere are we safe from this world's madness. The madness of bombs, of betrayals and lies. And so we must find what is true inside us, and love this the most. Love this in the best way we can.

A part of her felt that she should stay here, that she should lie down in the grass and sleep beside them. She remembered how, when her children were very young, she would awaken some mornings and find that they were sleeping in her bed. Something in the night had driven them to her and to their father. She used to think that to someone looking down on them, they would appear like survivors clinging to a raft.

Often in her life she had felt the urge to back away from what was difficult and sad in the world. But now at the grave, she had the sense that she had returned to a place where the sound of the wind was like a voice she recognized.

She saw where a spider was building its web under one arm of the white cross. As she watched the spider she remembered what her mother used to say to her when she misbehaved as a child: *You must be nice to me, Nora, because I grew you under my heart.*

Nora's mother had once concocted a theory that each new baby upon entering the world took its soul from a person dying at the same instant, the person closest. When Nora was twelve or thirteen she told her father this theory, laying claim to it, pretending she had thought it up herself. He was a practical man with a little half smile that was meant to dismiss the lazy and the inferior. They were having breakfast together. He didn't say anything in response to what she told him. Instead he took the occasion to show her how to butter her croissants. "Always turn them over and butter the flat bottom."

THE SKY CLEARED SLOWLY, then grew dark again. She bowed her head and closed her eyes. She pressed her lips against her arm, remembering how, as a child, she had always loved tasting the salt on her skin after coming out of the ocean.

A CAR PULLED UP to the black iron gate. A moment later James appeared across the field, beyond the stone wall that enclosed the cemetery. When she looked up, he was walking toward her. She watched him drawing near, the shape of him better defined with each step, and as he grew larger, what was already becoming the *memory* of him as well. His hands on hers when he taught her how to use the gun. The flat of her palm on his ribs when she helped the priest undress him. The kind of touch that can replace everything that happened before it.

"COLIN AND I HAVE BEEN COMING BY every hour. You're all right, then, Nora?"

"Yes."

"This is the end of it," he said. "Too many people have been hurt."

"And you've made plans for me?"

"I'm turning myself in. They're letting me drive you to Dublin first. To the airport." He glanced back at the road where she saw the second car, the car that would follow them, she presumed.

"I'm sorry," he said to her.

"I'm sorry, too," she told him. "I'm sorry about a lot of things."

"I knew about the bomb," he said, kneeling down beside her. "I was there when it was planned."

Though she had already been told this, her immediate reaction to his confession was the feeling that something sharp had scraped the inside of her lungs.

He went on. "There was nothing I could have done to stop it, and, in truth, I never believed it would come to pass. But I knew from the start."

She felt everything slowing down again. As if the lever of a powerful machine had been pulled, the gears grinding to a stop. "When I saw you in the coffee shop—" she said.

He didn't wait for her to finish. "That was when I knew what I was," he told her. "I admitted to myself that I was a coward."

He told her that he walked all the way up the hill and kept his silence. The people were moving against him, moving the wrong way. He kept his head down so he wouldn't see their eyes. Then he saw the mother with the baby in her arms, saw her reflection first in a puddle on the sidewalk. He expected to see fear in her eyes, but what he saw instead was the opposite. "I saw that she believed she and her baby would be safe by following our orders. I told her to turn around, that she was going the wrong way. Why would she believe me? A British soldier? So I did the only thing I knew would make her follow me up the hill."

A bird was singing somewhere above them, a shrill whistling. Nora tried to close her eyes and let her thoughts be lifted away on its taut wire of sound.

She heard herself saying, "Only men could plan such a thing. No woman would ever have agreed. A mother would not—as you put it—have kept her silence while those people were slaughtered."

Disconnected thoughts fell into her head. And one more memory. Her mother's new bed that she bought after the divorce, a twin bed to replace their double. It was made of clear red cedar. The manufacturer recommended keeping a small glass of water under the bed so the wood would soak it in and the boards would retain their pleasant scent. Once a week Nora would retrieve the empty glass and refill it for her mother, never failing to be enchanted by this.

He took her hand in his. "Even when I was running up the street with the baby, I was thinking that they might be right. This bomb, the horror of it, might end the killing here."

She didn't want to listen to any more of this.

"We're not without hope, are we?" he asked her.

He bowed his head over Avril Monaghan's grave. Nora saw that the toes of his shoes were salted with pollen.

They stood up together. "I will always come back to this church," she said, not really knowing what it meant.

"A part of us will never leave," he told her.

"Maybe it will work," she said. "Maybe it will be the last bomb."

He said nothing. She was trying to decide exactly how she would remember him. The small details that would define him. His voice. The accent that always made her think of a school headmaster. She wondered who would protect him after she had gone. A part of her wanted to show him her world. She couldn't help this. She wanted him to see that she would go on, living by herself if this was required of her, growing old and one day telling her love stories to a stranger from down the hall. Inventing what she must in order to make sense of what was never sensible.

She took him in her arms. A friendly embrace, that's all, laying no claim to him. "They have the mother, James," she said. "If we turn ourselves in to them, they'll protect us all."

"The IRA?" he said. He stopped and looked away, dismissing this possibility, she knew.

"We have to go," he told her.

She felt herself dropping down again. Her weight falling below the soles of her feet, through the surface of life that holds our coming and going from day to day, to the region of dreams and memory. We don't fall in love, we sink into it, into its stillness where it seems we are the only two people awake in the world, into its silence and the questions love never asks of us.

As soon as they were in the car Nora told them she wasn't going to fly home. "I'm not going to make it easier for you to give up," she said.

"Listen to her, James," Colin said.

She looked at him staring out the window as the car picked up speed. She turned back to Colin. "Can you get us to the boat?" she asked him.

He thought a few seconds. "Yes," he said. "I believe I can."

Chapter Thirty-seven

They drove south, and reached the outskirts of Dublin in just under two hours. Colin judged that his best chance to lose the car following them was in traffic, and when they came upon a street festival of some sort where two city blocks were crowded with maybe a thousand people on roller skates, he said softly, "Here we are, then."

He drove slowly, getting as close to the crowd as he could. He glanced once in the rearview mirror then said, "Go. And Godspeed."

Nora tried to persuade Colin to come with them, but he insisted the better chance was to keep the following car on him. If worse came to worse he planned to leave the car himself after eating up some time, and disappear on foot.

THEY RAN INTO THE STREET, ducking their heads and quickly disappearing among the people. Three-quarters of the way down the block they ran into a movie theater, passing the doorman, who called after them. They ran through the darkened theater, out an exit door near the screen. Then they caught a city bus heading east to the train station on Union Street.

They bought first-class tickets and had a private compartment just behind the dining car. Until the train was safely out of the station and running fast they kept the shades pulled down on the windows. By five o'clock they were coming into Portrush, three-quarters of an hour from where they would get off. They could smell the Irish Sea. "Tell me about the boat," Nora said. "Is she a strong enough boat to get us to Scotland?"

"Yes. But we'll be all night on the water."

"As long as it's not a motorboat," she said. "I'm no good at all around motors."

He smiled. "No motor at all," he said. "No radar. No automatic reefing. Not even a radio."

"You have a compass?"

"I have that."

"And if we're lucky there will be a few stars." She turned and looked up at the clouds. "Well, maybe stars are too much to hope for."

He told her that if the weather turned bad, it would be a punishing trip.

"Don't worry," she said. What could be better, Nora thought, than the feel of the sea rolling beneath her?

BUT FROM THE MOMENT she took the tiller in her hand she had a dreadful sense that nothing she had ever experienced in her life had prepared her for what lay ahead in the coming hours. She stood in the stern of the sloop and watched carefully as James hauled the sails from below onto the deck. She saw the exhaustion in his movements, how he paused to get his breath, though there wasn't a second to waste. Ahead of them was the sea, a blue-violet color, like no body of water she had ever seen before. And though there was a persistent bright light at the horizon, darkness had already begun to fall. Inishowen harbor was encircled by high hills, so well protected from the open sea that they wouldn't be able to tell the conditions of the North Channel until they had sailed well out of the bay and rounded the head. A hurricane could be awaiting them, for all they could tell from the harbor.

He was taking far too long attaching the sails, so Nora uncleated the main sheet and made her way forward along the oak deck. "I'll do the jib," she said. And he handed over that sail gratefully. While she fastened its bronze clips to the forestay she took note of the high-water line along the cedar posts that held the dock in place. The tide was going out. This small fact sent a chill through her. Yes, she had sailed all her life and she was confident of her abilities, but she had always been the most careful sailor. Even when she was in top form, enjoying the thrill of a high wind and rough seas, she never failed to calculate the risks in advance. In her home waters of Frenchman Bay, going overboard meant you had thirty minutes to live, usually less time than that, and she never would have sailed across the face of the open sea *at night* without the benefit of a returning tide and a following wind.

James was still threading the bottom of the big sail into the track along the boom. She wondered if she should tell him to take the tiller, and raise the sails herself. She considered telling him he was taking too much time, but a part of her wasn't yet willing to acknowledge how exhausted he was. How little help he might be to her. This, she knew, could very well turn out to be their fatal mistake.

She ran the jib sheets through the blocks along the port and starboard rails, tying figure eights into the ends of both lines. Then she went back to the tiller and waited for him to finish.

She tried again to get her bearings, but beyond figuring north, south, east, and west by the light on the horizon, and the direction of the wind by the way the other boats on moorings in the harbor were pointing, she was lost. And this troubled her. Near land, no two square miles of sea are the same. There are reefs and rocks, some murderously submerged just beneath the surface, narrows where tidal waters behave illogically, and caverns along the ocean floor that account for swells. She knew her home waters well enough to sail in pea soup fog, with a compass in one hand and the tiller in the other. But here, once darkness fell she would be sailing blind.

He called to her. "There's a lot to do down below, but I'd like to get out of the harbor first."

She agreed, and glanced behind her to the village. She was reluctant to keep her eyes on shore; if they were following her, she preferred not to know.

He raised the jib into a light breeze that caused it to flutter. He knelt down on deck to uncleat the main halyard. Then he raised the main, and the sight of the big sail, new enough to have only a few wrinkles and to be barely creased around its batons, encouraged her.

He cleated the halyard, and she recalled as she always did whenever she worked a line through a cleat, her father's telling her the very first time he took her sailing never to knot a halyard, always to cleat it simply so that you could lower your sails in an instant if you had to. This one thing, he had told her, may save your life someday.

She told James to take the tiller so she could cast them off.

She jumped onto the dock and unfastened the bowline. Then she pushed the bow off the wind with her foot before jumping back on board.

"You may have to back-wind the jib," she heard him call to her. She was already deciding to do this. The wind, though gentle, was coming straight at their bow, holding them in irons. She grabbed three or four feet of the jib sail and pulled it tight, directly across the face of the breeze. The bow began to turn at once. She looked back and saw James pulling in the main sheet. They were sailing.

She returned to the stern and sat beside him, reaching across him to pull in the jib sheet. "Are you all right, then?" he asked her.

She moved closer to him and took his hand in hers. He looked different to her, as if he were turning from new to familiar and back again in the same glance.

She turned to watch the shore receding. "I wonder if I'll ever come back," she said.

"Maybe after the peace has come," he said.

"Peace? Will it ever come, James?"

"It will have to come. I'm not sure I'll see it though."

IT DAWNED ON HER THEN that she hadn't looked to see the name of the boat. She leaned over the stern. "Margaret," she said.

"That would be my mother," he told her.

"That's nice. What would your mother say about me?"

"She would approve," he said. He looked into her eyes. "That first night, when I awoke in the backseat of the car and saw you, I remembered your face from the coffee shop and it seemed that we were meant to be together. And then you told me that you had seen me, in the street."

He stopped and turned them onto a port tack. What wind there was, was very light and coming straight through the mouth of the harbor, which meant they had to sail across it, one slow tack after another.

He looked behind them. "Jesus, will we ever get out of here?"

"We need more wind," she said. "My father taught me to whistle at the mast."

"Whistle?"

"Whistle for the wind."

"Don't whistle too hard," he said. "When we clear the head we may have all that we can handle."

He gave her the tiller and went below to get his chart.

When he was climbing back up to the deck she asked him how much wind he had sailed the boat in before.

"Oh, she can take a lot," he said. "It's me I'm worried about."

Nora looked up at the mainsail. There was a line of reef points three feet from the bottom of the sail. And a second line three feet higher. She went through the movements in her head, calculating how much time it would take to reef the sail. Tying the sail down in a big wind would be difficult. Five minutes, maybe. Far too long. There was a saying she had learned soon after she began sailing on her own: If you wait until the wind is howling to reef your sail, you've waited too long. In this sloop, one of them would have to stay at the tiller, holding the bow of the boat into the wind while the other uncleated the main halyard, lowered three or six feet of sail, and then tied that much of the sail around the boom. Maybe not five minutes, she thought. If it's done perfectly, maybe three minutes.

He sat next to her, unfolding the chart and spreading it across their knees. The point of sail was twenty miles due west once they rounded the head to the tip of Cara Island, leaving it on their starboard side. Then straight across the face of the Atlantic about forty miles, to Rhinns Island, a horseshoe-shaped island half a mile south of Nell's Ledge. Between the two was a narrow channel and a small point called Erin Point. That's where they would tie up. But before they could even reach the channel, they had to pass through one of the roughest bodies of water anywhere on the earth, Tiree Strait, just south of the Hebrides.

Nora was trying to calculate the distance. A total of maybe seventy miles. In a twenty-eight-foot sloop with all her sails raised to the wind, twelve hours, if the wind was favorable, blowing from due west or due east so they could hold the boat on a broad reach. If they had to beat into headwinds, it would take twice that long. And there was the tide running out. And there was the deadly combination of high seas and the retreating tide, and low winds, that would cause them to slip off course and drift helplessly out into the Atlantic.

"We reach here," he said, placing a finger on Erin Point. "There's a small airfield there, and someone I know with a plane. We'll have a fair chance of it."

"And where do we go from there?"

"Someplace warm," he said. "Someplace where we can talk about normal things."

She saw what he meant by this. All that was unknown would remain that way until they were safe. She thought of all that she hadn't told him about her life. She looked at their destination on the chart. She pictured them sitting before a peat fire in a cottage looking out to sea, with everything behind them.

When the first drops of rain struck the heavy paper of the

charts, James folded them quickly and slid them beneath his sweater. "I'd better get these down below," he said.

As he turned to leave, Nora said, "The rain—of course it will rain all the way across."

He apologized and looked up at the sky.

"Of all the things I want to remember to tell this baby," she said, suddenly feeling strong and hopeful, "I want to tell her how the sheep out in the fields change color in the rain."

He smiled again, and nodded. "The poor creatures in this country," he said. "Always so wet."

AN HOUR PASSED and they were still only halfway out of the harbor, still near enough to the dock behind them that the journey ahead wasn't yet real. Nora kept thinking of things they had to do. They had no running lights at all, no way for other boats to spot them in the night. James had two kerosene lamps below and he had just begun to lash one of these to the mast when Nora saw a gust of wind running across the water. She quickly pulled in both the sails to pinch a few degrees higher toward their point of sail.

Though the lamp was enclosed in glass, the flame wouldn't stand a chance in a high wind or in breaking waves. She asked him if he didn't think it would be better to figure out some way to lash them inside the cabin up against the port and star-board windows.

He waved his hand in acknowledgment and took the lamp back down into the cabin. At that moment, watching him descend the ladder stairs, she realized that she was just slightly ahead of him in each decision and that their passage to safety, to Cara Island, a place she had never heard of before and that existed only on a chart, was mostly in her hands. She watched him disappear below, the top of his head, his black hair matted by the rain. She saw his vulnerability. Maybe this was what had drawn her to him in the first place, the sight of him in the coffee shop in Omagh, the china cup in his shaking hand rattling against the saucer as he looked out into the street. It seemed possible to Nora that this *was* meant to be. Somewhere it had been decided years and years before that their lives would coincide, that the path of her life would intersect his exactly when it had.

She felt the wind tugging the main sheet in her right hand, the small force of it playing against the tiller in her left hand. *For what purpose?* she wondered.

Perhaps just to help him escape. It was a strange thought, but she turned it over in her mind, examining all its implications. Maybe life was really only a mystery that revealed itself in the smallest measures. This would make Steven an accomplice, and his cheerleader as well. Maybe all of their shared and separate history had been ordered around the single necessity of helping this man sail across the Irish Sea on an August night.

We cross borders of time and the person we once were, we leave behind. She knew this now.

A DOWNDRAFT from the rocky head pushed the boom and she allowed the boat to gently jibe. She glanced at her hand on the wooden tiller, then let go for a moment and felt the boat begin to turn up into the wind. She remembered teaching her children to sail. Sara took to it easily, but Jake was always wary. "Just let go," Nora had said to him. "Let go, and the boat will right herself. The boat will always come into the wind on her own. There's nothing to be afraid of. Trust me."

She took hold of the tiller and played with the jib until its belly filled, the way she had taught her children to coax the wind. A moment came back to her: There is Jake, barely two years old, standing on the boathouse dock with his shoulders pinned back and his little potbelly sticking out, his blond hair turned almost white by the summer sun. When Nora saw him standing there in his perfection, she knew it was a sight she would always recall. At the end of her life, if she could remember nothing else but that one moment, she would be satisfied. That night when she lay in bed beside Steven, he told her that he had seen her looking at their son on the dock. He told her that she looked as if she was falling in love. The expression on her face was the one Steven had seen when she was falling in love with him.

IN THE NEXT MOMENT James came up the ladder. "Are you all right?" he called to her. Nora was looking right at him, wondering why he was asking her this.

"I'm fine, yes."

"You're crying."

She hadn't known and she was embarrassed.

"Why are you crying?" he asked her.

She told him the first thing that came to mind. "Because it all went so fast."

He wanted to know what she meant, but she told him they needed to put something at the top of the mast so that other boats in the area with radar would be able to steer clear.

"Anything aluminum will work," she said.

He went down below and started searching. Then he held up various things for her to see. She chose a pie plate. James punched a hole through it, attached it to a halyard and ran it up the mast.

She watched him looking up at it. "When this is over," he said, "will you stay with me for a while?"

She thought about how to answer this. "How long would that be, James?" she said at last.

"Until you have to return to the States?" He smiled shyly, then looked away for a moment. "For as long as we have," he said. "Will you stay that long?"

Then it came to her, the thing she had been trying to decide. "I can't remember which one of us let go first," she said. "I think it might have been me, though, and I'm not proud of that."

He climbed another step higher on the ladder. "There are reasons why people let go," he said softly.

This startled her. She seemed to have forgotten for a second or two that she wasn't alone on the boat.

"Reasons," she said. "Yes. Yes, there were reasons. And you, James, you had your reasons too."

The expression on his face was like that of a little boy caught in a lie. He bowed his head and looked as if he was going to turn away from her and go back down the ladder.

"Good reasons, James?" she asked.

He told her that he didn't know anymore. "Once, I was sure. I believed it might finally be the end of all the sorrow."

She believed him when he said this. Whatever the world might never forgive him for, she knew that she would. If it came to this, she would be his last line of defense.

She told him that there was only one way for this to end. "Well," she said, "there are many ways, but only one *good* way." She told him what the man in Londonderry told her. "If we stand in front of the world and say what we know, it will be over."

He lowered his eyes and turned his watch around and around on his wrist.

He didn't answer her.

"You don't believe it," she said. "Funny, but I do."

WITH THAT THEY SAILED CLEAR of the head, where a cold wind took hold of the boat. It was work then. An hour tacking to the west and north to try to clear the big rocks outside the harbor. Behind the cold wind a thick fog rolled across the water from the open sea. Nora used a compass and set a course for 137 degrees, making their way from marker to marker. First the bell buoy at Rhinns Point. Then the nun at Drying Rock. Two hours later they came upon the bell at Crane Rock. They calculated their speed at just over four knots.

They listened in the stillness for the sound of breaking waves, which would tell them they were too close to shore.

The chart showed a low promontory of land fringed by large rocks. This was where boats were to steer clear of the wreck of HMS *Drake,* an armored cruiser torpedoed in 1916 two miles west of Holly Island. To clear it safely, the chart said, they must keep Rue Point open until Altacarry Light disappeared behind the high ground to the west light. But by then the fog was too thick for them to see the light. To be safe, they set their course twelve degrees higher to the north.

When the black whistle buoy at Wherryman Rocks came upon them more quickly than Nora had expected, though the wind had, if anything, fallen off, they both knew that they had fallen into the grip of the retreating tide.

It was the worst combination for a sailboat with no auxiliary power. A pulling tide and a weak wind. The only thing that could make it worse would be waves pushing the hull in the same direction as the tide.

· · ·

THEY MISSED THE SUNKEN LEDGE buoy completely. Though they listened for half an hour, they never heard it ringing.

Nora studied the chart again and again, trying to fix in her mind the point where they had drifted off course. She kept looking up from the chart and thinking that the fog was thinning. But it wasn't. And by now darkness had also overtaken them.

James set one of the kerosene lamps in the stern where they were sitting. "We're lost," Nora said to him. "If this compass is right and we follow it, I don't know which side of Sunken Ledge we're on. Do you see here, James, if we set our course and we're on the leeward side of the ledge we'll sail right on top of it."

They agreed that they must sacrifice their point of sail. Another hour or more passed. Nora asked him to take the tiller for her. She walked away, then climbed down into the cabin. The bunks were right there next to her. How nice to lie down and go to sleep. The bear sleeping through the winter— she remembered this.

She thought then that she had to write a note to Sara and Jake in case the ocean took her before the night was over. It didn't make sense, what were the odds anyone would ever find the note, but she did it anyway. She did it calmly. She poured what was left of a bottle of cider into the sink, rolled the note and slid it inside the bottle. All she wrote was her name and the address of Sara, and one sentence: *I am sailing across the North Channel of the Irish Sea tonight with a friend. August 22, 1998.*

She was suddenly sure of something: The person she had become was someone her daughter had never known. What had been returned to her these past eight days was what she had given away. Herself.

With twine she secured the bottle to one leg of the chart table. Before she climbed back on deck the thought came to her that they should turn back, but they had made so many changes in course by this time that there was no way to be sure what now lay between them and the mouth of the bay.

JUST AFTER MIDNIGHT, after three hours of drifting toward the open sea at about three knots, the wind came up more suddenly than Nora had ever experienced before. It was the first thing that told her that the Irish Sea was going to live up to its reputation. It was a sea that bore no resemblance to the sea she had sailed since she was a girl.

Before James could take a reef in the main, they had heeled over so hard that the starboard gunwale was in the water. The sails felt as if they were filled with concrete.

It was the noise that unnerved Nora. In fog, there were only sounds to go by, and now the sounds were obliterated by the rattling of their rigging and the sea smashing against the hull.

"How much wind?" she shouted to James. She was thinking twenty-five knots, gusting to thirty.

He just shook his head.

CONDITIONS KEPT BUILDING. Higher winds, bigger waves. There was such force below on the rudder that they had to hold the tiller together to keep on course. And they had no course, really, except a general idea now that the coast of Scotland was somewhere to their right. They were just trying to keep their bow headed into the waves that rose up at them from behind the wall of fog.

They were moving very fast, their sails filled with wind, the wooden mast and boom creaking like a flight of old stairs. And they were heeled over so far that the boat was taking on water. When Nora felt it sloshing around her feet she tried to spill some of their wind by beating closer to it so their sails luffed. A fisherman's reef was what she had always called this tactic. But the wind was so fierce now that luffing the sails put too much strain on the rigging. They had no choice but to sail full out.

What they needed, Nora suddenly realized, was a sea anchor, something to drag behind them to slow their momentum out into the open sea. A bucket tied to the end of a rope and trailing behind the stern would help.

When James left her side to go below and search for something, Nora felt her first sensation of terror. She tried to slow down her mind and to focus on something hopeful, but then a wave crashed over the combing and soaked her. She wiped the salt water from her eyes and called for James.

Climbing the stairs to reach her, he had his arms full of things from below to use in making the sea anchor. Before he reached the top step a swell rolled beneath the keel of the boat and knocked him off the ladder and down into the cabin. Nora jumped to her feet, calling to him. Standing, she was able to see to the front of the boat, and she watched the bow go completely under water. She yelled to James, "We're broaching the bow!"

When he didn't answer, she called his name again. She felt her body shaking with cold. It came into her mind that James was hurt and needed her help. But first she had to make a decision. The next swell might roll them over, filling the sails with water, the enormous weight pulling them 180 degrees, turning the boat upside down so that the top of the mast was pointing to the bottom of the sea.

She heard herself speaking to her son. "Jake, let go of the tiller, let the sheets loose, let go, let go." She had to make her left hand pull her right hand off the tiller. It required all of her concentration to begin this small act, and just as she was about to let go she heard a bell. At first she thought she was only imagining it. But then she heard it again, ringing dully beyond the crashing waves. *Up ahead somewhere,* she told herself. She tried to think clearly. She glanced down at the chart, now soaking wet and floating on the deck. *Which bell, which bell? No, it doesn't matter which bell, you're done sailing now. Yes! Tie up to the bell buoy and wait out this storm. That's it. That's it.*

She heard him telling her that he was all right, and the relief of this was so great that she felt like sitting down on the deck and closing her eyes. But if the bell was near enough for her to hear it, she was in danger of running into it. This new fear rose through her, and she knew at once that she had to get the mainsail down. She let go of the tiller and ran along the deck. The boat pitched sharply in a wave and she fell onto her hands and knees. She crawled along the deck until she reached the mast. She took the halyard in both hands and yanked it from its cleat. The sail didn't fall and this sent a new jolt of fear through her. She felt her breath rushing from her. *What? What?* She seemed to hear her father's voice yelling something to her. Another wave crashed over the starboard gunwale, the salt water blinding her momentarily. Then the sail began to fall. She looked back at the stern and saw James. She realized then that she had forgotten to uncleat the main sheet. James had it in his hands and the sail was nearly down.

She was about to uncleat the jib when she heard him hollering at her, motioning her to come back to the helm.

"The jib," she shouted.

"No, Nora," he cried back.

It took a few more seconds before she realized that he was right. Without the jib they wouldn't be able to steer the boat to the bell.

When she returned to his side, she could no longer hear the bell ringing and she thought that she had only imagined it.

He told her that he hadn't heard anything. "Nothing," he said.

He wanted her to go down below and get out of her wet clothes. *Maybe,* she thought. *Maybe I will.* But already forming in her mind was the idea of how they would be safe tied to the bell buoy. If they could sail to it they would have this chance. The waves behind them would smash the boat against the buoy, they had to sail *into* the waves and the wind, dropping the jib sheet a few yards from the iron buoy so they coasted up to it. Then tying to it from the bow and lowering the anchor from the stern.

If the bell was out there at all.

She saw the main sheet lying on the deck. She tied it around her waist as a safety and told James she was going up onto the bow to listen for the bell. He didn't want her to go.

She told him there was no other chance.

"If I find it," she called back to him, "you'll have to fall off, then circle up into the wind and the waves."

Finally he agreed.

THE BELL APPEARED through the fog so suddenly that Nora didn't have time to yell to him. But he saw it as it slipped past the stern and he knew just what to do. He tacked around it, running a little ways with the wind behind them, then tacking sharply again and making straight for it.

Nora jumped onto the buoy just as he was dropping the jib. It was rolling violently in the swells. She wedged herself between the metal fins while the buoy tipped over so far that her face was only inches above the water. She felt for something to tie the line to. And then she had it.

They kept the kerosene lamps burning while they sat below, waiting out the storm. James was asleep when the boat came upon them. Nora felt the vibrations of its engine just before its searchlight swept along their port side.

Chapter Thirty-eight

I t was a seventy-two-foot fishing trawler with a steel hull, sailing under the flag of Sweden. A unit of IRA soldiers had commandeered her when she was tied up in Londonderry undergoing repairs to her navigational system.

James and Nora were given dry clothes, thick brown bread, potato soup, and tea. The man in charge introduced himself as Nicholas McMahon. He wore a black wool fisherman's sweater with a turtleneck collar, an Irish pound coin on a silver chain around his neck.

In the ship's galley while Nora and James were eating, McMahon stood at the head of their table with one foot propped up on a chair, drinking tea himself. He told them that he had once been a librarian in Dublin. "Before the war," he said, looking squarely at James. He knew the poetry of John Keats and twice had visited his grave in Venice. He told James that if England had been content to export her literature around the world rather than her religion, a lot of innocent people, including the people of Omagh, would have been spared violent deaths.

A woman with wavy black hair that fell to her waist showed Nora to a room with a cot. She gave her a corduroy jumper, a denim shirt, and some dry socks to wear, telling her she was sorry she had no underwear to give her. On her way back from the ship's bathroom, Nora passed a wooden crate packed with straw and rifles.

JUST BEFORE DAWN they put in at Bishop's Harbor with the sloop in tow behind them. It was a fair morning with a light breeze that carried the faint scent of apples.

McMahon walked them down the dock to where a brown Mercedes and two women in black pantsuits were waiting. One sat in the backseat with James, the other up front with Nora while McMahon drove. With their perfume filling the interior of the car, it was difficult for Nora to think of the women as terrorists.

The affidavits were straightforward accounts of what had taken place in Omagh, Nora's beginning with the words "This is what I saw," and James's with "This is what I did."

Nora was still reading when she heard James ask, "Is it imperative that I name these other people?"

McMahon looked at him in the rearview mirror. "Is there something on those pages that is inaccurate?" he asked.

"It's not that," James said.

A moment of silence passed. "Your people have the mother," McMahon said, the muscles in his face tightening.

"You told me you had her," Nora shouted at him.

"I lied," he said. "And these people you don't wish to name, Captain Blackburn. They may have killed her by now."

He waited, then nodded almost imperceptibly, and the lawyers gave Nora and James pens to sign the documents.

When that was done, the woman in the backseat with James passed his affidavit to the woman in front, who placed both inside her metal briefcase.

"We're going to Stormont Castle," McMahon said. "There will be some reporters there to ask questions. Here's my advice: Tell the truth." He looked again into the rearview mirror. "In this case, only the truth can set you free. Your people will deny everything, of course, but if they were to harm either of you, it would be a confirmation of your testimony. You'll be free to walk away."

Nora turned and looked back at James.

"We'll take you wherever you want to go," McMahon said. And Nora wasn't sure if he was speaking to both of them or only to her.

They rode along in silence for a while. Then the two women and McMahon began speaking Gaelic among themselves. Nora noticed that he watched his rearview mirror as intently as he watched the road in front of them.

Somewhere north of Belfast he drove them off the highway and onto a winding, narrow road that led to a small cottage set in among the rounded hills, overlooking the river.

When the car came to a stop, the lawyers got out and opened the trunk. Nora suddenly thought that they were going to be shot here, now that the documents were signed. She turned to look at James. He had turned around completely in his seat and was intently watching both women and McMahon.

"Okay," McMahon said, "out you go."

Next to the open trunk stood a suitcase. One of the women held James's uniform on a hanger. Nora could see the surprise in James's eyes, but he said nothing.

"You can dress inside," McMahon told them. "Five minutes."

· · ·

THERE WAS A GLOBE on a table by a set of sliding glass doors that opened to a garden behind the cottage. James stood beside it, turning the globe on its bronze stand. Then he draped his uniform over it. In the light, Nora saw that the salt water had washed some of the dye from his hair.

"Five minutes," she said to him.

He turned to her slowly. "Will you do something for me, Nora?" he asked.

"Yes," she said, "anything."

"I can't wear my uniform," he said. "If you were to talk to McMahon, maybe he'd allow . . . I don't know."

"I'll try," she said.

OUTSIDE, SHE FOUND MCMAHON sitting on the trunk of the car having a cigarette with both the women.

When Nora put her question to him he looked confused. He placed the cigarette between his teeth. The smoke drifted up into his pale gray eyes. He thought for a moment. He looked as if he were about to say something, then in one movement he threw the cigarette onto the ground, stood up, and charged past her to the cottage.

NORA WAS HELD in an empty warehouse with a blanket tied over her head. Somewhere a church bell rang on the hour, seventy-two times in the three days before she was taken to the airport in Dublin. They made her get out of the car on the side of a busy highway. Just before the driver untied her hands and opened her door, he said to her, "Someday, when all of Ireland is one free nation, maybe you'll return."

It was a long flight home against a strong headwind. Nora watched the green land below her until it turned to blue ocean.

Chapter Thirty-nine

There was an Indian summer that year in New England, a succession of clement days that Nora spent on the beach with her daughter after the theater closed for the season. They would arrive just after noon with a picnic supper, staying until everyone else had left, until that time just before dusk when you can feel the seasons changing in the fading light above the sea and when the wind dropping down to just a sigh seems to mark the end of a journey. What you are feeling, of course, is the passage of time, rhythmic, benevolent, and sad.

On one of those autumn afternoons Nora placed Sara's hand on her belly to feel the baby move.

"An elbow!" Sara exclaimed.

"I think it's a knee," Nora said.

That was the day Nora was finally able to find the words to describe James's eyes, the look in his eyes when she first saw him in the coffee shop in Omagh on the morning of the bombing. She told Sara that in his eyes there was the pain of knowing something he had never wanted to know.

She saw the same look in his eyes as he stood beside the globe before he ran through the bluffs behind the cottage and they found nothing but his shoes and his footprints in the sand at the edge of the river.

"Knowing what?" Sara asked, her hand still on her mother's stomach.

"Maybe knowing about himself," Nora said.

WITH AN AUTUMN SO FINE, Christmas seemed to come at the end of one summer day, catching everyone off guard, and by the time Nora discovered that she needed more wrapping paper it was evening and Wal-Mart was the only store left open. In the parking lot just as she opened the car door she saw them coming down the cement exit ramp with a grocery cart filled with bags and boxes. By now Nora knew her name, but referred to her as Madame Bovary, the name Sara had given to her father's girlfriend. Nora watched them. How much he was in love with her, or she with him, no one from a distance would know. While she watched, Steven took the change out of his pocket as he walked along, separating the pennies and dropping them on the ground, a habit he had begun when he took his first real job after graduate school. Even from where Nora stood, she could hear the sound of the pennies striking the tarred parking lot, but Madame Bovary didn't acknowledge the sound, familiar as she would have been by now with all of his habits.

He walked a little ways behind her.

Waiting for them to pass and staring at the plum-colored horizon across the fields beyond the parking lot, Nora suddenly recalled Steven's lifting the children when they were small to the top of the Christmas tree to place the angel there. She tried, but couldn't remember when he had first begun this Christmas Eve ritual. The memory was incomplete, but vivid nonetheless, and it reminded her that this is the gift of small children. They provide you the chance to redeem your life in a moment's gesture. In a child's mind, all your failings and failures disappear when she feels your hands lifting her to the top of a Christmas tree.

Even as Steven passed before her with the woman who had replaced her in his life, Nora could see his goodness. She knew that this was how it would always be, a former life merging with her present one as if both were merely dreams.

And she also knew that what we remember at the end of a day, or at the end of a life, is usually something so *unexpected* that we will forever recall precisely where we were standing when it happened, and sometimes the particular color of the sky or the song playing on the radio or the scent of the air. There are never more than a handful of these unexpected events; in Nora's life there was the killing of Jack Kennedy. And then Martin Luther King, Bobby Kennedy, and John Lennon. The explosion of the *Challenger* shuttle in the sky over Florida. News from the doctor that her mother was dying. All losses, all sadness, as if she *expected* her life to be happy.

AND THEN, because she had certainly not expected a new story to begin in her life right then, the most unexpected thing of all. On a December morning with the first snowfall of winter, beautiful fat flakes swirling across the sky, there was a letter from James Blackburn, telling her that he was well. And enclosed with the letter a photograph of the Irish mother and her child, whom he had saved after all.

AFTER THAT, A YEAR PASSED. A busy, meaningful year. *Unexpectedly* busy and meaningful after twenty-one years without a baby in her house.

Just as unexpected was the way her daughter delighted in

this new baby, returning home for weekends and calling Nora every week from New York City, where she had enrolled at Columbia University in the General Studies Program. Because Sara had always been so much like her father, Nora had expected her to drift into Steven's new life, and she was constantly surprised and pleased by her sweet allegiance.

Jake was another story, equally surprising to Nora. He kept promising to fly home from the West Coast and to call more often, but it wasn't until the baby was six months old that he finally made the trip. By then, peace had come to Northern Ireland. The killing, after eight hundred years, was over, and Nora was about to return to see James Blackburn. In fact, Jake showed up the morning of Nora's flight. He drove her to Logan Airport, and they settled in for a long lunch at one of the restaurants in the International terminal. She was feeding the baby formula by then. He drank a bottle straight down, burped twice, and then fell sound asleep in his car seat on a chair between Jake and Nora.

"My brother," Jake said with a smile. "Stick a newspaper in his hands and you've got Dad at dinner."

"Fat and happy," Nora said.

Sounding so much like his father, Jake remarked that he was pleased to have a brother, an ally in this godforsaken wasteland of a country. "I mean," he went on, "when you think of it, what better thing can parents do than have big families? Surround each kid with a pack of brothers and sisters so at least he has a few friends."

As soon as he said this, he turned back to the baby, sticking out his lower lip and his stomach to mimic him. "Little King Tut."

He told Nora that he had been in touch with his father and

that Steven had recently sent him a collection of Thomas Wolfe's works. "He told me that Wolfe was so damned tall he used the top of the refrigerator for his desk. Is that true?"

Nora recalled Steven's telling her this once, but she said she didn't know.

"Anyway, I've been picking my way through the stuff," Jake said. "Dad told me he had always thought Wolfe was just full of himself, but he'd given him a second chance and he found that he'd been wrong."

"That's something, isn't it?" Nora said.

"I don't know. Is it? I mean I don't know what to think really. About Dad, I mean. He told me that during the ten years when Sara and I were small he had missed the miracle of little children. Putting down rails, is how he described it. He was breaking his back putting down rails and he never got to ride in the train."

Nora smiled at her son. "Do you suppose he's enjoying the ride now?"

Jake didn't really answer this. He told her instead that his coffeehouse was finally making money and he was investing every penny in what he called indulgences for the elderly.

"Indulgences for the elderly?" Nora said.

"Yeah, stuff for the baby boomers when they grow old. You know, wheelchairs, nursing homes, all that stuff. Because you see, the baby boomers are going to reinvent being old. They're going to want everything to be first class, just like they had everything else in their lives. Think of it—there's never been a more spoiled generation. When they get old, you think they're going to settle for standard-issue bedpans?"

They both laughed at this.

"What can you do with a bedpan?" Nora said.

"Hey, just wait and see," he told her. "Attached CD player with stereo headphones, maybe?"

"You're talking about me, then, aren't you?" Nora said.

"Well, let's see. You're forty-three? You were born in—yep, that makes you one of them, Mom. Big summer house on the ocean in Maine. Finished college without any debts."

Nora picked up the beat for him. "Spacious house in the suburbs. Two kids. Oops, make that three."

"Nice family vacations," Jake went on. "Junior League."

It was on the tip of her tongue—*Betrayed by husband.* But she kept her silence.

"What about *your* generation?" she asked. Maybe there was something in her tone that made Jake back off.

"Hey, don't get me wrong," he said. "When I think back to how we had it, I feel damned lucky. I mean, to have had a mother who was just a mother, you know? I don't meet anybody who had that. And for me, well, I always felt good about that. Coming home and knowing you'd be there." He looked down at his brother, and nodded his head. "Yeah, I was lucky."

THEY WERE STANDING at the departure gate when Jake held the baby and let her take a picture. He was looking into the baby's eyes when he began reciting a passage from one of Thomas Wolfe's novels: "There was a kind of dream which I can only summarize as dreams of guilt and time. The huge accumulations of my years of struggle. My brutal and unending efforts to record upon my memory each brick and paving stone of every street that I had ever walked upon, each face of every thronging crowd in every city with which my spirit had contested its savage and uneven struggle for supremacy—they all returned now—each stone, each street, each town."

"Don't quote me on that, little brother," he said, handing the baby back to her.

They kissed good-bye, Jake never asking her why she was going back to Northern Ireland. Nora turned once as she walked away to tell him she liked his long sideburns. She watched him wave and turn away. For the first hour of the flight, while she kept the baby sucking on his pacifier, Nora had the unsettling feeling that she had somehow gained a son and lost a son.

THEY MET AT the Maison Hotel, the place where James Blackburn's life had stopped twenty years before, where he had listed himself as a victim of the bombing there.

He carried their suitcases into the room. She handed him her son to hold while she made a bed for him in the bathtub. "He's a great baby," she told James. "Meaning he sleeps like a teenager."

He stood behind her. "Are you happy, Nora?" he asked.

She turned to look at him. "Yes," she told him. "I'm very happy."

THEN THERE WAS JUST a narrow space between them, a space of only a few feet to cross. She opened her arms to him, a gesture that would soon encourage her son to learn to walk toward her.

He dropped to his knees and laid his face against her thighs. She heard him sigh. She closed her eyes, and when she opened them she found James looking at her. She was thinking that maybe love is nothing more complicated than looking up to find someone looking at you, waiting to meet your glance.

She felt herself beginning to sway inside her body. She took his face in her hands and kissed his lips. She took his hands and placed them beneath her blouse, on her breasts. She reached down to the hem of her skirt and lifted it to her waist. *This will be the end of our being strangers,* she thought.

Taking his hands in hers, she felt in possession of herself. She leaned her head back and saw a blade of sunlight cross the ceiling. In another life she had forgotten the importance of touch. Forgotten, or discarded it the way we might set aside a map once we reach our destination. But now she remembered it. Remembered its deep recompense.

She could almost hear the country whispering its history to her. When she took him inside her and felt him shudder against her shoulders, she was committing the moment to memory. She had a vision of herself as an old woman in a room filled with silver-haired women. There is time to talk, and, no longer afraid to speak about sex, they speak of almost nothing else. The flowers of their youth. The scent and the blessed ache of it. In cars. On the floors of trains. By the ocean. In the limbs of trees. In tents collapsing under moonlight. On countertops. Their memories are identical. The way the warm night air fell against their necks. The back of a hand lying on a heart. The ground is common. *He was gentle and reluctant, so I ushered myself into the sanctuary of what he didn't know he desired, and I saved him.*

With him pressed against her, Nora leaned backward and set them both rolling down the hillside. Smiling to herself with the thought that we are essentially free to do what we choose in this world despite the requirements of life. We can put our clothes on in the middle of the night and walk off into a new life. We can reinvent ourselves. Find and refind ourselves. By tomorrow evening we can glimpse a pyramid.

They had one night together here. China in the room for their tea. Digestives on the bedside table, the ones covered in chocolate that Nora had loved twenty years before. Eventually there were stars at their window. It took some time before he understood that she wanted him to make love to her again. "You'll have to forgive me," he said. "I've been alone a long time. Forever, really."

"A long time maybe, but not forever." She put her arms around him and pulled him close, until she could feel the world withdrawing from her, dragging her heart across the wide ocean of time and memory, through the narrow corridor of shadows, toward the pale light of the moon.

And she saw something in that light. She saw that she was drawn out from the darkness of her history, here now to return to the belief in her own worthiness, and to love in the best way.

ACKNOWLEDGMENTS

This is a work of fiction; however, I am grateful to the real people of Omagh,
County Omagh, who opened their hearts to me in the days of despair that followed
the bombing in August 1998. I hope that this book will help the world remember
the victims, those who were killed and wounded and those who were made to suffer.

Two writers, James Sullivan and Jesse Workman, helped me shape the plot
of this novel. Lynn Nesbit, Victoria Wilson, and Richard Morris encouraged me
along the way, as did Brian Siberell. In the actual writing of the prose I was
inspired by the music of Juliet Turner and the work of the filmmaker Mark
Pellington.

People across Northern Ireland helped me research this book: library workers
in Enniskillen, Cookstown, Omagh, Londonderry, and Belfast; a cab driver in
Warrenpoint; a bus driver in Ballykelly; a priest in Donegal; the staff of the
marvelous Ashbury Hotel in Enniskillen; two IRA members in Portrush; three
golfers in Lurgan; a nun beside the River Foyle; and those indefatigable
historians, philosophers, and poets in residence at too many pubs to name here.

In chapter 26 James Blackburn talks about the place of numbers in the world
of nature; these ideas came from a magazine I was reading in December of 1999.
I can't recall which magazine it was.

A NOTE ON THE TYPE

The text of this book was set in Garamond No. 3. It is not a true copy of any of the designs of Claude Garamond (ca. 1480–1561), but an adaptation of his types, which set the European standard for two centuries. It probably owes as much to the designs of Jean Jannon, a Protestant printer working in Sedan in the early seventeenth century, who had worked with Garamond's romans earlier, in Paris, but who was denied their use because of Catholic censorship. Jannon's matrices came into the possession of the Imprimerie nationale, where they were thought to be by Garamond himself, and were so described when the Imprimerie revived the type in 1900. This particular version is based on an adaptation by Morris Fuller Benton.

Composed by Creative Graphics, Allentown, Pennsylvania

Printed and bound by Quebecor Printing, Martinsburg, West Virginia

Designed by Iris Weinstein